IRELAND'S TREES
MYTHS, LEGENDS AND FOLKLORE

ABOUT THE AUTHOR

Niall Mac Coitir grew up in a bilingual environment in Dublin with a love of Irish history, culture and nature instilled into him. An active member of the Irish Wildlife Trust, he works for Fingal County Council. His other books are *Irish Wild Plants – Myths, Legends & Folklore* (2006, 2015), *Ireland's Animals – Myths, Legends and Folklore* (2010, 2015) and *Ireland's Birds – Myths, Legends & Folklore* (2015, 2016).

ABOUT THE ILLUSTRATOR

Grania Langrishe's early childhood in Bermuda inspired her lifelong fascination with plants. Despite no formal training, she began painting watercolours, was elected to the Watercolour Society of Ireland in 1984 and exhibits annually with them.

IRELAND'S TREES

MYTHS, LEGENDS AND FOLKLORE

Niall Mac Coitir

Original Illustrations by Grania Langrishe

The Collins Press

PUBLISHED IN THIS FORMAT IN 2015 BY
The Collins Press
West Link Park
Doughcloyne
Wilton
Cork
T12 N5EF
Ireland

Reprinted 2016, 2018, 2021, 2022, 2023, 2025

© Text Niall Mac Coitir 2003, 2015

© Original colour illustrations Grania Langrishe

First published in hardcover in 2003
First published in paperback in 2003

Niall Mac Coitir has asserted his moral right to be identified as the author of this work in accordance with the Irish Copyright and Related Rights Act 2000.

All rights reserved.
The material in this publication is protected by copyright law. Except as may be permitted by law, no part of the material may be reproduced (including by storage in a retrieval system) or transmitted in any form or by any means; adapted; rented or lent without the written permission of the copyright owners. Applications for permissions should be addressed to the publisher.

To the best of our knowledge, this book complies in full with the requirements of the General Product Safety Regulation (GPSR). For further information and help with any safety queries, please contact us at productsafety@gill.ie.

A catalogue record for this book is available from the British Library

Paperback ISBN: 978-184889-248-4
PDF eBook ISBN: 978-184889-997-1
EPUB eBook ISBN: 978-184889-088-6
Kindle ISBN: 978-184889-089-3

Typesetting by The Collins Press
Typeset in Palatino 10 pt
Printed and bound by Oriental Press, Dubai, United Arab Emirates

The paper used in this book comes from the wood pulp of sustainably managed forests.

Black and white line drawings are taken from *Arboretum et Fruticetum* published by Longman, Brown, Green and Longmans, London in 1844.

Contents

Introduction			vii
Aspects of Tree Folklore			1
Folklore of the Trees:			
Birch	22	Furze	92
Rowan	28	Broom	98
Alder	34	Blackthorn	102
Willow	40	Elder	108
Cherry	46	Pine	114
Hawthorn	52	Ash	120
Oak	58	Elm	130
Holly	66	Aspen	134
Hazel	72	Yew	138
Whitebeam	82	Spindle	146
Apple	84	Juniper	148
Buckthorn	90	Arbutus	152

Ogham – the Gaelic Tree Alphabet	154
An Ogham Tree Calendar	184
The Months as Contrasting Pairs	201
Postscript: The Universal Inspiration of Trees	203
References	207
Bibliography	221
Index	227

*Do mo thuismitheoirí
Dónal agus Celia
de bharr an chabhair,
tacaíocht agus grá go léir.*

Introduction

This is a book all about trees, which is nothing unusual in itself, as there are many books on the subject. This book, however, is a bit different to most. Normally, books about trees concentrate exclusively on the natural history of each tree, with folklore consisting of a few remarks added in for a bit of colour. That is when folklore gets a mention at all. This is a book for all those frustrated by this state of affairs and who want to know more about the sorely neglected (and dare I say important) topic of tree folklore. This book therefore reverses the usual order of things by gathering together for the first time the folklore of all our native trees; and confining questions of natural history and practical uses to a few remarks. As such it is intended to complement existing books about trees, rather than replicate what can easily be found elsewhere.

Folklore did not always have such a lowly place. In ancient Ireland and in Europe generally, mythology and folklore were an integral part of the store of knowledge surrounding each tree. There was not the split we find today between folklore and natural history. There are abundant references to trees in early Irish poetry and many poems solely about trees. This book contains the most important of them, with the original Irish text when it is clear and accessible. Many of them are for the first time published outside of academic works (the translations are my own, unless otherwise indicated). The fact that the creators of the first Irish alphabet Ogam or Ogham named its letters after trees is also a testament to the regard with which trees were held. Ireland itself was once heavily wooded and as an example of this, it was alleged at one time that a squirrel could travel all the way from Killarney to Cork without once touching the ground!

Yet the special place of trees to the Irish changed dramatically over the last few centuries. Pressures of population as well as the use of timber for various purposes, particularly shipbuilding and charcoal, meant that the landscape was increasingly denuded. Even today Ireland remains one of the least wooded countries in Europe.

A measure of this is the shameful fact that Ireland must import ash timber from Scandinavia for making hurleys, as there are so few suitable Irish trees left. The result of all this is that, if anything, Irish people became hostile to trees, seeing them as a mark of privilege and the landed gentry. As Austin Clarke put it in his poem 'The Planter's Daughter': 'For the house of the planter/ Is known by the trees'. The rugged, treeless landscape of Connemara was held up as the landscape of the 'real' Ireland, just as its lifestyle was held to represent what was authentically Irish. This was unfortunate because beautiful as Connemara is, it is not representative of what Ireland looks like. It is rather like portraying the Lake District as the true image of the English countryside. Ireland is in fact mainly a country of rolling hills and broad valleys, and the lush pastures of Meath and Munster (once largely covered in dense forest) are a better guide to the average Irish landscape. The net effect was to create an unconscious idea in many Irish people's minds that heavily wooded countryside is somehow alien and 'unIrish'. Nothing of course, could be further from the truth.

Thankfully attitudes are changing, and efforts are underway to restore Irish woodlands to something of their former glory. Government grants are increasingly available for forestry, and for native broadleaf species as well as non-native conifers. Particularly worthwhile is the imaginative Millennium project undertaken by the government, whereby 1.2 million trees of native species have been planted at fourteen locations throughout the country. That is one tree planted in the name of every household in the state. It is to be hoped that these efforts to revive Ireland's forests will not only improve the natural environment, but also restore the traditional regard of the Irish for their native trees. If this book also helps to increase that regard by showing how deeply embedded trees are in our culture, it will have served its purpose well.

Finally, it should be noted that the definition of a tree used in this book is the same as that used by the ancient Irish in framing the Ogham alphabet, and so contains species like gorse and broom that today would not considered to be trees. The order of the trees as presented also follows that alphabet in a seasonal cycle.

Aspects of Tree Folklore

Trees have been important to mankind from the earliest times. Since the dawn of our species, trees have provided us with many of the commodities needed for survival. Their timber has been a source of raw material for a variety of uses, from implements (both peaceful and warlike) to furniture and construction. Even today we cannot build our homes without wood. Their fruit, leaves and bark provide food for ourselves and our livestock, and can often be a vital source of medicine. In the past trees provided transport, by chariot or coach, along with dyes for clothing and even forms of footwear. It is no wonder that trees have always loomed large in the human imagination and have been regarded by our ancestors as sacred.

But there is a dimension to trees other than their numerous practical uses. There is something about trees that gives them a symbolic importance.

The lifecycle of a tree from seed to sapling to maturity, to withered old age and death, mirrors that of man. Trees, like people, bleed when cut, even if it is sap that flows out instead of blood. The tree is a powerful symbol of our own life in its various forms. Psychologically it is recognised that trees represent 'the living structure of our inner self'.[1] According to psychological theory, in dreams the roots represent our connection with the physical body, the trunk the way we direct our energies through growth, sex, thought and emotion. The branches represent the abilities and directions we develop in life and the growing tips show our aspirations and personal growth. Taken together these different dimensions to trees have led to them being seen since ancient times as powerful symbols of fertility, and the living abode of gods. The result is that a rich complex of myth, legend and folklore has built up around trees which is still with us today.

This dual aspect, both practical and symbolic, to the significance of trees brings us to one of the most basic mistakes made about tree folklore. Many scholars are uncomfortable with the idea of trees being regarded as sacred, and so try to find a practical explanation to refute such a notion. This approach is incorrect, since presenting practical reasons to oppose the sacred is a false dichotomy. Taking an example unrelated to trees, the Plain Indians of North America regard the buffalo as sacred, since it provides them with food from its meat, clothing and shelter from its hide, and various implements from its bones. It is seen as a gift from the Creator, imbued with supernatural powers, sacred because of its many important practical uses, not despite them. In the same way the oak was regarded as particularly favoured by the gods due to its many valuable attributes. The distinction between the sacred and the practical, therefore, is a very modern approach and it is inappropriate to project the distinction onto people who would not have understood it.

An example of such a modern misconception is found in the scholar A.T. Lucas' treatment of the sacred tree or *bile* in his article 'The Sacred Trees of Ireland'. After examining the evidence in detail, Lucas concedes that many church sites were located near trees or groves sacred to pagans, no doubt as part of a policy of Christianising them. However, he then goes to offer an 'alternative' explanation, namely that pre-Christian sites may have been sited close to tall trees because of the latter's worth as lightning conductors. It is true that the value of trees in this regard was probably known by ancient people but this misses the point. For a tree to attract lightning onto itself and away from buildings would be a sign of its protecting power, and is therefore further evidence of its sacred status. Indeed, the tendency of lightning to strike both the oak and ash was noted since ancient times and is an important element in the mythology surrounding both of them.

Many 'practical' motives do not stand up to analysis. For example, it is commonly stated that the association of yews with churchyards is due to the need for a supply of bows for archers. It is true that several English kings did decree that yews be widely planted for this purpose in medieval times,[2] but there is no evidence that the yews growing around churchyards were ever used for this purpose.

In fact there is ample evidence that many of the church yews are the oldest to be found anywhere, having survived unmolested. Similarly, it is claimed that yew was planted to prevent cattle from straying into church grounds, because the yew is poisonous to cattle. Yet, as every farmer knows, the only thing that will prevent livestock from straying is a fence. Such explanations are probably stock answers that entered folklore simply to explain an otherwise mysterious phenomenon.

What lies behind many of these theories, however, is the desire to deny or downplay any pre-Christian origin to tree folklore, particularly anything that smacks of druidism and paganism. This is by no means a new attitude. All across Europe as Christianity spread, the evidence points to folklore being adapted to a Christian context to enable it to survive. For example, trees that appeared to have a malevolent aspect from pre-Christian times invariably became linked to the story of the crucifixion in various ways. The aspen, hawthorn, yew and elder are each said to be the tree upon which Christ was crucified. The elder has the added shame of being the tree upon which Judas was said to have hanged himself. In the same way, any tree with thorns such as the blackthorn, hawthorn and buckthorn, could hardly avoid becoming the tree from which Christ's crown of thorns was made. However, these trees already had a hostile reputation before this legend attached itself. The bramble, although thorny, did not attract the same story because it had a benevolent image. Instead the bramble became the rod which Christ used to ride his donkey into Jerusalem, and to drive the moneylenders out of the temple.[3]

In the same way, sites of pre-Christian significance were taken over to make them acceptable to Christianity. In Ireland, Lucas lists among others, Armagh, Derry, Clonmacnoise and Kildare as being associated with sacred trees or groves from before the beginning of Christianisation. Usually the trees then became linked to the particular saint credited with founding the church site, such as Colmcille with Derry, or Brigid with Kildare. According to legend, the saints themselves often recognised the ancient sanctity of the groves and saw no contradiction between venerating them and being devout Christians. Colmcille for example, is famously said to have dreaded more the sound of an axe in the oak grove of Derry than all the fears of death and hell. Naturally, there are plenty of St Patrick's bushes, usually whitethorn, located throughout the country at places with some connection to him, for example at Kilmogg, County Kilkenny and Milltown, County Carlow. Other examples include St Kevin's yew tree at Glendalough, and St Kevin's whitethorn near his monastery at Seir Kieran. Holy wells that were sacred in pagan times became linked to saints by a similar process, and so by extension did their associated sacred trees.

Lucas raises another important question in his explanation of the rowan tree's appeal in Irish folk custom; namely the extent to which tree folklore is borrowed from one country to another. Lucas offers the theory that the widespread use of rowan in Ireland in charms and superstitions is a borrowing from Norse settlers. He proposed that the veneration of the rowan began among the Norse because of the extensive use in Norway of rowan bark as fodder for livestock in winter, and that the Norse carried this regard over to Ireland where it was copied by the native Irish. This is Lucas trying too hard to find a practical explanation for the use of the rowan in popular magic. In fact all the evidence points to the power of rowan deriving from the perceived association in pre-Christian times of its flame-red berries with the element of fire, the supreme protector against evil. It is implausible to suggest the custom spread so deeply throughout Ireland from the relatively few Norse settlements. The majority of Norse arrived here as town-based traders, not cattle-owning farmers. This is an excellent example of looking in the wrong place for a more 'objective' cause for tree folklore.

But the Irish and the Norse did have similar customs concerning the rowan and evidence points to tree folklore being similar across Europe for most, if not all trees. It is a common heritage to all Europeans, certainly as old as our common Indo-European roots, and may be older still (for example many of the yew trees found at ancient church sites in Britain date from Neolithic times [4]). When and how the folklore spread is now lost to us but it must have been a long time ago to be so universal. The whole complex of folk beliefs and customs as practised by closely-knit farming communities is very enduring and resistant to change, and can survive the arrival of new peoples and religions largely intact. The deepest origins of tree folklore are thus based in pre-Christian beliefs of a world where all things were inhabited by gods and spirits, and in its core it has probably changed little for millennia. There are exceptions, like the lore about the weeping willow deriving from the bible; and perhaps the image of the apple in Irish tales, which may have been influenced by classical sources. But these later layers co-exist with earlier ones, rather than replacing them entirely. Therefore, it is legitimate to use examples from other countries to complement the evidence from Ireland about tree folklore.

THEMES OF TREE FOLKLORE

The folklore of trees can be divided into two main themes. The first is the role of the tree as a marker and magnifier of an important place to the community, such as a royal inauguration site, or a holy well. This role of trees is the one which has the most prominent place in myth and legend. The second is the role that different species of tree play as sources of magical power in folk customs and superstitions. This aspect is the one most often found in popular lore. Although there is naturally an overlap between the two, it can clearly be seen that most trees are connected with one role more than the other. Only a few trees are sufficiently important to play a strong part in both areas.

With regards to the important place of the sacred tree in Ireland, there is even a special word in the Irish language to describe it, namely a *bile*. Examples of the *bile* marking an important place can be found all over Ireland. Particularly noteworthy is the link between sacred trees and royal inauguration sites. In these cases the tree acted as the symbolic tribal centre and local *axis mundi*, often known as the *Bile Buadha* or Tree of Power or Victory. As the sacred tree was therefore seen as symbolic of the tribe's power, efforts were often made by rival tribes to destroy it. So in the Annals of the Four Masters for the year 982 we read that the *bile* of Magh Adhair at the inauguration place of the kings of Dál gCais was uprooted by Mealseachlainn of Meath.[5] Similarly in 1111 the sacred trees of Tullaghoge, County Tyrone, the inauguration place of the O'Neills, were uprooted by a County Antrim tribe. The *Ruadh-bheitheach* or

'Red Birch' of the chiefs of the Ui Fiachrach Aidhne in Killeely, County Galway also suffered this same fate when it was cut down by the men of Munster in 1129. It appears, however, that new trees were often planted (or allowed to grow) to replace those destroyed, as the Annals record the destruction of trees in the same place on different occasions.

It follows from this that a sacred tree was a common feature to be found adjacent to a royal residence or fort. Many of the early Irish tales involve the hero coming to a kingly rath or fort and seeing a fine *bile* standing on the green before its door. For example, the famous king Conn Céadchathach, after journeying through a magic mist, comes to 'a kingly rath with a golden *bile* at its door'.[6] The phrase *Bile Rátha* or 'Tree of the Rath' appears in placenames and seems to have been a common term in ancient Ireland. Even today many of the 'lone bushes' are found beside the remains of these forts, which are generally regarded as the abode of fairies and places of otherworldly power. Another word occasionally used to denote a sacred tree was *craebh* (literally branch), and it was sometimes used interchangeably with *bile* for the same tree, e.g., *Craebh Daithi* or *Bile Daithi*.

In ancient Ireland there were five great trees considered by legend to be sacred above all others. These were the *Bile Tortan* near Tara, *Craebh Daithi* at Farbill, County Westmeath, *Craebh Uisnigh* at Uisneach, County Westmeath, *Eo Mugna* at Moone, County Kildare, and *Eo Rossa* at Old Leighlin in County Carlow. All five stood at or near important royal or sacred sites. The first three were ash trees, and the last two were an oak and yew, respectively. A poem in the *Metrical Dindshenchus* (a collection of old Irish poems concerning the lore of placenames) gives an account of the qualities of all five and their collective fate:

TREE OF ROSSA, TREE OF MUGNA
How was the Branch of Daithi laid low?
Its gentle shoots bore many blows.
An ash tree of the skilful hosts,
Its wind-lashed top bore no lasting growth.

An ash in Tortan, recount it well,
An ash in Uisneach where the troops dwell,
The branches fell; the truth is plain,
In the time of the sons of Aed Slane.

Oak of Mugna, bountiful treasure,
Nine hundred bushels, its great measure.
In Dairbre southwards it did fall,
On Ailbe's plain of the cruel war.

Yew of Rossa, yew of the graves,
Plentiful its wooden staves,
Tree without any hollow or flaw,
O noble yew, how was it laid low?

We have already seen how sacred trees came to be associated with ecclesiastical sites, and by extension with the saints that founded them. Another important link between saints and sacred trees is the association both have with holy wells. According to Lucas,[7] it has been estimated that there are more than 3,000 holy wells in Ireland dedicated to saints, and the majority have a tree or bush growing alongside them. Generally on the saint's feast day they were the focus of gatherings of the faithful called 'patterns' or 'patrons' after the patron saint of the well. A major feature of the pattern was the leaving of offerings on the tree, especially in the hope of a cure. These offerings usually consisted of rags or scraps of clothing, but objects such as rosary beads, miraculous medals, pins, nails, coins, buttons or combs were also left. As a result the branches of such trees often became thickly festooned with objects. A widespread legend has it that such trees sprang out of the saint's staff which he or she stuck into the ground beside the well. This is the story told about St Mullen's Well, County Kilkenny, St Brandon's Well, County Kilkenny and St Patrick's Well, County Roscommon. Of a survey of 210 holy wells throughout the country Lucas found that of the trees beside them, 103 were hawthorn, 75 were ash and the rest were randomly distributed among various species. Typically, Lucas denies that there might be any symbolic reasons for this, but on examination of the lore surrounding ash and hawthorn refutes this.

Considering their symbolic importance it is not surprising that tribal names were often derived from trees. For example, in Gaul the Eburones were the yew tree tribe, while the Lemovices were the people of the elm.[8] Of course, not only single trees were considered sacred; groves were as well, and were known throughout the Celtic world by the name *nemeton*. The most famous of these was at Drunemeton in Galatia. Similarly Nemetona, the goddess of the sacred grove, was worshipped in Bath. In Ireland, the term was *fid-neimheadh* which was usually, but not always, attached to a church site and considered a place of sanctuary under Irish law. [9]

The second aspect of tree folklore is the use of trees as sources of power in charms and superstitions. The main purpose of the majority of these is to act as increasers and protectors of fertility, particularly in livestock (especially dairy), and in crops. The house and property are also to be protected, and vulnerable people, like children and the sick, are to be kept safe from the fairies. As well as protecting animals against harm trees could also keep away harmful animals. For example, hazel and ash are said to protect against snakes. The reason may be that both are connected with water and wells but other similar trees like alder, willow and hawthorn do not share this characteristic. Trees could also be useful in protecting against various ailments, and to effect cures through folk magic. For example, a good cure for ague, or shaking illness, was to blow three times into a hole in a willow tree. Occasionally there are examples of trees being used for harmful purposes. One story in the Annals of the Four Masters tells of elder being used by a queen to curse her rival.

It is interesting to note that whether a tree is regarded as being lucky or unlucky (benevolent or malevolent) varies from place to place. At first sight this might seem to suggest that the folklore is arbitrary and without any great depth but there is something else at work. The fact is that notions of 'lucky' and 'unlucky' are very much two sides of the same coin. If a tree was perceived as having a particular attraction for hostile forces, it followed that in the right context the tree's powers could be 'harnessed' and used against those forces with particular effect. For example, the elder is a tree loved by witches but planted near the house or barn it is also one of the best trees to guard against witches. Most of the trees with a malevolent reputation have this dual aspect, which results in them being regarded as benevolent or 'lucky' in some places.

It is widely believed that it is unlucky to bring blossoms or catkins into the house. Sickness, misfortune, or even death will surely follow.[10] The hawthorn is particularly mentioned in this regard, perhaps because of the smell of its blossoms, but the prohibition applies to many flowers, even non native ones like lilac and garden daffodils. It is hard to discern what exactly lies behind this idea but it seems to have something to do with the notion that such blossoms are a threat to the human 'flower' of the household, either the woman of the house or a child (in parts of England hawthorn was known as 'mother-die'). This can be seen a little more clearly in a superstition about the willow. In parts of England willow catkins are called 'goosy goslins' or similar names on account of their resemblance to goslings. To bring them into the house, however, will cause any real goslings not to be hatched. As always, of course, in some places it is actually considered lucky to bring blossom indoors.

Another aspect of trees that is important to consider is the question of how well the timber of each tree functions as firewood. Again, as in all aspects of folklore, this practical question is also bound up with the lucky and unlucky aspects of each tree. Trees like rowan, birch, ash and pine are good trees to burn; rowan because of the association with its flame red berries; pine, birch and ash because of the bright, pure flame they produce. In the case of pine, in particular, the white flame of its resinous wood is the main reason it is considered a tree of good fortune. On the other hand, the negative aspects of elder are amplified by the fact that it does not burn when put on a fire but merely smoulders. This association does not work with every species, however. For example, aspen is considered a good species to burn, despite its unlucky associations.

There are two very important caveats in all of this, however. The first is that no matter how valuable a species of tree is for firewood, to cut down a tree considered sacred or special is taboo. It may be acceptable to use a tree of the same species growing in a hedgerow or some other unremarkable spot, but to use a tree marking a holy or otherworldly location is to invite the most terrible misfortune. Irish folklore is full of tales of people suddenly dying, being disfigured, or losing their wits after cutting down a sacred tree, for whatever purpose. The second is that an unlucky tree is on no account to be used for fires marking a special occasion, whatever about everyday use. In the Scottish Highlands, for example, according to the folklorist, Carmichael, blackthorn, 'wild fig' (bird cherry) and aspen were to be avoided as wood for the St Michael's Eve (midsummer) fire. Bonfires were a very widespread way of marking seasonal festivals and particular trees were favoured for these. For example, in Scotland the midsummer 'needfires' were usually made of oak, and rowan was considered best to use at Maytime.

In a story called, 'The Death of King Fergus', a poem about the properties and folklore of various kinds of Irish timber is recited by Iubhdan, King of the Leprechauns. Iubhdan has come to call on King Fergus and while in his court, observes a servant throw a piece of woodbine twisted around a length of wood onto the fire. Shocked by the servant's ignorance of the ill fortune of doing such a thing, Iubhdan recites the poem in order to warn and educate him. There is the added implication that the burning of the woodbine in some way foreshadows or contributes to King Fergus' death later in the tale. The poem is a good summary of the merits of most Irish timber, with some valuable pieces of folklore added in for good measure:

LAOI IUBHDAN
A fhir fhadós teine ag Fergus na fled,
Ar muir ná ar tír, ná losc ríg na fed.
A irdrí feda Fáil, im nach gnáth sreth sluaig,
Ní fann an feidm ríog sníomh im gach crann cruaid.
Dá loisce an fid fann bud mana gréch nglonn,
Ro sia gábad renn, nó bádad trén tonn.
Ná loisc aball án, na ngéag faroll faen,
Fid man gnáth bláth bán, lám cháich na cenn chaem.
Deorad draigin dúr fid, fid nach loiscenn saer,
Gáirid elta én tréna chorp cid cael.
Ná loisc sailig sáir, fid deinim na nduan,
Beich na bláth ag deol, mian cáich an cró caem.

Caerthann fid na ndruad, loisce caemchrann na gcaer,
Seachain an fid fann, ná loisc an coll caem.
Uinnseann dorcha a dath, fid luaite na ndroch,
Echlasc lám lucht ech, a cruth ag cládh chath.
Crom feda deín dris, loisc féin an ngeír nglais,
Fennaid gerraid cois, srengaid nech ar ais.
Bruth feda dair úr, ó nach gnáth nech seím,
Tinn cenn tís ó a dhúil, tinn súil ó a ghrís ghéir.
Na fern urbadb fheda, an crann is teo i ngliaid,
Losc go derb do deoin, an fhern is an sciaig.
Cuilenn losc a úr, cuilen losc a críon,
Gach crann ar bith becht, cuilenn as dech díob.
Trom dana rúsc ruad, crann fírghona iarfíor,
Loisc go mbeidh na gual, eich na sluaga siod.
cid na fharrad faen, béithe ba blad buan,
losc go deimin derb, coinnle na mbalg mbuan.
Léíg síos madat maith, crithach ruad na rith,
Losc go mall go moch, crann is a barr ar crith.
Sinnsear feda fois, ibar na fled fis,
Déna ris anois, dabcha donna dis.
Da nderntá mo thoil, a Fhir déadh dil,
Dot anam dot chorp, ní bud olc a fhir.

IUBHDAN'S LAY
O servant to king Fergus, make sure the fire's good,
On land or on sea, do not burn the king of woods.
High King of Irish woods, that no army can hold,
It is no weak service tough trees to enfold.
But burn the weak woodbine and warning cries will sound
Of danger at spear point, or strong waves to drown.
Do not burn the pleasing apple, drooping its spread,
Loved its white blossoms; all touch their fair heads.
Hardy outlaw the blackthorn, that no craftsman will burn,
Although scanty, bird flocks cry out from its form.
Do not burn the noble willow, enduring in verse,
Bees the blossoms suck, all love its graceful curves.
Rowan the druids' tree, burn the fair tree of berries,

But avoid the weak wood, the fair hazel, for fires.
Ash, dark in colour, wood for chariot wheels,
Horsewhip in horseman's hands, shaft on the battlefield.
Bending wood the vicious briar, burn it sharp and fresh,
Cuts and flays the foot, keeps everyone enmeshed.
Smouldering green oak wood is hard on everything,
Headache comes from liking it, strong embers make eyes sting.
Alder, great scald crow of woods, hottest in the fight,
The alder and the hawthorn, burn both as you might.
Holly burn it fresh, or holly burn it old,
Name the worth of any tree, holly is tenfold.
Elder with its tough bark, truly wounds the most,
Burn it into charcoal, steed of the fairy host.
Though it feebly droops, birch that is so good,
Burn it certain sure, stem of the swelling bud.
Lay down a good staff; aspen racing without stop,
Burn it late or early, tree of the shaking top.
Senior of eternal woods, yew of the learned feast,
Make with it now, brown vats of the best.
O good and faithful servant, if you carry out my will,
Your body and your soul will come to no ill.

Having examined the various aspects of the myth and folklore of trees, it is an interesting exercise to classify Irish trees in order of their importance in these respects. To do this, each species of tree must be assessed under two categories, namely its place in myth and legend, and its place in popular folklore. I believe the following best fits the evidence. I accept that some would not agree with my choices but the list is not intended to be final and definitive. Also, there is no doubt that outside of Ireland the list would be somewhat different. Pine, for example, would occupy a much higher place, probably in the second class.

First come the trees which are important in both categories. This first class can be called the 'big four' – ash, oak, hazel and yew. All four have myths involving them as a protector or marker of important places in a sacred and social sense, while also having much folklore attached to them. There are no grounds for saying that any one tree among them was valued above any of the others. Second come trees that have a significant place in folklore, and can occasionally also appear in the myths as important. This class includes birch, rowan and hawthorn. Third come trees that are important in terms of their place in myth and legend but that only occasionally appear in folklore. The apple is the only tree in this class because despite its strong place in myth, it is curiously lacking in popular folklore. Fourth come trees that hold an important place in popular folklore but no significant place in myth. This class includes holly, elder, blackthorn and willow. Fifth and finally come trees that occupy a place of lesser importance in folklore and do not appear in any significant way in myth, including alder, pine, cherry, elm, aspen, furze and broom. It is of note that there is a correlation between a tree's worth in practical terms and the value placed on it in folklore.

Trees in Early Law

In ancient Ireland the importance of trees meant that they were classified into various categories, with a series of laws governing their use and fines for damaging or cutting trees without the landowner's permission. These laws are found in the eighth-century legal tract *Bretha Comaithchesa* or the Laws of Neighbourhood, but they may ultimately derive from an earlier, and now lost law tract *Fidbretha* or Tree Judgements, which is mentioned in a work dating from the seventh century. The laws recognise a hierarchy of four classes of trees or bushes: the *airig fedo* or nobles of the wood, *aithig fedo* or commoners of the wood, *fodla fedo* or lower divisions of the wood, and *losa fedo* or bushes of the wood. Each class consists of seven different species of tree or bush, and each species owes its position to its perceived economic worth. This in general depends on the value of the tree's timber so the classes are usually related to the size of the tree when fully grown. There are exceptions to this of course, like apple and hazel, which owe their position in the top class due to the importance of their fruit as food.

The law tracts give the following reasons as to why the Nobles of the Wood occupy their exalted position:

Oak: *a mes agus a saíre* – its acorns and its dignity

Hazel:	*a mes agus a cháel* – its nuts and its rods
Holly:	*fer for araili innsin agus feirtsi carpaid* – grass for another and chariot shafts
Yew:	*a haicdi sáera* – its noble artefacts
Ash:	*folach rigsliasta is leth arad airm* – support of a royal thigh and half material of a weapon
Pine:	*a bi a tulcuma* – its resin in a bowl
Apple :	*a mes agus a rúsc* – its fruit and its bark

The reference for holly to 'grass for another' is believed to concern holly's use as fodder, while the reference for ash to 'support of a royal thigh' probably refers to the fact that ash was a favourite wood for making chairs and stools. The full list appears as follows:

THE OLD IRISH TREE LIST

AIRIG FEDO
Nobles of the Wood

Daur	Oak
Coll	Hazel
Cuilenn	Holly
Ibar	Yew
Uinnius	Ash
Ochtach	Pine
Aball	Apple

AITHIG FEDO
Commoners of the Wood

Fern	Alder
Sail	Willow
Scé	Hawthorn
Cáerthann	Rowan
Beithe	Birch
Lem	Elm
Idath	Cherry

FODLA FEDO
Lower Divisions of the Wood

Draigen	Blackthorn
Trom	Elder
Féorus	Spindle
Findcholl	Whitebeam
Caithne	Arbutus
Crithach	Aspen
Crann Fir	Juniper

LOSA FEDO
Bushes of the Wood

Raith	Bracken
Rait	Bog Myrtle
Aiten	Gorse
Dris	Bramble
Fróech	Heather
Gilcach	Broom
Spín	Gooseberry*

* 'Wild Rose' according to Kelly.

Naturally the penalties relating to damage done to the trees vary according to their class and the four classes carry the following graduated fines due to the owner of the land where the trees stood:

Nobles of the Wood – for branch cutting one *dairt* (year-old heifer), for fork cutting one *colpthach* (two-year-old heifer), and for base felling one milch cow. The fine for removing the trees altogether was the economic equivalent of the value of two and a half milch cows. This was a more serious act than base selling because there was no prospect of the trees re-growing.

Commoners of the Wood – for branch cutting one sheep (some sources have one *dairt*), for fork cutting one *dairt,* and for base felling one milch cow, and for removal, the price of two and half milch cows.

Lower Divisions of the Wood – for base cutting one *colpthach* and for removal, one *dairt*. There do not appear to have been any penalties for cutting anything less.

Bushes of the Wood – the laws state that 'their single stems are not entitled to a penalty', i.e., cutting a single stem of a neighbour's bracken etc. will not mean having to pay anything. However, for *earba* or extirpation, i.e., cutting down all the bracken, the fine is one *dairt*.

The situation in Wales paralleled that of Ireland, with penalties under native Welsh law for damaging or felling trees. The laws of the Welsh king Howel Dda (Howel the Good) date from around 1200 AD and outline various fines for felling different types of tree. As under the Irish laws, some trees carried heavier fines than others, but the classification is not as detailed. The laws state as follows: 'A yew of a saint is a pound (240p) in value. An oak is six score pence (120p) in value. Whoever shall bore through an oak is to pay three score pence (60p). A branch of mistletoe is three score pence (60p) in value. Every principal branch of the oak is thirty pence in value. An apple tree is three score pence (60p) in value. A crab tree is thirty pence in value. A hazel tree is fifteen pence in value. Fifteen pence is the value of a yew of a wood. A thorn is seven pence halfpenny in value. Every tree after that is four legal pence in value except a beech tree. That is six score pence (120p) in value. Whoever shall fell an oak on the king's highway, let him pay a fine of three kine directly to the king, and the worth of the oak; and let him clear the way for the king; and when the king goes by, let him cover the stock of the tree with cloth of one colour. If a tree falls across a river and things get entangled in the tree, the owner of the land whereon the stock of the tree may be, is to have the find whatever way the river may have turned the top branches of the tree.' The amounts of the fines are given in the decimal system of money where one pound (sterling or Irish) was equal in value to 240 pence.

The ranking of different trees is obvious enough, with oak occupying a pride of place, and apple and hazel having a high status due to their fruit. The highly valued 'yew of a saint' no doubt refers to the importance of certain landmark trees venerated for their connection with some local saint and/or church. The importance attached to mistletoe is probably connected with its perceived properties as a powerful healing plant.

Also from Wales comes the poem the '*Cad Goddeu*' or 'Battle of Goddeu', in which appears a list of trees. The battle is not a real one of flesh and blood but an enchanted one of poetry between the various letters in the form of trees. The poem is a play on the different meanings of the word *gwydd,* for in Welsh the word means both tree and letter. This is exactly the same as in Irish with the related word *fid*. It is tempting to see the poem like Robert Graves did, as an example of encoded Ogham lore, but this is not sustainable. The list of trees is too different, leaving out vital trees like apple and elder, and including others like raspberry and laburnum which do not feature in connection with any of the letters. Nevertheless, the poem does contain important pieces of genuine tree lore and is a testament to the importance of trees in Welsh folklore.

From THE BATTLE OF GODEU

Now the alders, at the head of the line,
Thrust forward, the first in time.
The willows and mountain ash
Were late joining the army.
The blackthorns, full of spines –
How the child delights in its fruit

And their mate, the medlar
Will cut down all opposition.
The rose marched along
Against a hero throng.
The raspberry was decreed
To serve most usefully as food,
For the sustenance of life –
Not to carry on strife.
The wild rose and the woodbine
And the ivy intertwined.
How greatly the poplar trembles
And the cherry dares.
The birch for all its ambition,
Was tardily arrayed,
Not from any diffidence, but
Because of its magnificence.
The laburnum set its heart on the
Dingles rather than on bravery.
The yew is to the fore,
At the seat of war.
The ash was exalted most
Before the sovereign power.
The elm, despite vast numbers
Swerved never a foot,
But fell on the centre,
On the wings, and the rear.
The hazel was esteemed,
By its number in the quiver.
Hail blessed cornel tree
Bull of battle, king of all.
By the channels of the sea,
The beech did prosperously.
The holly livid grew,
And manly acts he knew.
The whitethorn checked all
Its virus aches in the palm.
The vines, which roofed overhead

Were cut down in battle,
And their clusters plundered.
The broom, before the rage of war
In the ditch lie broken.
The gorse was never prized,
Thus was it vulgarised.
Heath that promotest obstruction
Thy multitude has been enchanted:
Easily ensnare the pursuer.
Before the swift oak darts
Heaven and earth did quake.

translated by J.G. Evans

TREES IN PLACENAMES

Placenames derived from trees are abundant in Ireland. For example, according to the botanist, Charles Nelson, in his book *Trees of Ireland*, more than 1,600 townlands in Ireland contain the word *Doire* or oakwood, reflecting how widespread oak forests once were. The best known of these of course is Derry city, or in Irish *Doire Cholmcille* – Colmcille's oakwood. Other examples include Dunderry (*Dún Doire* – fort of the oakgrove), County Meath and Edenderry (*Éadan Doire* – brow of the oakwood), in Counties Offaly and Antrim. *Dair*, meaning a single oak, also appears in placenames. Examples include Kildare (*Cill Dara* – church of the oak) and Durrow (*Darú* – Oak plain). Another common name is *Sceach* or hawthorn. It appears on its own, anglicised simply as Skeagh in Counties Antrim, Cavan, Cork, Donegal, Down, Fermanagh, Kildare, Laois, Monaghan, Roscommon and Tipperary. Other versions such as Skea, Skagh and Ska also appear.[11] Some of these names can be quite poetical, including Skenarget (*Sceach an Airgid* – the silver hawthorn), County Tyrone and Skeheenarinky (*Sceichín an rinnce* – hawthorn of the dancing place), County Tipperary.[12]

Also quite common in placenames is *Beith* or birch appearing in such names as Glenbeigh (*Gleann Beithe* – glen of the birch) and Beaghmore (*Beitheach Mór* – large birchland), County Tyrone. Names including *Iúir* or yew are also widespread. Examples include Newry (*An tIúir* - the yew), County Down, Terenure (*Tír an*

Iúir – territory of the yew), County Dublín and Gortinure (*Gort an Iúir* – field of the yew), County Derry. The willow is well represented in names such as Clonsilla (*Cluain Saileach* – Meadow of the willows), County Dublin and Sallins, (*Saileáin* – place of the willows), County Kildare. Examples of placenames involving other trees include Oulart (*Abhall Gort* – Orchard), Counties Wexford and Kilkenny; Ferns (*Fearna* – place of the alders); County Wexford; Trim (*Baile Átha Troim* – town of the ford of the elder), County Meath; and Lucan (*Leamhcán* – place of elms) County Dublin. Names which include *Bile* and *Craobh* also appear, for example Moville (*Má Bhile* – plain of the sacred tree), County Donegal and Creeveroe (*Craobh Rua* – red branch/tree), County Armagh. Finally, there are numerous examples of the generic words for wood i.e. *Coill, Fiodh* and for tree, i.e., *crann*. Examples include Kilnamanagh (*Coill na Manach* – wood of the monks), County Tipperary, Fethard (*Fiodh Ard* – high wood), Counties Tipperary and Wexford, and Cranagh (*Crannach* – place abounding in trees), Counties Galway, Mayo, Laois, Roscommon and Tipperary.

TREES IN EARLY IRISH POETRY
Early Irish poetry is famous for its fresh and vivid evocation of nature, and it is only to be expected that trees should be a feature of it. The life of the early Christian scribes, living close to nature as monks or hermits, lent itself to a keen appreciation of the beauties of the natural world. In a seventh-century Irish poem, the hermit, Marbán, tells of how he lives out his life in a hut in the woods, with an ash tree on one side and a hazel on the other. Along with extolling the beauty of the flora and fauna around him, Marbán lists the fruits which provide him with nourishment. Alongside fruits like whortleberries (fraughans), wild strawberries and blackberries, he lists the produce of various trees. As well as the obvious hazelnuts and apples, these include rowan berries, sloes, yew berries, cherries, juniper berries, haws, and acorns.[13]

The most famous of the nature poems involving trees, however, is attributed to Mad Sweeney or Suibhne Geilt. Sweeney was a seventh-century king cursed by St Ronan after a dispute. The curse took effect at the battle of Mag Rath when the horrors of battle drove him mad and he fled the company of men, preferring to live wild in the woods. It is therefore appropriate to finish with Sweeney's eulogy to the forest trees, which captures the essence of the Irish woodland in a way which has not been bettered since.

LAOI SHUIBHNE	SWEENEY'S LAY
A dhair dhosach dhuilledhach,	Thou oak, bushy, leafy,
At ard os cionn crainn.	Thou art high beyond trees,
A cholláin, a chraobhacháin,	O hazlet, little branching one,
A chomhra cnó cuill.	O fragrance of hazel nuts.
A fhern, nidot naimhdidhe,	O alder, thou art not hostile,
Is alainn do lí.	Delightful is thy hue,
Ní dat cuma sceó sceanbaidhi,	Thou art not rending and prickling
Ar an mbeirn a mbí.	In the gap wherein thou art.
A dhroighnéin, a dhealgnacháin,	O little blackthorn, little thorny one,
A áirneacháin duibh,	O little black sloe tree.
A biorair, a bharr ghlasáin,	O watercress, little green topped one,
Do brú thobair luin.	From the brink of the ousel's spring.
A mhinen na conaire,	O *minen* of the pathway,
At millsi gach luibh,	Thou art sweet beyond herbs,
A ghlasáin, a adhghlasáin,	O little green one, very green one,
A lus forsa mbí an tshuibh.	O herb on which grows the strawberry.
A abhall, abhlachóg,	O apple tree, little apple tree,
Tren rotchraithenn cách,	Much art thou shaken,
A chaerthain, a chaeirecháin,	O quicken, little berried one,
Is alainn do bhláth.	Delightful is thy bloom.
A dhriseog, a dhruimnechóg,	O briar, little arched one,
Ni damha cert cuir.	Thou grantest no fair terms,
Ni ana gum leadradhsa	Thou ceasest not to tear me,

Gursat lomlán d'fuil.	Till thou hast thy fill of blood.
A iubhair, a iubhracháin,	O yew tree, little yew tree
I reilgibh bat reil.	In churchyards you are conspicuous
A eidhinn, a eidhneacháin	O ivy, little ivy,
At gnáth a choill cheir.	Thou art familiar in the dusky wood.
A chuilinn, a chlithmharáin,	O holly, little sheltering one,
A chomhla re gaoith.	Thou door against the wind,
A uinnes, a urbhadach,	O ash tree, thou baleful one,
A arm lámha láoich.	Hand weapon of a warrior.
A bheithi blaith bennachtach,	O birch, smooth and blessed,
A bhorrfadaigh bhinn.	Thou melodious, proud one,
Alainn gach craobh cengailteach,	Delightful each entwining branch,
I mullach do chinn.	In the top of thy crown.
Crithach ara criothugadh,	The aspen a-trembling,
Atchluinim ma seach.	By turns I hear,
A duille for riothugadh,	Its leaves a-racing
Dar leam is í an chreach.	Meseems 'tis the foray!
Mo mhioscais i fidhbadhuibh,	My aversion in woods –
Ni cheilim ar chách,	I conceal it not from anyone –
Gamhnach dharach duilleadhach,	Is the leafy stirk of an oak
Ar siubal go gnáth.	Swaying evermore.

TRANSLATED BY J.G. O' KEEFFE

Birch – Beith

Betula pendula - Silver birch
Betula pubescens-Downy birch
1st consonant of the Ogham Alphabet

27 December -23 January
3rd month of Ogham Tree
Calendar

 B

The Birch, with its pale white bark and graceful sweeping habit, is renowned for its beauty. It is the first forest tree to colonise new ground, and its twiggy branches are ideal for use as a broom. These qualities have made it a symbol of birth and rebirth, youthfulness, love and purity.

FOLK BELIEFS AND CUSTOMS

Birch was widely associated with birth and young children.[1] Birch was put over cradles to protect babies in the Hebrides, and in Wales cradles themselves were often made of birch. In the Scottish Highlands a cross of birch twigs was used in Bride's Eve (31 January) ceremonies, which after Bride (or St Brigid) was invoked, was placed in the cradle to represent either a child or a *dealbh bríde* – 'the form of Bride'. Alternatively, a rod of birch or other suitable wood (such as willow or broom) was placed in the cradle beside a straw figure. This rod was known as Bride's wand or Bride's birch. Another variation was a bed of birch twigs made especially for St Brigid. In many parts of Europe birch saplings were placed in houses and stables to promote fruitfulness, and young people and cattle were struck with birch twigs. A Scots Gaelic rhyme states that to strike cows with birch twigs would lead to them calving.

Birch features strongly as a symbol of love in Celtic lore.[2] The warrior Diarmuid made a bed for himself and his lover Gráinne out of soft rushes and birch tops, once at Doire Dá Bhaoth and again at a place called simply Beith or Birch. In the tale 'The wedding of Maine Morgor', green leaved birch branches and rushes were strewn on the floor to welcome Maine to his marriage to Ferb. In later Irish Gaelic poetry birch was often compared to a beautiful

Folklore of the Trees

young woman – *finnbhean na coille* or 'the fair woman of the woods'. In Wales the lovers' bower was traditionally beneath a birch tree and wreaths of birch were given as a love token. A birch twig given by a boy to a girl as a love token meant constancy. This association of birch with love was a constant in Welsh poetry. The fourteenth-century Welsh poet Dafydd ap Gwilym asks a nun with whom he is in love: 'Is it possible, the girl that I love, that you do not desire birch, the strong growth of summer?' Later he calls on her to come with him to the spreading birch.

Given its associations with youthfulness and love it is not surprising that birch features prominently in summer time festivities in many countries.[3] Frazer, in his seminal book on folklore *The Golden Bough*, gives plenty of examples in his account of Maytime and St John's Eve customs. In many countries likeEngland, France and Germany, birch was one of the favourite trees to use as a maypole, or the maypole was itself bedecked with leafy birch boughs. In Sweden boys made the rounds of the village on May Eve singing songs, with each carrying a bunch of fresh birch twigs, and in parts of Germany a wooden frame covered in leafy birch twigs hid the 'May King' whose identity had to be guessed by the other villagers.

In Wales dancing and playing games around a birchen maypole was a feature of the festivities. In south Wales the Morris dancing around the maypole was known as *dawns y fedwen* – 'the birch dance'. This could also be done on St John's Eve. In Cheshire groups known as May Birchers went around people's doors on May Eve leaving humorous messages. In Cheshire it was also the custom to fix a birch twig over a sweetheart's door on May Day. In Scotland birch kindling was used to set alight a ritual fire at the rising of May's first sun, and birch branches were hung over doors on Midsummer Eve. Strangely there seems to be no evidence of birch being used in similar customs in Ireland.

Birch is also a symbol of purity and protection against evil.[4] Birch was used throughout Europe at the New Year or Winter Solstice to 'beat the bounds' of the parish to expel evil spirits, and birch garlands were generally known to keep away demons. For example, in Herefordshire, new birch twigs were put outside the house and outhouses, and a maypole of birch was erected to keep

Birch – Beith
Betula pubescens

Rowan – Caorthann
Sorbus aucuparia

Alder – Fearnóg
Alnus glutinosa

Goat Willow – Saileach
Salix caprea

away witches. Also, of course, birch rods were used to beat the evil out of miscreants. In Ireland the fairies were not supposed to like birch, and indeed the very first use of Ogham cautioned Lugh that his wife risked being taken by the fairies 'unless birch guard her'. In Scotland a catkin of birch twined into a cord and placed under milk would protect it from any harm. One Scottish folk story tells of how a man is saved from being taken away to hell by a phantom horseman called 'Headless Hugh' by hanging on to a birch sapling until the first cockcrow.

LEGENDS AND MYTHOLOGY

Perhaps because of birch's perceived purity and grace there is evidence of a link between birch and church bells. One story concerns St Molasius who left a bell in Rome. When Molasius returned to Ireland the bell was hanging outside his house on a birchen bough. Three times Molasius returned the bell to Rome and each time it returned to Ireland.[5] In *The Life of St Patrick* the saint was said to have a handbell which, in a fit of anger, he threw under a bush. A birch tree subsequently grew up through its handle. On being rediscovered the bell was christened the Bethachán or Betullanum - 'the little birch of iron'. Suibhne Gelt or Mad Sweeney described the birch as: *A bheithi blaith bennachtach/a bhorrfadaigh bhinn* or 'O birch, smooth and blessed/thou melodious, proud one'. Perhaps this belief in birch's purity explains the reference in the Welsh poem the '*Cad Godeu*' (the Battle of Godeu) to birch being late to battle because of, and not despite, its greatness.

But not only was birch a symbol of birth in this life, it was also a symbol of rebirth after death.[6] The ritual for a departed person in Ireland involved a feast followed by funeral games and the carrying of the body to the grave in a covering of *strophais* or 'green bushy branches of birch'. A similar example was a Celtic chieftain found buried at Hochdorf in Germany. The chieftain was dressed in robes of silk and was wearing a hat made of birch. This custom of birchen hats must have been known until recent times because it is mentioned in the Scottish poem 'The Wife of Usher's Well', where a mother's three sons return to her from the dead on the eve of Martinmass, each wearing a hat 'o the birk' which grew at the gates of paradise. The resurrecting abilities of birch may also account for the cryptic reference in the '*Cad Godeu*' which states: 'We have emanated from birches/He who disenchants will restore us'.

Birch's qualities of youthfulness and love suggest that it was associated with the Celtic god of love, Aongus. Aongus was the *mac óg* – 'the young son' – whose beauty was so great that four of his kisses were said to follow him around in the form of birds. Aongus also provided help to the lovers Diarmuid and Gráinne to escape the pursuing Fianna. Aongus' Nordic equivalent, the god Baldur, may have a connection with the rune letter called Berkana (or birch). A Norwegian poem about the rune states simply that Loki, the Norse god of mischief, was fortunate in his deceit. As Loki's most infamous act of deceit was to have Baldur killed with a spike of mistletoe, the poem may be a cryptic reference linking Baldur to the rune. In Ireland other youthful heroes have references to birch.[7] In the story of Cúchulainn's boyhood deeds his hair is described as having 50 tresses between one ear and the other and being 'bright yellow like the top of a birch tree'. Again Lóeguire, one of the chief warriors of the Ulaid, is described as having 'short reddish hair that shone like the crown of a birch tree at the end of autumn'.

SEASONAL PLACING

Another link between the birch and Aongus is that both are associated with the sun. We have seen how birch featured in many summer time festivities and it is not hard to see how its shining white bark would link it with the sun. Aongus also has a link with the sun as his chief residence was in Brú na Bóinne or Newgrange, famous for the winter solstice sun penetrating its inner chamber. Aongus was born at Newgrange, just as the new sun is 'reborn' there each winter solstice. It was considered in Ireland that Christ was born in midwinter.[8] Is this through an association of Christ with Aongus? Birch is linked with the winter solstice in many places through the custom of the 'beating of the bounds', and Ireland may have been no different. The customs of Gaelic Scotland certainly link birch strongly with the festival of Brigid at the beginning of spring, so there can be little doubt in any case that birch was particularly associated with the beginning of the year in Gaelic culture. Birch is associated with the Ogham letter *Beith* which itself means birch. The birch is also the first tree to have colonised open ground, making it a suitable tree to begin the alphabet, with the added virtue of B being the first consonant of the Latin alphabet.

THE USES OF BIRCH

In early Irish law birch was classified as an *Aithig fedo* or Commoner of the Wood. Apart from making brooms, dye made from birch bark was used for tanning leather and for preserving fishermen's lines.

Rowan – Caorthann

Sorbus aucuparia - Rowan

2nd consonant of the Ogham Alphabet

24 January-20 February
4th month of Ogham Tree Calendar

The rowan or mountain ash has always been considered a tree of formidable magical and protective powers due to its bright flame red berries. An alternative name, 'quicken', refers to its 'quickening' or life giving powers, while the Irish name caorthann *derives from the word* caor *which means both a berry and a blazing flame.*

FOLK BELIEFS AND CUSTOMS

There are many examples of the protective powers of rowan against evil forces.[1] According to A.T. Lucas the rowan was hung in the house to prevent fire-charming, used to keep the dead from rising, and tied on a hound's collar to increase its speed. Above all it was used to protect milk and its products from supernatural harm, was kept in the byre to safeguard the cows, and put in the pail and around the churn to ensure that the 'profit' in the milk was not stolen. In Scotland rowan was placed over the lintels of the barn, stable and other buildings to keep away witchcraft, and a twig of rowan made into a circlet was placed beneath the milk boynes to keep the milk from being spirited away. The berries were used to safeguard animals and guard against mishap. A poem about a black mare which was 'a kicking and a running' recommends a 'handful of red rowan berries to safeguard her'. In the Isle of Man crosses of rowan were tied to the tails of cattle and in Yorkshire whipstocks were made of rowan.

In Scotland it was also believed that rowan wood should be used for the cross beams of the chimney, and for various implements including the distaff, the churn staff, the peg of the cow shackle, and the pin of the plough or water mill. Highland women wore necklaces of rowan berries as a charm. A rowan tree was also commonly planted at the door of the homestead to keep witches away. So strong was this particular custom that it was carried on in New Zealand by Scottish settlers. In Ireland it was believed that rowan in the house prevented fire. In Scotland flail rods were also made of mountain ash to keep the witches from threshing the corn and carrying away the grain.

In Wales rowan was considered to give protection against demons and rowan trees are often found planted in Welsh churchyards. In Scotland a coffin made of rowan, or a coffin bier carried on spokes of rowan, was treated with special reverence. In Ireland a walking stick of rowan offered good protection against the fairies and one tale describes how a stick of green rowan wood allows a man to enter a fairy fort safely to steal a magic drinking horn. Rowan was also placed on hats to keep away the fairies. In a similar Scottish tale, a person is advised to wear a cross of rowan on his clothing to enable him to enter a fairy hill to rescue his brother. It was also believed in Scotland that a person held captive dancing in a fairy ring could be pulled to safety by holding out a pole of rowan for them to grasp onto. A Scottish charm against witchcraft recommends a tuft of rowan twigs tied up in a red thread. One Irish folk tale tells of how a boat which was sinking due to a hag's curse was saved by a sprig of rowan.

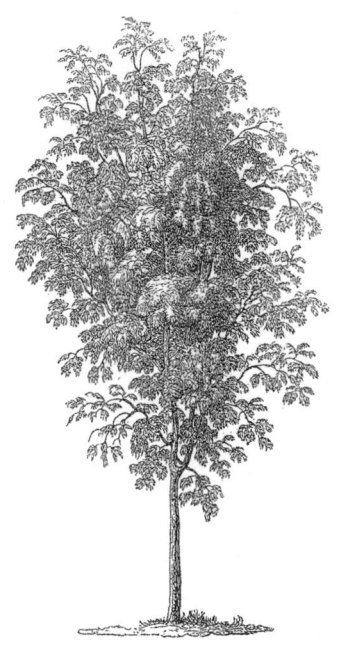

Lucas speculates that all these magical uses may have come from Viking settlers, as rowan bark shavings were used as fodder in

Scandinavia, but I think he is trying too hard to find a 'practical' origin for rowan's magical uses. It is clear from the evidence that it was the rowan's red berries which gave it power. The fact that the rowan was considered magical in both Ireland and Scandinavia is not evidence in itself that one place borrowed directly from another. The tree folklore of all of Northern Europe is very similar in many respects, as we shall see.

Given its connection with livestock and fire it is not surprising that rowan should be particularly associated with the month of May.[2] In ancient Ireland at this time livestock were driven between twin fires to keep away evil influences. Homes, crops and cattle were believed to be particularly at risk on May Eve. The first smoke from a chimney on May morning should be from a fire of rowan, in order to thwart any mischief that witches might be planning. A piece of mountain ash was put in the crops, and cattle going out that morning were struck with a switch of the wood. On May Eve a loop of rowan was put on the tails of livestock, especially cows, to protect them from the fairies. Alternatively red rags or thread were used. Rowan was a favourite for use as May boughs. On May Eve sprigs were put on window sills and door steps and roofs and could also be set up in fields and farmyards for protection. In the Isle of Man twigs of rowan were also set up around the house on May Eve. In Scotland on May Eve sheep and lambs were made to pass through a hoop of rowan. However, rowan was also associated with other times of the year.[3] In Scotland sprigs of rowan were burnt on the doorsteps of the byre on the first day of the quarter, on Beltane and Hallowmass; and bannocks were toasted on a fire of rowan wood on St Michael's Eve and the Feast Day of Mary (15 August). Houses were also decked with rowan on New Year's Day. In Wales people wore Easter crosses made of the wood.

LEGENDS AND MYTHOLOGY

Rowan was also noted for its life-giving properties. 'The Pursuit of Diarmuid and Gráinne' features a famous rowan called 'The Quicken Tree of Dubhros' whose berries had many virtues. The berries gave both the exhilaration of wine and the satisfaction of rich food, and no sickness or disease hit anyone who ate three of them. So life giving were they that if someone 100 years old tasted them, they would return to the age of 30. In the story the tree is guarded by a one eyed giant called the 'Searbhán Lochlannach' or the Surly Scandinavian, whom Diarmuid has to kill before he can fulfil Gráinne's request to get some of the berries. In the story 'The Cattle Raid of Fróech', Ailill demands that Fróech swim across a river, and bring him back a branch from a rowan growing there whose fruits were supposed to prolong life and heal illness. I believe that both trees in these tales, however, may actually have been cherry trees in the original versions. The *Lays of Fionn* make mention of the Rowan Tree of Clonfert, under which the warrior Iollan stayed awake for 'seventeen day-thirds' having taken but one draught of clear water and five berries of the rowan. Another Lay concerning the *caorthann cas* or 'wry rowan' explicitly credits the red colour of the rowan's berries with its power. The Lay claims that one look at the colour of the berries would satisfy a person who had gone nine days without food.

Iubhdan's poem about the properties of different woods calls rowan *fid na ndruad* or 'the druid's tree' and it is not hard to see why. In the tale 'The Siege of Knocklong' druids on both sides made immense fires of rowan, cut and lit ritually and with incantations, to put a sinister influence on the opposing side. The outcome of the battle was seen in the smoke and flames of the fire.[4] Keating's *History of Ireland* tells how the druids used the hides of sacrificial bulls stretched over a construction of rowan branches for the purposes of divination. *The Book of Invasions* recounts how the Philistines used skewers of hazel and rowan to slay the demons fashioned by the Tuatha Dé Danann, by thrusting them behind their necks. In the tale 'The House of the Quicken Trees', Fionn and his men are trapped through enchantment by an enemy in a house of that name. The *Metrical Dindshenchus* also has a story in which a warrior named Eochaid (rider) set the head of the son of Conn of the Hundred Battles on a spike of rowan outside Tara. This led to his banishment into Leinster because this action was taboo. An ancient druidic ordeal for a woman clearing her name was to rub her tongue to a red hot adze, which would be heated in a fire of rowan or blackthorn wood. [5]

Rowan's powers could be used by witches. In the tale 'The Wooing of Étain', Étain's rival Fúamnach strikes Étain with a wand of scarlet rowan, turning her into a pool of water. In the Lay known as 'The Headless Phantoms', Fionn and his men take shelter in a sinister house where a churl kills their horses and roasts them on spits of rowan. They are then attacked by three phantoms who seek to avenge the death of their sister. In the tale concerning Cúchulainn's death, the hero is offered dog meat to eat by three hags who have been cooking it with charms on rods of rowan. It is taboo for Cúchulainn to eat dog, but also taboo to refuse offered food, so he loses some of his strength in accepting the meal. An Irish tradition states that the first woman sprang from a mountain ash. [6]

One legend tells of how St Patrick banished a fire spitting monster called the Caorthannach. St Patrick had pursued the monster from Croagh Patrick and she had quenched all the wells which she passed on the way. St Patrick, overcome with thirst, prays for water and the Hawkes Well in Sligo springs up beside him. Suitably refreshed, he is able to banish the monster with a single word.[7]

Seasonal Placing

Rowan shares with St Brigid an association with fire and the protection of livestock, so it is logical to link rowan with her. St Brigid 'of the flame' had a perpetual fire in Kildare which was tended by Brigid and nineteen nuns, and she was credited in tales with the power to multiply milk, butter and bacon. These attributes were undoubtedly transferred to the saint from the older goddess, thereby placing rowan with the feast of Brigid at the start of spring in the tree calendar. The rowan berries may also be still on the tree at this time of year, making it a more suitable choice than May time. Rowan is associated with the Ogham letter *Luis* which means 'flame'.

The Uses of Rowan

In early Irish law rowan was classified as an *Aithig fedo* or Commoner of the Wood. In medieval times rowan berries were used either as food or fermented into a drink resembling perry. Rowan wood is tough and was used for a variety of implements.

Alder – Fearnóg

Alnus glutinosa - Alder

21 February-20 March
5th month of Ogham Tree
Calendar

3rd consonant of the Ogham Alphabet

The alder, because it was traditionally used to make shields, and because its wood when cut turns from white to blood red, was considered to be a tree of war and death. Alder is associated with both fire, on account of its red colour, and water, because it grows in marshy places.

FOLK BELIEFS AND CUSTOMS

According to an old Irish tradition it was believed that the first man sprang from an alder.[1] However, in Irish tradition the alder is an unlucky tree which is best avoided, and it is especially unlucky to pass an alder during a journey. The Irish do not like felling the wood because it soon changes from white to red, like blood.[2] This association was shared by the Germans and Goethe's famous poem 'Erlkonig' (properly translated as the 'Alder King') refers to a Danish legend about an alder king who carries away children to their deaths.[3] Two Scottish stories also link alder with death.[4] One tells of a bridegroom who has apparently died and been buried, and returns to tell his bride that he has in fact been taken by the fairies. After he is rescued from them his tomb is opened and there is nothing inside but a log of alder wood. A similar story tells of a woman being abducted by the fairies and a log of alder left in her place. Alder is also believed to be beloved of water spirits in Ireland, especially the white fairy horse.[5]

LEGENDS AND MYTHOLOGY

Mad Sweeney, the seventh-century king, seems to be out of step with these negative images, as he has this to say: 'O alder you are

not an enemy/delightful is your hue/you are not rending and prickly/in the gap where you are'. Perhaps Sweeney feels an affinity to the alder as a fellow outcast, or else it is some kind of reference to alder's protective use as a shield. There are some instances of alder's warlike nature being miraculously tamed. Gerald of Wales in his account of Ireland relates how Cormac Mac Cuileannán planted an apple-bearing alder tree. The life of St Brigid tells of how the saint blest an alder so that it bore two-thirds apples and one-third sweet sloes.

Alder is noted for its use in making shields and huge Bronze Age shields made of alder wood have been found in Ireland. In the Welsh poem the '*Cad Godeu*', of a large number of trees hastening to the battle the alder is 'at the head of the line/thrust forward the first in time', which is probably a comparison to a shield. There are numerous references in literature to red and fiery shields which may well have been made of alder. In the story 'The Battle of Ventry', the king of Norway had a shield which had red flames shooting from it. In 'The Martial Career of Conghal Cloiringhneach', Conghal, who is described as 'son of Rudhraighe, the red', has battalions armed with 'red, beautifully coloured shields'. In the tale 'The king of Norway's sons' two champions fight with 'two handsome, flower red, speckled, lastingly lettered shields' (is this last a reference to Ogham inscriptions?). A well-known folk-tale links alder to flame.[6] A farmer is cutting branches off an alder, which overshadowed an ancient holy well, when he sees his cottage in flames. When he rushes home his house is fine and so he returns to cutting the tree. Again he sees his cottage in flames, and, rushing to the spot, again sees nothing. The third time he ignores the sight of his flaming cottage, and returning with his bundle of wood he finds his cottage burnt to the ground.

There is evidence to believe that alder was the 'red branch' of the Red Branch Knights or Ulstermen.[7] The Ulstermen's original family name was Clann Rudhraighe and from this the word *ruadh* or red came to be linked to them. Medieval writers interpreted the term *Craobh ruadh* or 'red branch' to mean that the palace of the Ulstermen was supported by posts of red yew. However, the alder, with its warlike connotations, would make a better candidate, and it does appear several times in connection with the Ulstermen. In the story 'The Intoxication of the Ulaid', the druid Cromm Deróil speaks of seeing from afar the advancing 'red-armoured company' of the Ulstermen. He then goes on to recite a poem with the following lines: 'If they were a grove of alder trees/over the wood of a cairn/ they would not follow a deceptive path/they being dead' and later: 'men of triumphs these men of alder shields/ red their weapons'. Geoffrey Grigson, in his anthology of poems *The Cherry*

Tree, quotes an early version of Yeats' poem 'The Death of Cúchulainn' where Concobar, the king of Ulster, commands his druids to cast a spell to make Cúchulainn vent his rage at the unwitting killing of his own son Finmole on the waves of the sea. The druids cast a spell by chanting and holding 'tall wands of alder and white quicken wands'. In another story, the warrior Ulaid called Celtchar killed a ferocious dog by thrusting a hardened alder stick into its mouth. When the dog locked onto the stick Celtchar shoved his hand down the dog's throat and ripped out its heart.

In the Welsh tale 'Branwen daughter of Llyr', Branwen, sister of Bran, the king of Britain, is married to the king of Ireland Mallolwch. Their young son, Gwern (literally 'alder') is invested with the kingship of Ireland in order to bring peace between Ireland and Britain. No sooner is this done, however, than the Welshman Evnissyen takes the boy and thrusts him head first into a fire. In the ensuing battle most warriors on both sides are killed. The precise significance of this is not clear but it links alder to the motif of a king's death, to war, and to fire. Robert Graves, in his book on folklore *The White Goddess*, quotes a reference from the *Myvyrian Archaiology* where Bran's name is guessed because of alder: 'The high sprigs of alder are on thy shield/Bran thou art called of the glittering branches' and again: 'The high sprigs of alder are in thy hand/ Bran thou art, by the branch thou bearest'. This is probably because Bran is also the name for a raven, a bird associated with war, blood and death, like alder. Iubhdan in his poem about different woods describes alder as *fern úrbadb fheda, an crann is teo i ngliaid* – 'Alder, great scaldcrow of woods, hottest in the fight'.

Alder was associated with the Celtic cult of the head, involving Celtic warriors keeping the heads of those slain in battle. The ancient Celts believed that the head was the seat of a person's soul and the source of power. The Roman author Lucan in his poem 'Pharsalia' describes a famous druidic grove at Marsalia known for its atmosphere of gloom and dread. Among the trees described as growing there were yew, cypress, ash and alder, and according to Lucan, severed heads hung from the trees. In the *Táin* Cúchulainn smites off the heads of his enemies and arranges them on stones. Bran's severed head is kept by his warriors and buried at the hill of

London to protect Britain from its enemies. Cormac's *Glossary* has the story about the fool Lomna warning Fionn of his wife's infidelity in a cryptic message, where he uses alder to symbolically refer to a man. Lomna is later beheaded and his severed head speaks to Fionn. As the cult of the head is intimately linked to the themes of war and death, it is not surprising that alder should appear in the same contexts.

There is evidence of the alder being considered sacred.[8] A name of an ancient Celtic tribe was 'Guerngen' or 'son of the alder'. In Ebchester, near Hadrian's Wall there is a dedication to the god Vernostonus, the personification of the alder tree. Vernostonus is a variant of the god Cocidius, whose name derives from 'red'. Cocidius was the local war and hunting god equated with Mars and Silvanus, the Roman god of woodland.

The alder's associations with kingship, war and death seem to link it with Donn, the god of the underworld and his variations, particularly figures like Da Derga. In the story 'The Destruction of Da Derga's Hostel', the king Conaire on his way to the hostel meets three red creatures. Not only are they dressed in red, with red shields and spears, but their teeth and hair are red as well. Greeting Conaire they inform him that their name is also Derg (or Red) and make the following extraordinary speech: 'We ride the horses of Donn Tétscórach of the Síde. Although we are alive we are dead. Great omens! Cutting off of lives, satisfaction of crows, sustenance of ravens, din of slaughter, whetting of blades, shields with broken bosses after sunset. Behold!' This is an omen of Conaire's own death. He is attacked at the hostel and after a fierce fight is beheaded, and, after being given a drink from a sacred gold cup, his head then recites a poem.

SEASONAL PLACING
Frazer recounts many customs from European countries about the

king of the old year, or death, being symbolically killed around Easter or Maytime to make way for the king of the new year or summer. Whether alder's seasonal placing in spring has anything to do with this is a matter of conjecture. In any case spring is a suitable time to place alder as this is when the alder produces its catkins and the red sap begins to swell its purple buds. Alder is associated with the Ogham letter *Fern* which itself means alder.

THE USES OF ALDER

In early Irish law alder was classified as an *Aithig fedo* or Commoner of the Wood. Apart from shields, alder wood was used to make bowls and other containers and for making charcoal. The catkins and bark were used to make a black dye.

Willow – Saileach

Salix caprea - Goat willow
Salix Cinerea - Grey willow

21 March-17 April
6th month of Ogham Tree Calendar

4th consonant of the Ogham Alphabet

The willow, with its honey-providing catkins, its quick growing nature and habit of growing next to water is a symbol of fertility and life. Another name for the willow is the Sallow or Sally, which has the same origin as the Latin name Salix.

FOLK BELIEFS AND CUSTOMS

The willow, particularly the weeping willow, is nowadays firmly linked to grief in the popular mind. According to Roy Vickery, in his book *A Dictionary of PLant Lore*, this association of willow with grief probably stems from Psalm 137: 'By the rivers of Babylon we sat down and wept/when we remembered Zion./There on the willow trees/we hung up our harps.' In the sixteenth and seventeenth centuries the custom of jilted lovers wearing wreaths or caps of willow became widespread, and many poems about unrequited love mention the willow. However, Vickery states that recent biblical scholars have stressed that the trees mentioned in the psalm were actually poplars rather than willows. This makes sense, as the aspen, the native Irish tree of the poplar family, is associated with misfortune.

Certainly in Irish folklore the associations of willow could not be more different.[1] Suibhne Geilt or Mad Sweeney calls the willow *sail ghlann grinn* or the 'bright cheerful sallow'. Iubhdan in his poem of Irish woods says: 'Do not burn the noble willow, enduring in verse/bees the blossoms suck, all love its graceful curves'. In Ireland it is lucky to take a sally rod with you on a journey and a peeled sally rod placed around a milk churn will ensure good butter. In Cairbre in west Cork if the butter was not coming, rods of

willow were put around the churn, after which the butter would be sure to come. On St Patrick's Day in Cill Rialaig in Kerry, everyone would wear a '*cros cipín dóite*' or 'cross of charred pin' made of burnt sally twigs on their right arms, and this was the custom throughout east Kerry. A variation of this in County Cork involved the burnt rods simply being used to mark a cross on the right arm. That this might have something to do with increasing fertility is strengthened by the folk cure that willow charcoal can bring back the hair on an animal where it had been rubbed off.

Willow features in the customs of other countries also.[2] In many parts of Europe willow was traditionally used instead of palm on Palm Sunday and in some parts of England it was considered unlucky to bring flowering willow indoors before Palm Sunday. White willow was also one of the woods which was used in Scotland as 'Bride's Wand' in the Bride's Eve ceremonies. In Essex willows kept away witches if planted near the door and willow twigs hung on the door kept away marsh witches. In Herefordshire, willow brings good luck if brought into the house on May Day and is potent against the evil eye. However, a young animal or child struck with a sally rod will cease to grow afterwards. In Shropshire ,willow catkins are thought to resemble young goslings and should never be brought into the house. If they are, any real goslings will never be hatched. According to the Scottish folklorist Carmichael, the woolly catkins of the willow were particularly good for protecting milk. The catkin wool was spun while the following verse was recited: 'I will pluck the catkin wool/as plucked the Mother of God through her hand/for luck, for kine, for milking/for herds, for increase, for cattle'. The wool, twined into a cord, was then placed under milk to protect it from evil spirits.

Willow is well known for its long, pliable shoots, which are used in basket making and wickerwork. Robert Graves states that the words 'wicker', 'witch' or 'wych' (as in wych elm) derive from the same root but this is not strictly true. The words all derive from an Old English word meaning 'to bend or yield', but the other word 'witch' (as in a woman with magical powers) has a different origin. Graves is right though when he quotes the seventeenth-century herbalist Culpeper's comment about willow, i.e., 'the moon owns it'. In Scotland it was believed that withes of willow or hazel should never be cut while the moon was on the wane as the wood would be brittle and dry.[3] Perhaps it was willow's reputation as a pliant and supple wood that gave rise to the curious belief in Ireland that willow could create an uncontrollable inclination to dance. By placing a willow wand over the lintel of a door , the inhabitants could be made to dance without stop.[4] Something similar may be involved in the Welsh tradition that willow was considered good for curing the shaking ailment ague. The cure involved breathing into a hole in the willow three times.[5]

LEGENDS AND MYTHOLOGY

Even if the trees mentioned in Psalm 137 were poplars, the mention of harps in connection with the willow does have parallels in Ireland. The Irish harp was traditionally made of willow, and the most famous Irish harp of all, Brian Boru's Harp in Trinity College Dublin (which actually dates from the fourteenth century), is made entirely from willow.[6] In Keating's *History of Ireland*, mention is made of a willow harp in the well-known story of the Leinster king Labhraidh Loingseach. The story goes that Labhraidh Loingseach had horse's ears instead of human ones, and as a result he always wore his hair long to hide them. A youth who had been ordered to trim Labhraidh's hair discovers the truth but is sworn to secrecy on pain of death. The burden of keeping the secret causes the youth to fall ill, and he is only cured when on advice he whispers his secret to a willow tree growing near his home. The tree is later cut down and made into a harp by a harpist of the royal court, and brought before Labhraidh for its first playing. However, when the unfortunate harpist tries to play a tune, the only sound the harp will make is to cry out: 'Labhraidh Loingseach has horse's ears!' Word of Labhraidh's secret then spreads the length and breadth of the kingdom.

The association of willow with milk also comes out in a story told by Gerald of Wales in the *History of Ireland*, which concerns a miraculous willow tree that grew near the cell of St Kevin of Glendalough. The story goes that St Kevin took pity on a local boy who was sick and prayed for his health. A nearby willow tree then began to produce miraculous fruit which was health giving to the boy and any others who were sick. The fruit was white and oblong in shape and was nourishing rather than pleasant to the taste. The fruit of St Kevin, as it became known, was later credited with curing many diseases. The suspicion that the fruit was some kind of 'milk-fruit' is reinforced by the story that the ravens of Glendalough, because they had spilled the milk of the sick boy, are forever prohibited from resting or taking food on the Saint's Feast Day.

According to the scholar Miranda Greene in her book *Dictionary of Celtic Myth and Legend*, the willow features in two important Celtic carvings found on the continent.[7] The Paris sculpture features on one side a woodcutter hacking at the branch of a tree above the inscription ESUS, while the other side features leaves accompanied by a bull and three cranes, and the inscription TARVO TRIGARANUS (Bull with Three Cranes). The second carving from Trier shows a woodcutter chopping at a tree, in which is the head of a bull and three cranes. The exact meaning of all this is unknown, but Greene points out that both cranes and willow have an affinity with water, while the close cousin of the crane, the egret, has a close relationship with cattle through its eating of parasites from their hides. Greene speculates that the willow may here represent the Tree of Life that is periodically cut down at winter and reborn at spring. All of this is plausible but I believe a strong case can be made that the tree depicted in the carvings is in fact an ash (see *Ash*). The willow, because of its link with water, milk and cattle, would seem to be particularly associated with river goddesses like Bóinn. Bóinn was pictured in mythology as a great cow with the milk from her udders flowing out to form the rich waters of the river Boyne.

SEASONAL PLACING
The customs linking willow to St Patrick's Day and Palm Sunday, and the importance attached to its catkins, mean there is no difficulty placing willow seasonally in the middle of springtime. The willow is associated with the Ogham letter *Sail* which itself means willow.

THE USES OF WILLOW
In early Irish law willow was classified as an *Aithig fedo* or Commoner of the Wood. Apart from wickerwork and harps, willow was also used to make various household implements.

Cherry – Silín

Prunus avium - Wild Cherry
5th consonant of the Ogham Alphabet

The cherry, with its beautiful blossoms and sweet-tasting fruit, is a symbol of youthfulness, beauty and love. The gum from its bark is also believed to help the complexion.

FOLK BELIEFS AND CUSTOMS

In England the cherry tree is associated with the cuckoo.[1] An old English proverb states that the cuckoo never sings till he has thrice eaten his fill of cherries. In Yorkshire children sing around a cherry tree 'cuckoo cherry tree, come down and tell me how many years I have to live'. Each child then shakes the tree and the number of cherries which fall betoken the years of its future life. In the north of England generally, on hearing the cuckoo the following is said, 'Cuckoo, cuckoo! Cherry tree, good bird, tell me how many years before I die?' Alternatively the questioner asks 'how many years shall I be before I get married?' Cherry stones were used by children in a counting rhyme to foretell when a wished for event would come to pass: 'This year, next year, some time, never.'

A traditional English ballad called 'The Cherry Tree Carol' sheds some light on this connection with the cuckoo. The carol tells of St Joseph and the pregnant Mary walking through a cherry orchard. Mary asks Joseph to pick a cherry for her and Joseph bitterly replies, 'Let him pluck thee a cherry that brought thee with child'. At this the infant Jesus speaks from within his mother's womb and commands the tallest tree to bow down to Mary's hand so that she can gather the fruit. At the sight of this Joseph repents his harsh words.[2] The clear implication is that Joseph is piqued because he feels cuckolded and this suggests that the cherry, like the cuckoo, is a symbol of love outside wedlock. No doubt this explains

why in the north of England cherry blossom, particularly wild cherry, was considered an unlucky decoration to have for a wedding![3]

The fruit of the cherry has a sweet taste but a relative lack of nourishment, and this made it a symbol of the fleeting nature of youth and life's pleasures. In medieval England cherry fairs or feasts were held in cherry orchards in July, and they became a symbol of the short stay of man on this earth. A poem of that time states 'This lyfe, I see, is but a cheyre feyre / All thing is passen and so must I'.[4] Perhaps this view of the cherry as a symbol of the death of youth explains the above mentioned children's rhymes where the cherry is asked to tell how long the child will live.

Legends and Mythology

Similar themes are found in Celtic lore.[5] According to Rees and Rees in their acclaimed book, *Celtic Heritage*, in Welsh poetry May was the month of love and extra-marital relations. The husband in these poems is the despised *Yr Eiddig* - the jealous one or cuckold, who is usually portrayed as a older man who prefers the sterility of winter. The poems make frequent reference to the green leaves, birdsong and the cuckoo. In Ireland the cuckoo had similar associations and the Irish word for cuckoo *cuach* is a term of endearment – *mo chuach thú* - 'you are my darling'. It is interesting to note that the rival of the Irish god of love Aongus is similarly called Ealcmhar or 'the envious one'.

The old Irish word for cherry appears to have been 'Idath' and later 'Fidach',[6] and as such it appears in the old Irish tree lists as an 'Aithig Fedo' or 'Commoner of the Wood', the second highest category. There are many examples in the Irish tales of handsome youths with the name 'Idath' or 'Fidach' who are rivals in love with an older man. The best known of these is in the 'Cattle Raid of Fraoch' which tells the story of Fraoch son of Idath (later Fidach) – literally Heather son of Cherry. The story tells how Fraoch, the handsomest warrior in Eriu and Albu, sought the hand of Findabair, the daughter of Ailill and Maedhbh. Out of jealousy, Ailill demands that Fraoch bring him the branch of a rowan tree that grew on a riverbank, knowing that a monster lived in the river. For Findabair seeing Fraoch in the dark water with 'the branch of red berries between his throat and his white face' was the most beautiful thing she had ever seen.[7] The monster attacks Fraoch while he is in the water and Findabair throws him a sword to help him. In some versions of the tale Fraoch dies, while in others he kills the monster and survives to marry

Findabair. Although the tree mentioned is a rowan, it is plausible that the original oral version of the tale merely involved a tree with red berries, with Fraoch's full name signalling that it was a cherry tree. The tree could have easily become identified with the more common rowan in further re-tellings.

Something similar may have happened in the story of 'The Pursuit of Diarmuid and Gráinne' concerning the famous rowan tree called the 'Quicken Tree of Dubhros'. In the story, Fionn Mac Cumhaill demands that two warriors called Aongus and Aodh get some of the berries of the tree for him. Diarmuid is reluctant to help until Gráinne says that she will not lie on a bed again and will die unless she gets a taste of the berries. Diarmuid is then forced to fight the guardian of the tree and kill him to obtain them. The theme of a youth obtaining the berries to help out a woman has echoes both of the Cherry Tree Carol and the story of Fraoch, so it seems plausible that the outline of a story originally involving a cherry was borrowed. In this case Fionn is the bitter elder rival and Diarmuid (whose name means '*Dí-Fhormaid*' or 'without envy') is the handsome youth. It is worth noting how the sweetness of the Quicken tree's berries is strongly emphasised in the story. Although rowan berries are edible they are rather tasteless, and this is the only instance in a tale where they are described as being good to eat.

Youths with the name Fidach appear in other stories.[8] In the tale 'The Wooing of Becfola', Becfola falls in love with a handsome youth called Flann (red) grandson of Fedach who: 'in the firelight, in his armour and raiment, had the loveliest appearance in the world'. Flann defends the island of Fedach against his brothers until they are all killed, and then he and Becfola become man and wife. A handsome, youthful hero called Fidach, son of the King of the Bretons, dies an untimely death in the Fianna story 'The Battle of Ventry'. Fidach is praised by Fergus of the True Lips, one of the Fianna, but he dies shortly afterwards in battle when a flail goes into his 'comely mouth' and kills him outright. Meadhbh, the mythical queen of Connaught, was wooed by a Fidach Mac Féig, but he was intercepted and killed by one of Maedhbh's future husbands, Tinne Mac Connrach.

In addition, the boyhood deeds of Fionn Mac Cumhaill mention his killing with a spear an otherworld warrior called Cúldubh son of Fidgha, 'the very fair'. In another tale involving Fionn, a warrior called Ceithearn with whom Fionn had been staying went to woo a beautiful otherworld maiden at Sídh Éile. The attempt was abandoned when an otherworld warrior called Aedh Mac Fidaigh killed some of Ceithearn's men. In retaliation Fionn then kills Aedh Mac Fidaigh by casting a javelin at him. Fionn is told that Aedh killed all those who came to woo Éile, 'because he himself loved her'. Another Aedh Mac Fidaigh is killed by Fionn's grandson Oscar because he had been given a woman called Niamh whom Oscar loved.

All these stories suggest that the cherry was linked to some version of the story of Aongus the god of love, involved in a struggle with an older rival. This struggle has seasonal overtones with the young hero symbolising summer battling against an older rival who symbolises winter for the goddess of the land. This is the basis of the Diarmuid and Gráinne story.[9] There are also echoes of the Greek legend of Adonis, the short lived handsome youth who dies and is resurrected every year. Like Diarmuid, Adonis was killed by a wild boar. The scarlet anemone is said to have sprung from the blood of Adonis,[10] and this parallels the red berries of the cherry.

Seasonal Placing

The cherry is placed seasonally in late spring and Maytime when it is in bloom and is associated with the Ogham letter *Nin* which means 'Branchfork'.

THE USES OF CHERRY

In early Irish law the cherry was classified as an *Aithig fedo* or Commoner of the Wood. Cherry fruits were gathered as food in Ireland since ancient times and cherry stones have been found in excavations of a late Bronze Age crannog in County Offaly. There is little evidence of cherry wood being used in Ireland in ancient times but its wood is strong and durable, with a colour like mahogany, and was frequently used in furniture making in more recent years.

Hawthorn – Sceach Gheal

Crataegus monogyna - Hawthorn, Whitethorn or May tree

6th consonant of the Ogham Alphabet

18 April-15 May

7th month of Ogham Tree Calendar

|H|

The hawthorn, whitethorn or Maybush, with its white blossoms and thorns is a symbol of Maytime, and of magical powers and the 'little people' or fairies. As such the hawthorn, especially the 'lone bush', has always been regarded with a mixture of fear and respect.

FOLK BELIEFS AND CUSTOMS

There are many stories of harm and even death coming to those who interfere with the fairy thorn, especially the 'lone bush', growing by itself in the open.[1] For example, one story tells of a man who had uprooted a few hawthorn bushes from a fairy circle was found paralysed in his bed the next morning. In another tale a man who took thorn bushes to build his house from the churchyard in Cill Rialaig in Kerry was visited night after night by the fairies, until he returned them. An Ulster story tells of a farmhand who gathered fallen branches from under a fairy thorn to use on the fire. As soon she threw the twigs on the fire the farmer's best red cow fell down in a fit. The girl gathered up the twigs at once and returned them to the bush, and the cow then recovered. Another possible danger told of was that the passer by might get enticed by enchanted music coming from the fairy thorn or rath and be taken away. But one story tells of how the fairies could be generous. A farmer who heeded their warning not to build on a fairy circle was told to build between a certain pair of whitethorns. As he dug the foundations he found a pot of gold.

A widespread belief in Ireland, and elsewhere, was that hawthorn blossom was unlucky. A recent survey carried out by the Folklore Society in Britain found that hawthorn flowers were

considered to be the most unlucky of plants, with death resulting if brought into a house. Recently it has been shown that a chemical present in the early stages of tissue decay is found in hawthorn blossoms, so perhaps an association with the smell of death is the cause.[2] In common with other 'unlucky' trees it was widely held that whitethorn was the tree upon which Christ was crucified, and Christ's crown of thorns was also supposed to be made of whitethorn. In west Cork it was wrong to hit anyone with a stick of hawthorn as it was believed that there was a temper in the tree. If a stick of hawthorn was brought into the house there would be trouble as long as it was there.[3] Similarly in Kerry hawthorn was supposed to have a poison or venom in it. One story from Connaught tells of blood spurting from a lone bush when felled and the person who witnessed this dying.[4]

Whitethorn was also known for its general magical and protective powers.[5] In Scotland the work of a cattle thief was thought to be made easier by waving a wand of hawthorn and chanting a rhyme which called on 'every beast that bears milk' to come to him.

Similarly, if a neighbour in Ireland used a whitethorn stick to drive his cattle, he was suspected of the worst. An old custom was that the first milk of a newly calved cow was taken and poured under a fairy tree as a tribute. Hawthorn was planted around houses to keep away witches. In Wales hawthorns of a huge size are often found near old houses. Hawthorn was also known for its powers of fertility. At a stone circle near Naas, County Kildare called Longstone Rath, girls hoping to get married hammered pins into a hawthorn tree growing inside the ring. An English tale tells of how, when a certain thorn bush was cut down no chicken would lay eggs, cow would calf, or woman have babies. The situation was only rectified when a new bush was planted.

The hawthorn featured heavily in Maytime customs both in Ireland and abroad.[6] Throughout Ireland a suitable bush, usually hawthorn, was cut down and brought before the house or other conspicuous spot and decorated with flowers, ribbons, eggshells, and other bright scraps of material. Sometimes candles or rushlights were attached to the bush and lit at dusk on May Eve. In Dublin in particular the festivities were marked by rival groups trying to steal each other's hawthorn bushes. In many places bonfires were lit beside the bush, and at the end of the festivities the bush would be thrown into it. In some places the tradition of leaving small gifts of food and drink at the foot of a lone bush or fairy fort was carried out. In Kerry the custom of some older people was to leave hawthorn blossoms on the dresser during the month of May to keep away evil. In Laois sprigs of whitethorn which had been sprinkled with holy water were stuck down in the field on May Day to prevent the fairies from taking the crops. In Pembrokeshire, in Wales, on May Eve people would turn out in troops bearing hawthorn branches in full blossom. The branches would be stuck outside the windows of the houses. However, it was unlucky to bring the branches indoors. In Carmarthenshire it was customary on May Eve to plant a whitethorn tree by the door of the house, and in Gwent a cross of birch or whitethorn over the door on May Eve was the commonest way of counteracting a witch's spell. In Cornwall the maid servant who brought a hawthorn branch inside of the house on 1 May was entitled to a dish of cream.

LEGENDS AND MYTHOLOGY

The whitethorn is closely associated with holy wells.[7] A survey carried by A.T. Lucas of 210 randomly chosen wells found that 103 had hawthorns present at them. Usually the wells were known for their healing properties and pilgrims often left offerings of rags hanging on the tree. One famous example is St Kieran's well at Clonmacnoise. On the saint's day people would hang offerings of rags on the whitethorn next to the well while they circled the well and prayed. Another such was All Saint's well near Banaher, County Offaly where offerings were also left on the trees. St Patrick's well in Downpatrick has a thorn bush growing beside it and was believed to overflow and effect cures on Midsummer Eve. A well associated with St Colmcille was called *Tobar an Deilg* (well of the thorn). The legend says that the saint had a thorn in his foot which he bathed at the well. The thorn came out and grew into a tree. In Listerling parish in County Kilkenny a thorn bush beside a holy well is believed to have grown from St Moling's walking stick. There are also many well-known 'lone bushes' which do not grow beside wells.[8] The Maguire chiefs were inaugurated at a thorn tree in Lisnaskeagh fort, County Fermanagh. In County Kilkenny there was a St Leonard's Bush, a sprig or chip of which was believed to guard against shipwreck. In County Offaly there is a whitethorn associated with St Kieran which stands in the middle of the public road because the local authority dared not cut it down when the road was being widened. In England a famous hawthorn which was said to have grown at Glastonbury was believed to have sprung from the staff of Joseph of Arimathea.

Eugene O'Curry describes an old Irish method of satire known as *Glam Dichenn* or 'Satire from the Hill Tops' involving the hawthorn.[9] A poet fasted on the lands of a king on whom the satire was to be uttered and then joined six other poets at sunrise to visit the top of a hill where a hawthorn was growing. Their backs were to be turned to the tree, with a north wind blowing. Having a perforated stone and a thorn in both hands, each man sang a satirical verse. All seven then laid their stone and thorn under the hawthorn. If they were in the wrong the ground would swallow them up, but if the king was in the wrong then this fate would befall him and his wife, son, steed and hound. In Cath Maigue Tuiread (battle of Moytirra) the poet Cairpre, son of Étain, declares he will carry out this procedure in order to satirise his opponents the Fomhoire. The magician Merlin is also linked with the hawthorn. An early Welsh poem describes the abode of Merlin as being in a bush of whitethorn laden with bloom,[10] while according to Breton legend Merlin lies in an enchanted sleep in the forest of Broceliande under the shade of a hawthorn tree.[11] The Welsh poem the '*Cad Godeu*' says: 'the whitethorn checked all/its virus ached in the palm'.

Ysbaddaden Pencawr or 'Hawthorn Chief Giant' features in the Welsh tale of Culhwch and Olwen. Ysbaddaden is the jealous father who sets seemingly impossible tasks for the suitor Culhwch. He has one huge eye which requires attendants to raise his eyelids by means of forks, and is the Welsh equivalent of Balor of the Evil Eye. This image of the huge single eye is believed to symbolise the scorching sun. Similarly Ysbidinongyl is a giant's castle in the Welsh tale of Peredur, which means something like 'thorny castle'. In Norse mythology Odin's father, who is a giant, is called Bolthorn or 'evil thorn'. In Indian legend the thorn tree was believed to have grown from a claw and feather of the god of lightning Agni who assumed the form of a falcon.[12] It is commonly believed in many regions of England today that thorn trees provide certain protection from lightning. The evidence suggests a link between the hawthorn and the god Belinus who is the Celtic Apollo. Belinus, like Apollo, was a solar god associated with healing, and many healing wells and springs on the continent were known to be dedicated to him. The name Belinus meaning 'bright' or 'brilliant', is related to Balor in origin and the Irish name for May, 'Bealtaine', is believed to derive from 'Bel-Tine' or 'The Fire of Bel'. Also, the smith god Goibhniu, who is a variant of the sun god, features strongly in Irish folklore. Smiths were traditionally feared for their ability with spells

Cherry – Silín
Prunus avium

Hawthorn – Sceach Gheal
Crataegus monogyna

Oak – Dair
Quercus robur (showing lammas [August] growth)

Holly – Cuileann
Ilex aquifolium

and charms, and Goibhniu is invoked in an old Irish charm to remove a thorn: 'Very sharp is the awl of Goibhniú, let Goibhniú walk away from it'.[13]

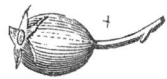

SEASONAL PLACING

All of the evidence clearly places hawthorn in the season of Maytime and the start of the bright half of the year in Irish tradition. Hawthorn is associated with the Ogham letter *hUath* which means 'Fear'.

THE USES OF HAWTHORN

Hawthorn was classified in early Irish law as an *Aithig fedo* or Commoner of the Wood. Although hawthorn's wood is tough, it does not appear to have been used much in Ireland. The haws have been eaten but usually only when there is no other food available.

Oak – Dair

Quercus petraea - Sessile oak
Quercus robur - Pedunculate oak
7th consonant of the Ogham Alphabet

13 June-10 July
9th month of Ogham Tree Calendar

The oak provides strong and excellent timber and a plentiful crop of acorns which provides food for many animals. This, together with its stately bearing and long life, make it a symbol of strength, fertility, kingship and endurance.

FOLK BELIEFS AND CUSTOMS

The oak was used for kindling the bonfires or 'needfires' of May time and midsummer in Scotland and Wales.[1] In North Uist in Scotland a sandy plain bore the name of 'Sail Dharaich'or 'Oak Log'. A beam of oak lay there from which the people produced the need fires. Similar customs existed on the islands of Skye, Mull and Tiree. The Beltane fire was kindled by rubbing a drill made of oak in a bore hole of an oak plank and similar customs were followed in Wales. A Scottish custom involved the toasting of a bannock on St Michael's Eve on a fire of rowan or oak wood. Perhaps these customs explain the description in a Scots Gaelic poem of the oak as being 'of the sun'. In Wales May Day fires were kindled by rubbing two bits of oak together over kindling consisting of nine different types of wood. This association of oak with fire had a more sinister side. J.W. Campbell states in his book on the folk tales of the Scottish Highlands that whenever a man is to be burned for some evil deed, faggots of green oak are used for the task, and recounts a tale of how a king, on learning of his sons' cowardice calls for faggots of green oak for a fire to burn them.[2] In Wales the May Day festivities generally also involved gatherings on the village green around a small mound called a *twmpath*, which would often be decked with oak branches. A musician, usually a harpist or fiddler sat on the mound

while playing. These festivities often also occurred at other times throughout the summer.[3] Interestingly, the Dagda possessed a harp called *'Daur Dá Bláo'* or the Oak of Two Meadows, on which he played peaceful, sorrowful, and joyful music.

The oak has associations with magic and the otherworld.[4] In Scotland a highlander would draw a circle around himself with an oak sapling to protect himself from the fairies. In Brittany a piece of oak wood is used as a talisman. In the *Táin*, Cúchulainn writes a piece of Ogham on an oak sapling while adopting a magical posture, and twists it around a standing stone in order to hinder the armies of Maedhbh. He later lays a great oak tree in a gap and writes Ogham on it for the same purpose. A poem in the *Metrical Dindshenchus* about the Slige Dála talks about the ancient lore of Samhain being learned in oakwoods 'from spirits and fairy folk'. In

'The Pursuit of Diarmuid and Gráinne', the pair stop at a place called *Doire Dá Bhaoth* (Oakwood of the Two Fools) and Diarmuid cuts seven doors of wood from the grove to protect them. These may have had magical significance as the Fianna are unable to pass through them, and are forced to wait for Diarmuid to come out. There is also a play on words here between *doire* (oak grove) and *doirse* (doors).

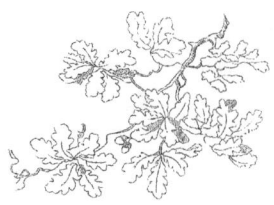

LEGENDS AND MYTHOLOGY

The oak is nowadays seen as the supreme tree of the druids. This image derives mainly from the Roman naturalist Pliny who wrote as follows: 'The druids .... hold nothing more sacred than the mistletoe and the tree that bears it, always supposing that tree to be an oak. But they choose groves formed of oaks for the sake of the tree alone, and they never perform any of their rites except in the presence of a branch of it; so that it seems probable that the priests themselves may derive their name from the Greek word for that tree.' Pliny then went on to describe the much quoted ritual of the Gaulish druids cutting mistletoe from the oak tree with a golden sickle after sacrificing two white bulls. The Greek scholar Maximus of Tyre, writing in the second century, commented that the Celts worshipped the lightning god Zeus in the form of high oak trees. There is archaeological evidence to back up these assertions.[5] A column erected near Stuttgart to the Celtic Jupiter by Romanised Celts is adorned with oak leaves and acorns, and a depiction of the Celtic sun god at Séguret in Provence is accompanied by an oak tree with a serpent twined about it. The Gaulish god Apollo Vindonnus had offerings of oak objects made to him at a healing spring sacred to him near Burgundy. Near Scarborough, at a funeral mound at Gristhorpe, there was found a bronze age oak coffin covered in oak branches together with the remains of mistletoe, an old man's skeleton, and in Brittany many megalithic tombs contain a bedding of oak leaves. Also, according to the Greek scholar Strabo, the Galatians (Celts living in Asia Minor) had their central meeting place at Drunemeton or 'the oak grove sanctuary'. The *'Cad Godeu'* has this to say about the oak: 'Before the swift oak darts/heaven and earth did quake' and 'Oak saplings ensnared us/by the incantation of the oak-priest'.

This would appear to be strong evidence that the oak was considered by the druids to be their most sacred tree but the argument has flaws. In the first place, it is now considered by most scholars that, contrary to Pliny's assertion, the name 'druid' most likely comes from the Celtic *dru-vid* meaning 'very knowledgeable'.[6] Secondly, while the evidence points to the oak being associated with the Celtic Zeus or Jupiter, this does not mean that other deities and their associated trees were not considered as important. Strong evidence points to the equal importance of the Celtic mother goddess and her associated trees, the ash and yew. Lastly, this tells us nothing about what tree or trees were considered important to the druids *as druids*, and here the evidence contradicts Pliny's assertion that the oak was needed for every druidic rite. The rowan and whitethorn were prized for their magical properties, and the hazel for the mystical power of its nuts.

Nevertheless, the oak was a very important tree to the Celts, and its lore is rich and complex. In Ireland, several well-known Christian sites are associated with oak groves which were probably chosen for their pre-Christian significance.[7] Among them are Daire Calgaich or Derry founded by Saint Colmcille, and the monastic school at Maigh Daireach (Oak Plain) or Durrow. So great was his regard for his oakwood at Derry that Colmcille declared that he was more fearful of the sound of axes in it than he was of death! Another site was Cill Dara (the Church of the Oak) or Kildare, founded by St Brigid. The high oak tree there was considered blessed by her and remained for many years as a source of miracles.

The oak is a symbol of kingship, because of its connotations of strength and fertility.[8] The word for oak in Irish also means a chief and the same is true in Welsh. The *Annals of Connaught* for the year

1442 describe the children of the king Ardgar Mor Mag Mathgamna as 'fragrant trees and mighty oaks of bounty' for their generosity in distributing horses and treasure, money to every suppliant. In the story of Cormac Mac Airt's visit to Manannán Mac Lir, he sees a man kindling a fire by throwing a thick oak tree upon it. But by the time the man arrived with a second oak, the first one would be burnt out. Manannán later explains that this represents a young lord who is more generous than he can afford, with everyone but himself benefiting from his largesse. The sons of Tuireann praise the king Tuis as the oak above the kings: 'that is, as the oak is beyond the kingly trees of the wood, so are you beyond the kings of the world for open handedness and for grandeur'. Keating's *History of Ireland* tells of the king Fachtna Mac Seancha Macuill who had a direct link with the land's fertility. If he gave a bad judgement at harvest time, all the acorns would fall off the trees. However, if his judgement was a good one, the oaks retained their fruits.

The most famous oak tree in Irish legend, the Oak of Mugna (Moone County Kildare), was closely associated with kingship. It was planted by the mythical figure Fintan Mac Bóchna but remained hidden from view until it appeared at the time of the birth of the legendary king Conn Céadchathach. The oak was enormous in size, being 30 cubits in girth and 300 in height, and bore three crops a year, one of acorns, one of nuts and one of apples. Naturally, the crops were prodigious, with apples 'wonderful, marvellous', nuts 'round, blood red' and acorns, 'brown, ridgy'; and one poem mentions a crop of 900 sackfuls of acorns.[9] It finally fell southward across Magh Ailbe in the time of the sons of Aedh Sláne. One version has it that this was because wind had also felled the Ash of Tortan, while another version claims that it was destroyed by the poets. The *Metrical Dindshenchus* contains the following two poems about it:

PLAIN OF MUGNA
O Mugna, host to a tree so fine,
That God fashioned in ancient times.
A tree so greatly blest with favour,
With three fruits so choice in flavour.

Acorn and slim nut so brown
And apple, wild and sweetly grown.
The king would get without let up
Three times a year a mighty crop.

Tree of Mugna, great its worth,
Thirty cubits full in girth.
From far and wide a glorious sight,
Three hundred cubits full its height.

So the pure branch was brought down,
As wind broke the Tree of Tortan.
Thus life's quarrels pass away,
Like the ancient tree of Mugna's plain.

TREE OF MUGNA
Tree of Mugna, great and fair,
Highest its top beyond compare,
Thirty cubits, no small count,
The measure of its girth's amount.

Three hundred high, tree without stain,
A thousand could gather in its shade.
In the Northeast hidden from sight,
Until Conn of the Hundred Fights.

A hundred score warriors, no idle boast,
A thousand and forty more at most
Could gather there with raucous noise,
'til the satire of poets it destroyed.

There is also evidence of oaks standing near royal sites. A poem about the fort of Rathangan calls it 'the fort by the oak trees'.[10]

Recent excavation at Navan Fort, the old site of Emain Macha, found a large oak post in the centre of a massive circular structure, the purpose of which is believed to be primarily ritual. It is thought that the post may have been the focus of ritual activities to the Celtic Jupiter, as a sacred symbol of tribal integrity.[11]

The oak is connected with certain animals, particularly the stag, bull, pig and eagle.[12] One story which concerns the adventures of the eagle Leithin tells of the stag Dubhchosach who stands beside a bare oak spike. The stag was born beside the oak when it was only a sapling, grew into a mighty stag as the oak grew into a mighty tree, and stayed with it until it was nothing but a stump. In the *Lays of Fionn* a lay called 'The Enchanted Stag' tells of an occasion when the Fianna were out hunting and were killing 100 stags from every oak grove all around. They come upon a huge stag in one and give chase. During the chase the stag reveals he is king Donn and challenges the Fianna that they will not kill him so long as there are deer in Ireland, as he Donn, was the herdsman of all the deer. Nevertheless, the Fianna succeed in killing him in the end. Another lay mentions the Fianna starting a huge stag from the fresh brown (*donn*) oakwood. In another story about the Fianna, Fionn, Oisín and Caoilte are hunting in a wood at Feeguile, County Offaly when they are confronted by a headless spectre who demands that they give him one of their heads unless his own be found. Nothing daunted, Oisín and Caoilte strike at an oak tree with their swords and the spectre's own huge head falls from its branches. The spectre is a version of the god Donn. Donn is the underworld aspect of the Dagda and has links with the horned hunting god Cernunnos, who was also the patron of wild animals. Mad Sweeney says about the oak: *binni leat fo bharr doiri/ crónán dhaimh dhuinn dhamhghoiri* (more sweet wouldst thou deem under the oak wood the belling of the brown stag of the herd).

The oak and the bull are linked in some folk tales. One folk tale tells of how first a serpent, and then a bull are bested by the hero and then tied to an oak. The hero beats the bull into submission with an uprooted oak. Another tells of a mighty bull that uproots an acre of land in one go and then throws up a mighty oak until it almost reaches the sky. Another tells of how a bull caught Cúchulainn in the ribs and threw him against a great oak tree. A Scots Gaelic rhyme states that to carry an oaken staff produces heat in cattle. Mad Sweeney makes this enigmatic statement: 'my aversion in woods/I conceal it not from anyone/is the leafy yearling (cow) of an oak/swaying evermore'. Again, the bull is linked to the god Donn. Whitley Stokes recounts a delightful story from the *Bodeian*

Dinnshenchus about an oakwood in the west of the plain of Macha that was so fertile it drove the swine of Ireland mad. The wind would blow the scent of the oakwood all over Ireland and whichever part of Ireland it drove the scent into, the swine would rush to seek it in droves. In the Welsh story of 'Math, son of Mathonwy', Lleu the rightful lord who has been ousted, is found in the form of an eagle taking refuge in an oak tree. A variant of the horned animal motif is found in the tale 'The King of Norway's Sons'. The hero Cod slays a giant who has two goat's horns and a garment of hornless deer and roebuck skins about him. The sound of the giant's falling was said to be like that of a prime oak in the forest.

Frazer shows how the oak was a symbol of the sky god, and the god of thunder and lightning, among the peoples of Europe, including the ancient Romans and Greeks, the Germans and Slavs, as well as the Celts.[13] In *Cath Maige Tuiread* (Battle of Moytirra) the daughter of Indech forbids the Dagda to go to the battle, pledging to be a giant oak in every ford and pass that he will cross. The Dagda replies that he will pass and in token of this, the mark of his axe will remain in every oak forever. The author adds: 'and people have remarked upon the mark of Dagda's axe'. It seems probable that the Dagda's axe is a symbol of lightning, similarly capable of splitting open a tree. The axe was an offering to the sky or sun god, and axes are found in earthworks and burials all over Europe.[14] In the Irish context, it is clear that the oak was sacred to the Dagda, and the underworld god Donn, both forms of the Celtic Jupiter.

SEASONAL PLACING

The oak's associations with May time, midsummer, with fire and the sun, clearly place the oak seasonally in summer. The oak is associated with Ogham letter *Dair* which itself is the Irish for oak.

THE USES OF OAK

In early Irish law the oak was classified as one of the seven *Airig fedo* or Nobles of the Wood. Oak timber was used for numerous purposes from constructing buildings and ships to barrels and furniture. In addition, the bark of oak was used for tanning leather and for making a black dye.

Holly – Cuileann

Ilex aquifolium - Common holly

8th consonant of the Ogham Alphabet

11 July-7 August
10th month of Ogham Tree
Calendar

 [T]

The holly with its tough wood, prickly evergreen leaves and red berries is a symbol of the strength and ability of the champion, and of protection, magical power and purification.

FOLK BELIEFS AND CUSTOMS

The English name Holly comes from 'Holy' and originates in the belief that the holly's scarlet berries like drops of blood, along with its prickly leaves, are symbolic of Christ's sufferings.[1] This and the fact that the holly is evergreen and has scarlet berries in the winter means that it has long been associated with Christmas and New Year.[2] It is used to decorate houses, often with the idea of protecting the house against evil spirits during the season. Indeed, in some parts of Wales, holly is an unlucky tree at all times other than Christmas. Holly features in St Stephen's Day customs from various parts of Ireland about the wren boys. One custom involved going from house to house with a wren which they had caught and killed, attached to a holly bush decorated with ribbons. The custom in Wales was 'holly beating' on St Stephen's Day, when men and boys would beat the arms of the local women until they drew blood. Also, the last person to arise on that day would be whipped with a bunch of holly and made to do chores. It is believed that the custom arose from the supposed beneficial effect of bleeding which prevailed in former times, coupled with the notion of the stimulating effect of the strengthening sun at this time. Similar customs took place in the Scottish Highlands, and took the form of boys beating one another with holly branches on New Year's Eve. It was believed that for every drop of blood that was lost through the beating, a

clear year of life was assured to the loser of it. Children were also thrashed with a holly branch as a remedy for chilblains 'to let the chilled blood out'. For New Year's Eve in Scotland the house was also decorated with holly to protect it, especially from the fairies.

Holly was widely believed to have protective powers.[3] The Roman naturalist Pliny stated that holly, if planted near a house or farm, repelled poison and defended it from lightning and witchcraft; and that the wood, if thrown at any animal, even without touching it, had the power to compel that animal to return and lie down beside it. In Ireland holly is a *crann uasal*, a 'gentle' or 'noble' tree and you annoy the fairies when you misuse it, for example by sweeping the chimney with it. In Scotland the holly is believed to be hated by witches, and holly and rowan berries were used to keep people and animals safe from evil influences. A garland of holly and the bittersweet plant hung around the neck would cure a hag-ridden horse. In England to cut down a holly tree is to bring bad luck, and holly was planted near houses and in churchyards to protect against witches. In England holly was also believed to protect against lightning and thunder.

Unlike other trees with protecting powers, holly seems to have no powers of fertility, perhaps because it is essentially a warrior tree.[4] Indeed, in County Tyrone it was believed that holly bushes planted near a house meant that the daughters of that house would never marry, or if they did would be childless. In Donegal to strike a milch cow with a holly was bad luck as it could lead to the cow passing bloody urine. In a Scottish *Lay of the Fianna*, Fionn tells Oscar that: 'No fleshly heart was ever in my breast, but a heart of the holly spikes, all overclad with steel'. The '*Cad Godeu*' has this to say: 'the holly livid grew, and manly acts he knew'.

LEGENDS AND MYTHOLOGY

Holly's protective powers are also often linked to saints.[5] In Brittany the Irish hermit St Ronan had a protecting circle of holly bushes around his hut in the woods. One story tells of how it protected him from being assaulted by the wife of the local master, who hated him, by preventing her approaching due to its mysterious force. A Breton folk tale also tells of a man who is able to enter the realms of the dead and return alive (if insane!) by carrying a branch of holly dipped in holy water.

The holly could also be used for magical purposes.[6] In one tale Fionn is confronted by three hags at the cave of Keshcorran who weave enchanted yarn on crooked holly sticks. The hags reel out the yarn around the cave and the warriors of the Fianna become weak and helpless when they pass through it. The hags are only defeated when Goll Mac Morna kills them in battle. In the tale 'The King of

Norway's Sons', the tutor to the king's son rescues him by riding on a harrow wheel of holly to where the son is held captive, surrounded by a dark fog.

Holly was used to make spears and darts and this features in many tales.[7] When Colmcille came to what is now Glencolmcille the devil threw a holly spit at him, killing his servant Cerc. Colmcille hurled the holly spit back, lifting the fog which shrouded the valley and casting the devil out. The spit immediately sprouted into a fresh holly tree which is reputed to survive to this day. Mannanán Mac Lir appears in one story at the court of The O'Donnell dressed as a clown and carrying three spears of holly scorched and blackened. Holly appears to have some link to Mannanán as he also met his death at the battle of Maigh Cuilenn or the Plain of Holly, while in another story Fionn was cured of an enchantment which had turned him into an old man by a Cuilinn of Cuailgne (Holly of Cooley) who we are told, was the same person as Mannanán. In 'The Pursuit of Gruaidhe Griansholus', Cúchulainn is armed with holly spits that he uses successfully to kill birds. The Welsh *Romance of Peredur* begins with Peredur in the forest throwing holly darts.

The holly features several times alongside Cúchulainn in the *Táin*. The first reference occurs when Cúchulainn comes upon the charioteer of Órlám cutting chariot poles from a holly tree. Cúchulainn helps him to strip the poles, and rubs them with his hands until they are polished, slippery and smooth – 'so smooth that a fly could not stay on them'. When he has done this, however, he immediately strikes off Órlám's head. Shortly after Cúchulainn is attacked by a warrior called Nath Crantail who fires 27 ('thrice nine') spits of holly sharpened, charred and pointed by fire at him. Of course Cúchulainn is able to fend them all off easily. Later Cúchulainn kills a warrior called Fer Báeth by throwing a shoot of holly over his shoulder at him. According to the folklorist Daithi Ó hÓgáin in his book *Myth, Legend and Romance*, the name Cúchulainn may mean something like 'chariot warrior', and this would explain his linkage with holly as we saw earlier. In the medieval English romance *Sir Gawain and the Green Knight*, which involves a ritual beheading game, the Green Knight is armed with a holly club. The story, in which Sir Gawain's life is spared by the Green Knight, is

Irish in origin and involved Cúchulainn instead of Sir Gawain.

Cúchulainn is linked to the god Lugh, and several references in stories hint at an association between Lugh and the holly tree.[8] A Scottish folk tale called *An Ceathairneach Caolriabhach* (The Slim, Swarthy Champion) features a champion who uses a stick of holly to kill a large number of men, while carrying in his other hand a grey hand-plane (for planing wood). The champion also displays magical powers of healing and can control music by destroying harps and making them whole again. It is noteworthy that the champion's skills mirror those of Lugh. Both are great warriors and skilled at carpentry, the harp and healing. The story is an old poetic composition of Irish origin, so it is possible that it was inspired by lore surrounding Lugh. In one tale called 'Fionn Mac Cumhaill and Seven Brothers' a giant called Curacha is killed and his head brought to Fionn. Fionn puts the head on a holly bush and it immediately burns the bush to the ground. This echoes a popular folk story of how drops of blood from Balor's severed head (which Balor had advised Lugh to let fall onto Lugh's own head) fall onto a stone which immediately burns or breaks due to the blood being poisonous. In another Irish folk tale the hero Bioultach is struck down by two champions who are sent by a giant, and becomes a grey flagstone heaped with ice and snow with a holly tree growing out of it. Bioultach is restored to his former self when a 'ragged green man' cuts a handful of flesh from the giant and squeezes it onto the stone. Finally, a tale concerning the death of the king Fearghus Mac Róich tells of him being killed by a giant with holly darts shot from a bow. This is a later version of a tale which had Fearghus being killed with a javelin cast by a blind poet called Lughaidh. It is noteworthy that in many of these stories the opponent of the hero is a giant, just as Lugh is opposed to Balor.

Seasonal Placing

Despite its strong links with Christmas, the identification of holly with chariots and the god Lugh place holly seasonally at the festival of Lughnasa, the time of chariot races. Its use for making implements may also link it to this time of year. A widespread tale of the Cailleach Bhéarra (a mythological figure who is a version of the goddess of the land) tells of how she gave advice on threshing, recommending that a flail should have holly for a handle and hazel for a striker.[9] The holly is associated with the Ogham letter *Tinne* which means 'Iron Bar'.

The Uses of Holly

In early Irish law holly was classified as an *Airig fedo* or Noble of the Wood. Apart from spears and chariot poles, the fresh shoots of holly were used as fodder for livestock.

Hazel – Coll

Corylus avellana - Common hazel

9th consonant of the Ogham Alphabet

8 August-4 September
11th month of Ogham Tree
Calendar

Also 2nd supplementary consonant of the Ogham Alphabet

The hazel, with its nourishing nuts and habit of growing near water, is a symbol of fertility, wisdom, kingship, poetic inspiration and mystical knowledge.

FOLK BELIEFS AND CUSTOMS

The hazel is noted for its powers of protection against evil.[1] When travelling at night a hazel stick was regarded as good protection against evil spirits. One story relates how a dark creature 'like a black pig' was successfully beaten off with a stick of hazel because: 'the hazel is blessed, and no wicked thing can stay when it is touched by it'. It was believed that a piece of hazel tied to a horse prevented the fairies from abducting it. An Irish folk tale describes how a man rescues his wife from the fairies by carrying a black handled knife in one hand and a stick of hazel in the other. A story in *Lebor Gabála Erenn* (The Book of Invasions) describes how the philistines killed demons fashioned by the Tuatha Dé Danann by thrusting skewers of hazel and rowan wood behind their necks. Hazel branches were found inside the Loose Howe Bronze Age tree trunk burial in Yorkshire and hazel nuts and bark have been found in several other graves, perhaps to protect against evil spirits. In Colchester in Britain the god *Silvanus Callirius* or 'god of the hazel wood' was worshipped probably by local hunters for protection. Hazel could also be used for magic. An English medieval charm says that to make oneself invisible one ought to carry a

FOLKLORE OF THE TREES

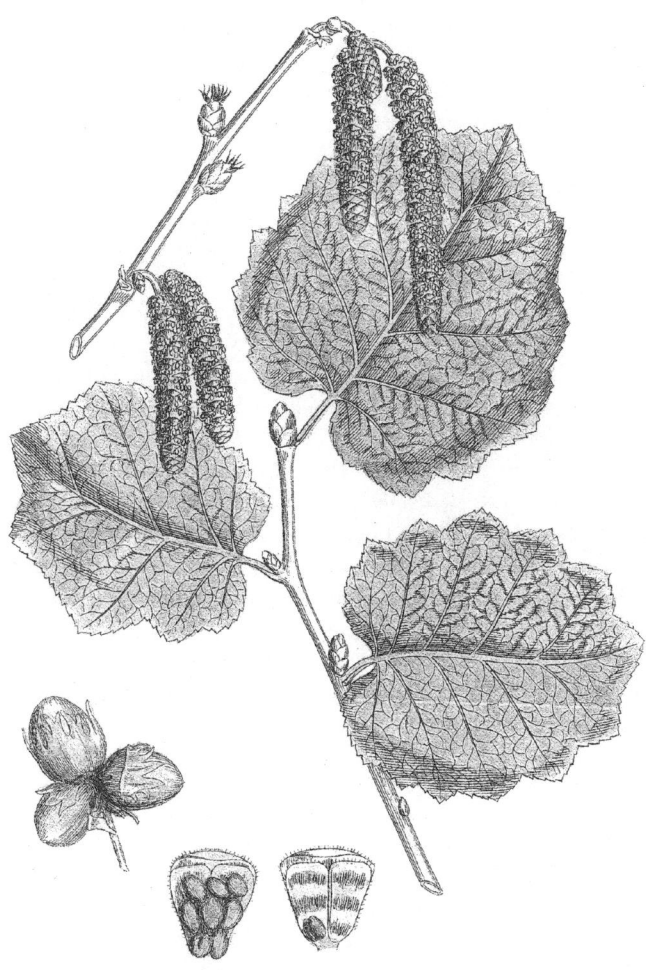

hazel rod with a green hazel twig inserted in it. Fionn's wife Sadbh was turned into a fawn by Fear Doiche, the Dark Druid, using a hazel rod, because she would not return his love.

In the Scottish Highlands two nuts naturally joined together were called *cno-chomblaich* and were considered to be effective against witchcraft.[2] Another name for this double nut was St John's nut. In Scotland the night before Roodmass or *Féille Róid* (14-26 September) was known as 'the night of the holy nut' when popular belief held that the devil went nutting.[3] In Scotland, children who were born in autumn were given the milky centre of the green nut as their first food, often mixed with honey. In Wales a stick of hazel given to a girl meant a change of attitude or the breaking off of an engagement.[4] Interestingly, this custom is explained as meaning 'be wise – desist'. Hazel is noted for growing beside water and hazel twigs are often used by diviners or dowsers to seek water or hidden veins of metal.[5] Perhaps the link with water explains why in Wales a cap of hazel leaves and twigs was worn for good luck by sailors. In folklore everywhere, hazel sticks were considered to be poisonous to snakes.[6] When the Irish emigrated to America and Australia they often brought a bundle of hazel rods with them to kill any snakes they might encounter. This is probably because hazel was considered to have power over snakes as both were associated with water. In Welsh tradition for example, snakes are associated with sacred wells and a well-known legend speaks of a Pembrokeshire well whose treasure was guarded by a serpent. In other countries snakes had similar powers to the Irish Salmon of Knowledge. In German folk tales a *haselwurm* or snake found under a hazel was a source of mystical wisdom. Perhaps a salmon took the place of a snake in the Irish version because of Ireland's well known lack of snakes.

The hazelnut, with its round, hard shell and nutritious core is a symbol of the heart, and its nourishing and life-giving qualities link it to the earth. The heart is frequently portrayed in folklore as being similar in nature to a nut.[7] In the tale 'The Cattle Raid of Cooley' it relates how, after Erc, son of Cairpre was killed, his sister Acaill wept for him for nine days until her heart broke like a nut inside her. Similarly, the Rennes *Dindshenchus* states that after the warrior Lugaid Láigde fell in battle, his daughter Findabair's heart broke in her like a nut for sorrow when she heard the news. In the *Metrical Dindshenchus* it tells how the warrior Gabrán died after hunting a wild pig, his heart bursting like a nut from his exertions.

FOLKLORE OF THE TREES

 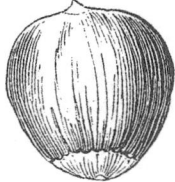

LEGENDS AND MYTHOLOGY

Various versions of a sacred well of knowledge, surrounded by nine hazel trees of wisdom, appear in Irish myth. It is found either under the sea, in the otherworld, or at the source of the main rivers of Ireland. The Tuatha Dé Danann had such a well below the sea where seven streams of wisdom sprang from it and turned back to it again. Elsewhere it is called Connla's Well in Tír Fá Thonn (Land Under Wave) and is the source of the Shannon and the seven chief rivers of Ireland. It appears again as the Well of Segais at the source of the Boyne or Shannon, from which also spring seven streams of wisdom. Here we are told that the hazel trees are those of Crimall the Sage. It is not clear who this is but it is interesting to note that Fionn Mac Cumhall's uncle is called Crimall. When Cormac the king visited Mannanán Mac Lir, King of Tír Tairngire (the Land of Promise) he saw a similar well on the green of a royal dun, this time with five streams flowing out of it and 'the sound of the flowing of the streams was sweeter than any music that men sing'. He is told that it is the well of knowledge, and that the five streams represent the five streams through which knowledge go, ie. the five senses.

The various descriptions of the well are similar. The nine hazel trees are of wisdom, inspiration and the knowledge of poetry. The leaves, blossoms and nuts of the trees would break out in the same hour and fall into the well in a shower that raised a spray or purple wave. Five salmon living in the well would eat the nuts and for every nut they ate a red spot would appear on their skin, and any person who ate one of those salmon would know all wisdom and poetry. The hazelnuts would also raise bubbles of inspiration in the water of the streams, which would flow out all around to be drunk by people of many arts. A well of knowledge surrounded by hazel trees seems to be at the centre of Gaelic cosmology. It echoes Mimir's Well in Norse mythology which also dispensed wisdom to those who drank from it.

Two poems from the *Metrical Dindshenchus* about the river Shannon describe the well of knowledge at its source. The following are the relevant extracts from each of the two poems:

From Sinann I*
Here the inspiration of Segais is found
At the true spring's excellent ground.
Over the well of the graceful flow
Where the hazel of musical poetry grows.

The spray of Segais spreads its mantle
Over the well so strong and gentle
When fall the nuts of Crimmall fair
On its royal bosom true and rare.

Altogether so abundantly heavy,
Spring forth from the tree so lovely
Leaf and flower and nut in plenty
Not a one in any way scanty.

In the same fashion, as is good reason
They fall again in their own season
Into Segais' much loved well
In a display where all excel.

From Sinann II
The nine hazels of Crimall the wise
Drop their fruits where the wellspring lies
Through the power of magic they stay,
Under a dark druidic spray.

Together in a way not known
Both their leaves and flowers grow.
A marvel is this noble power

When they ripen in the same hour.

When the nuts form a ripe crop
Down into the well they drop,
Where they scatter on the bottom
And the salmon wait to eat them.

From the nuts' juice no puny portion,
That make bubbles of inspiration,
Which every moment can be seen,
Gushing down the verdant streams.

*The River Shannon

Another story describes how St Senan, under the direction of an angel, dug a well with a hazel stake in order to relieve a drought. He set the stake by the well and the next morning it had grown into a sacred tree or *bile*.[8]

The Gaelic hero Fionn Mac Cumhaill has a strong connection with the hazel.[9] Fionn acquired his powers of wisdom from the salmon of knowledge fed on hazelnuts which had dropped into the Well of Segais. The story goes that the seer Finnéigeas caught the salmon and left Fionn to guard it while it cooked. Fionn burst a blister on the salmon's skin and burning his thumb, he sucked it to relieve the pain. In that moment he instantly acquired knowledge of all things. When Finnéigeas saw what had happened he christened the boy Fionn for the first time. The original idea behind the story involved a young seer acquiring wisdom from an older version of himself, essentially through contact with the dead. In other words Finnéigeas and Fionn are ultimately the same person. The name Finnéigeas itself means nothing other than 'Fionn the Seer'. The name Fionn or Finn means whiteness and derives from a word originally meaning wisdom or insight, and inspiring revelation.

Fionn had further connections with hazel. His shield was made of wood from the Dripping Ancient Hazel. The story goes that after Lugh had slain Balor he set his head in a fork of hazel. The poison dripping from the severed head caused the hazel to split in two and for all its leaves to fall off, and for it to drip poisonous milk from then on. Fifty years later Mannanán was passing the spot on Whitehazel Mountain when he saw the hazel and had it dug up. The wright Lucra created a shield from it and after many owners it passed into Fionn's hands. This hazel was supposedly that which the king Mac Cuill had worshipped. Robert Graves' remark in *The White Goddess* that the hazel shield symbolised the poisonous power of the satiric poem may be accurate. Fionn's musician was a dwarf called Cnú Dheireóil or the Little Nut, who played music so sweet and beautiful that wounded men could fall asleep to it and be healed. This is perhaps a play on the nourishing and otherworldly properties of the hazel nut. Cnú Dheireóil was supposedly a son of Lugh. In Fionn's house in Almha he also possessed 'thrice fifty goblets of white silver that held the hazel mead of May' and one of the trials of the Fianna involved a warrior being put in a hole with a shield and hazel rod, and having to fend off nine spears cast at the one time. Another character with a variation of the name Fionn was Fintan Mac Bóchna, a mythical seer who survived the flood and lived for hundreds of years. He is described as 'Fintan of the hazel wood'.

A Scottish version of the tale of Fionn Mac Cumhaill and the Salmon of Knowledge concerns a man called Farquhar (Mac Fhionnlaidh in Scots Gaelic) who went, on the advice of a doctor, to a certain hazel bush from which he cut some boughs. Then he waited while six brown snakes emerged from the bush. The seventh was white and he caught it. He made a fire of the hazel sticks and boiled the snake in a pot, making sure that no steam escaped. However, a stream of steam began to emerge from one side of the pot and Farquhar put his finger to it to stop it, sucking his finger as it was wet. As soon as he did so he immediately gained knowledge of all medicine. The doctor was furious as he had hoped to gain the knowledge for himself.[10] It is interesting to note that a snake is involved here rather than a salmon.

A Welsh tale describes the encounter between a saint called Collen (or Hazel) and the king of the fairies Gwyn son of Nud.[11] Gwyn is the Welsh version of Fionn Mac Cumhall, and the name is of the same origin. The story relates how Gwyn summons Collen and offers him riches, fine food and clothing, everything due 'a white-headed man of wisdom' such as Collen. Collen, being a saint, turns him down as ungodly and banishes him with holy water. Although the Christianised story shows Collen, who signifies wisdom, as being hostile to Gwyn, it does demonstrate a connection between the two.

The hazel is also associated with poetic inspiration. Cormac's *Glossary* contains the entry *Caill Crínmón* or the Hazels of Scientific Composition, referring to the hazels from which come, or from which is broken, a new composition. The hazel here stands as a metaphor for acquiring knowledge ie. breaking through the hard exterior to get at the nourishment inside. In the Welsh poem 'The Battle of The Trees' or '*Cad Godeu*' the hazel 'was esteemed/ by its number in the quiver'. The quote is probably a reference to the large vocabulary in the hazel's 'armoury' as the Battle is one of words not weapons.

Hazel's association with wisdom and truth links it to kingship.[12] The English name hazel itself derives from an Anglo-Saxon word meaning 'authority or kingship' while the Irish word *Coll* also had the meaning of a chieftain. In Wales a folk tale relates how a hazel tree grows over the cave where King Arthur and his men sleep. Many a sacred site was originally a hazel wood. A hazel named after St Patrick is found in the district of Coillrige, near the church of *Domhnach Sratha*. According to Robert Graves hazel was the *Bile Ratha*, 'the venerated tree of the Rath'. Aedh, the grandson of the Dagda, was called 'Aedh of the Poets' because of the number of the poets that gathered at his Rath, which was described as having in it 'golden-yellow apples and crimson pointed nuts of the wood'.

The three things put by the Tuatha Dé Danann above all others were the plough, the sun and the hazel tree.[13] Indeed, the last Tuatha De Danann kings of Ireland were called Mac Cuill (Son of Hazel), Mac Cecht (Son of Plough) and Mac Gréine (Son of the Sun), whose wives were the goddesses Fodla, Banba and Ériu respectively. One story relates how Mac Cuill killed Lugh at Uisneach. It seems this triad of plough, sun and hazel is related to the three functions of Celtic society noted by the Celtic scholar Georges Dumézil, namely the priestly class, the warrior class and the peasantry. The plough represents the peasantry or farmers whose function is fertility. The sun represents the warriors and nobility whose function is physical force and the exercise of power. The hazel here represents the priests and the sovereign power of kingship whose function is the sacred one of mediating with the gods and acting as keepers of knowledge. According to Dumézil this threefold division is ancient and has parallels in Hindu cosmology.

SEASONAL PLACING

The hazel is linked seasonally with autumn and the festival of Samhain when its nuts are ripe. It is associated with the Ogham letter *Coll* which itself is the Irish for Hazel. It is also associated with the Ogham letter name Emancholl which means 'twinhazel'.

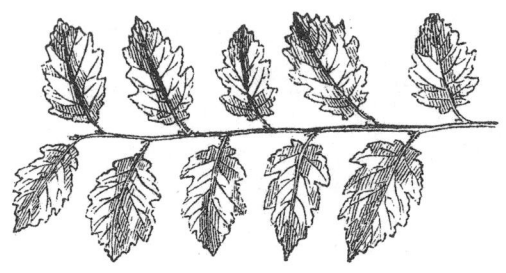

THE USES OF HAZEL

In early Irish law hazel was classified as an *Airig fedo* or Noble of the Wood. Hazel nuts have been eaten as an important food source in Ireland from the earliest times. Hazel wood has also been used in making furniture, fencing and wickerwork.

Whitebeam – Fionncholl

Sorbus aria – Common Whitebeam
Sorbus hibernica – Irish Whitebeam

As well as the hazel proper there is another species of tree considered by the ancient Irish to be a form of hazel. This is fionncholl *or 'white-hazel', or in modern English the whitebeam.[1] Whitebeam in reality is related to the rowan rather than the hazel but its leaves bear a passing resemblance to those of the hazel. It usually has scarlet berries like those of rowan but in some species they are brown and could be considered to look like hazel nuts. Whitebeam's leaves have white undersides and its timber is also white in colour, which accounts for the name 'whitehazel'.*

LEGENDS AND MYTHOLOGY

The whitebeam is a symbol of royal authority and 'the king's truth'.[2] In the story 'The Wooing of Étaín', the king Elcmar presided over the feast of Samhain with a forked stick of whitehazel in his hand. In the *Táin* the royal messenger Mac Roth approaches Cúchulainn carrying a staff of whitehazel. In the Colloquy of the Ancients (*Agallamh na Seanóirí*) Saint Patrick and *Caoilte* of the Fianna are twice approached by messengers of the king of Ireland who signal their status by carrying staffs of whitehazel. A white or silver rod generally was also a symbol of authority. Conchubar king of Ulster kept a silver rod at Emhain Macha while Ailill, the husband of Queen Maedhbh, did the same at Cruachan. The *Metrical Dindshenchus* describes a part of the Boyne as 'the stream of the whitehazel'.

THE USES OF WHITEBEAM

In early Irish law Whitebeam was classified as a *Fodla fedo* or one of the Lower Divisions of the Wood. Whitebeam wood is hard and durable and was probably used for making staves as legend would indicate. The fruit of whitebeam is edible, if not very tasty. In

FOLKLORE OF THE TREES

20 ft. high, 3¼ in. diam.

England the brown fruits of the Devon whitebeam (*Sorbus Devoniensis*) were picked and eaten and the tree was known locally as 'French Hales' a name apparently derived from hazel.[3]

Apple – Úll

Malus sylvestris - Crab apple

10th consonant of the Ogham Alphabet

5 September-2 October
12th month of Ogham Tree Calendar

The apple, with its beautiful blossoms and nourishing fruit, is a symbol of the delights of the otherworld, and of fertility, replenishment and healing.

Folk Beliefs and Customs

In Ireland many games involving apples were played on Halloween, while in Cornwall Halloween was known as 'Allan Day' or 'Apple Day' and children went to bed with an apple under their pillow.[1] In England at Halloween a mixture of hot spiced ale, wine or cider with apples and bits of toast in it was drunk. This was called 'Lamb's Wool' which comes from the Irish *lá maois úll* or 'Apple Gathering Day'.[2] In apple growing areas of England, especially in the south west, orchards were traditionally 'wassailed' at the New Year to keep the trees fruiting productively. This involved placing cakes and cider on the best producing trees and toasting their health.

Legends and Mythology

The Irish god of the sea Mannanán Mac Lir lived in a beautiful otherworld region often thought of as an island to the east of Ireland which was variously called *Magh Meall* ('the Pleasant Plain'), *Tír Tairngire* ('the Land of Promise') or *Eamhain Abhlach* ('the Region of Apples'), an island full of trees bearing the most beautiful golden apples. *Eamhain Abhlach* is essentially the same as the Avalon of Arthurian myth. Trips by mortals to this eternal realm are the subject of numerous tales. In the best known of these Mannanán appeared to Cormac Mac Airt at Tara as a warrior carrying on his

shoulder a branch with nine apples of red gold. When the branch was shaken the music the apples made was so beautiful that the listener would forget all troubles and tiredness. Later Mannanán took Cormac to the Land of Promise where he presented him with a Cup of Truth. The lovers Deirdre and Naoise were said to have sent their children, Gaiar and Aebgréine, into the care of Mannanán in Eamhain Abhlach. In another tale a fairy woman from the Land of Promise appeared to Connla, son of Conn Céadchathach, and presented him with an apple. Connla lived off the apple for a month, taking no other food or drink, and despite his constant eating the apple grew no smaller in size. At the end of the month when the woman returned, Connla sailed away with her forever. A later tale describes the adventures of the hero Tadhg Mac Cian in the otherworld where he met Connla and the fairy woman on an island where the apple tree which produced the everlasting apple also grew.

St Brendan and his companions reach the Land of Promise at the end of their voyage which is again described as full of fine apple trees in fruit. [3] In the voyage of Maol Dúin, he and his brothers last for 40 days on three apples that miraculously grew on a rod that Maol Dúin had picked on the journey.[4] The compensation paid to Lugh by the sons of Tuirill for the death of his father Ethland included the harvest of apples that are under the sea, 'near to the island of Caire Cendfinne which is hidden between Éire and Alba'.[5] The apples are said to be the colour of burned gold, the size of a month-old child's head, to have the taste of honey and 'they do not leave the pain of wounds or the vexation of sickness on anyone that eats them, and they do not lessen by being eaten for ever'. A twelfth-century poem declares that the Lugh himself was reared in Eamhain Abhlach.[6] In an early British poem about Merlin entitled 'The Apple Trees', the wizard addresses a 'sweet apple tree', one of seven score and seven (147) apple trees growing in the forest of Caledon in southern Scotland; praising at length the beauty of its yellow fruit and white blossoms. Merlin in this poem is the British equivalent of Mad Sweeney, having fled to the forest after losing his reason in a terrible battle. The region of apple trees appears to be a version of Avalon or *Emhain Abhlach*, hidden in a great forest where no one could find them, instead of on an island.

There are several examples of saints being associated with apple trees.[7] Adamnán's life of St Colmcille tells of an apple tree at the monastery of Durrow which had been bearing bitter fruit. At the saint's command it changed its ways and bore sweet apples from that moment on. St Brigid on the other hand cursed an apple tree which had been very fruitful, making it barren. However, she also blessed an alder tree, changing its warlike nature so that it bore fruit, two-thirds apples and one-third 'sweet sloes'. The Bishop of Cashel, Cormac Mac Cuilennán, was similarly supposed to have planted an apple bearing alder tree. St Mochuda proved his holiness to a druid by blessing an apple branch four times, the first time causing it to bear leaves, the second time blossom, then sour fruit and finally fruit as sweet as honey. He also used apples to effect cures. On one occasion he cured a child with a withered hand by holding out an apple to her. As soon as the child grasped the apple her hand became whole. He performed the same cure on a pregnant woman who subsequently gave birth painlessly. St Patrick was reported to have planted an apple tree at a spot called *Achadh inna Elta* (Field of the Doe). In Scotland St Servanus flung his staff across the Firth of Forth, and where it landed it took root and blossomed into an apple tree.

The apple features in many folk tales.[8] In the story of the doomed lovers Baile Mac Buain and the princess Aillin a yew tree grows out of Baile's grave with a likeness of his head in the branches and an apple tree grows out of Aillin's with her likeness in it. Writing tablets are made out of each tree and when the tablets are brought close they spring together and cannot be separated. In the tale 'The Story of Conn -Eda' or 'The Golden Apples of Lough Erne' the prince, Conn Eda, after many adventures succeeds in getting three golden apples from a tree that grew by a castle of the king of the Fir Bolgs at the bottom of Lough Erne. He plants the apples in his garden and a great tree grows up bearing similar golden fruit. Consequently the district around the tree becomes very fertile, bearing an exuberance of crops and fruit. In the folk tale 'Fionn Mac Cumhaill and Conán Maol' a strange giant gives apples to all the company. Conán says of this: 'May every curse be on me if ever I have had such sweetness from music as from the taste of this apple'. Another Irish folk tale concerns a hero called Blaiman Son of Apple who is conceived when his mother, a princess, plucked the only apple from a tree and ate it. He is born with a golden spot on his poll and a silver spot on his forehead and was very beautiful in form. Some folk tales have Mannanán appearing in the form of a fool, performing miraculous tricks and feats of magic and playing the most beautiful music on his harp. The only food he would accept for this was a vessel of sour milk and a few crab apples.

Apples, like hazelnuts, have royal associations.[9] The Rath of Aedh of the Poets had 'golden yellow apples in it and crimson-pointed nuts of the wood'. Aongus son of the Dagda bid the three sons of Lughaidh Menn, King of Ireland to stay with him at Brú na Bóinne and when they left he bade them to bring with them three apple trees from the oakwood nearby, one in full bloom, one shedding its blossom and one covered with ripe fruit. In his royal house of the Red Branch King Conchubar of Ulster had a silver rod with three golden apples on it, and when he shook the rod or struck it, all in the house would be silent. Caoilte of the Fianna had a magic goblet with an apple of red gold in the centre of it, which when filled with water would give to the king whatever drink he chose.

The otherworld nature of apples is also seen in several references linking them with feats of magic or trickery. In the tale 'The Destruction of Da Derga's Hostel', the fool Tulchoine juggled nine swords, nine silver shields and nine apples of gold at the same time and their movement was 'like that of bees going past each other on a beautiful day', while in the tale 'Bricriu's Feast', Cúchulainn entertains the women of Ulster with a similar trick. Elsewhere Cúchulainn is described as having 50 gold apples playing over his head, performing tricks on his breath.

As well as being linked to Mannanán Mac Lir, the apple's association with fertility also ties it to goddess figures.[10] At Cirencester in Britain a stone statue from Celtic times depicts a seated mother goddess figure with three apples in her lap as a symbol of fertility, while another stone in East Stoke depicts a goddess holding a bowl of apples in front of her. This recalls the Norse goddess Iduna who kept apples in a chest to give to the gods so as to maintain youth and health.

SEASONAL PLACING

Seasonally apples are ripe in late autumn in time for Samhain, the great otherworld feast with which it is associated. The apple is associated with the Ogham letter *Cert* which means 'Bush'.

Hazel – Coll
Corylus avellana

Whitebeam – Fionncholl
Sorbus aria

Crab Apple – Úll

Malus sylvestris

Purging Buckthorn – Ramhdhraighean
Rhamnus catharticus

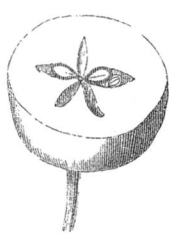

THE USES OF APPLE

In early Irish law the apple was classified as an *Airig fedo* or Noble of the Wood as its fruit has been an important food source since earliest times. Apple bark was also rarely used to dye wool yellow.

Buckthorn – Ramh-dhraighean

Rhamnus catharticus - Purging buckthorn
11th consonant of the Ogham Alphabet

 M

The buckthorn, with its purging berries and bark, was an important medicinal tree from ancient times up to virtually the present day. There are several names in Irish for buckthorn, each of which link it to the fruit of other trees. Ramhdhraighean *seems to mean 'purging blackthorn', if* ramh *is taken to be a variation of ruibh, 'sulphur' or 'venom' or derive from ramhán, a fit or spasm.* Paide bréan *seems to be a variant of the name* Prunus Padus, *the bird cherry, meaning something like 'rotten cherry', while another name* Bréan Úll *similarly means 'rotten apple'. These names put buckthorn in the same category as other important fruits, even if in a negative way.*

FOLK BELIEFS AND CUSTOMS

There is little folklore about the buckthorn.[1] At the festival of the Commemoration of the Dead celebrated in mid March in Athens, the dead were believed to rise from their graves and go walking about the streets. Their entry into homes and temples was barred by a combination of buckthorn, ropes and pitch. In England an old superstition states that Christ's crown of thorns was made of buckthorn. These suggest that buckthorn was considered as similar in nature to blackthorn, a malignant tree, yet also effective in protecting against evil. Perhaps the dearth of folklore is because buckthorn's use was something people did not wish to dwell upon!

SEASONAL PLACING

Buckthorn can be placed seasonally in the autumn when its berries ripen, and the name *bréan úll* or 'rotten apple' suggests a contrast with the previous Ogham letter *Cert* and the apple, a fruit with similar, if more pleasant, healing associations. Buckthorn is associated

with the Ogham letter *Muin* which means 'Thicket'.

THE USES OF BUCKTHORN

Buckthorn was an important medicinal plant throughout these islands.[2] The first recorded Irish reference to buckthorn as a medicinal plant was made by Dr Caleb Threkeld in the early eighteenth century, who noted that the berries were widely used at that time by apothecaries and physicians. The Dublin herb market at that time was supplied by berries harvested in large numbers in the then King's County (County Offaly). In England buckthorn was mentioned by the Anglo-Saxons in their medical writings and Welsh physicians of the thirteenth century prescribed the juice of buckthorn berries mixed with honey as a laxative. Similarly, when the Benedictine abbey of St Alban's was excavated in the 1920s, considerable quantities of buckthorn seeds were found in the monks' latrines. Buckthorn continued to be taken in a syrup form in Britain up until the nineteenth century. Buckthorn's close relative the Alder Buckthorn (*Frangula Alnus*) was considered the best shrub for making charcoal for gunpowder, and the bark and berries were used for making dyes (the bark yellow and the berries green).[3] Like buckthorn itself, alder buckthorn's bark and berries are an effective purgative.

Furze – Aiteann

Ulex europaeus - Common Furze
Ulex galii - Mountain Furze
12th consonant of the Ogham Alphabet

The furze, gorse or whin, with its golden yellow blossoms seldom out of bloom, its evergreen branches used for food and fuel, and its habit of springing up quickly after being cut or burned, is a symbol of wealth and the fertility of the land itself.

FOLK BELIEFS AND CUSTOMS

It is not surprising then that an old Irish saying states: *An t-ór fé'n aiteann, an t-airgead fé'n luachair agus an gorta fé'n bhfraoch* (Gold under furze, silver under rushes and famine under heather), and there are several folk tales which connect furze with gold and money in general.[1] Likewise, in Yorkshire a similar saying has it that 'where there's bracken there's gold; where there's gorse there's silver; where there's heather there's poverty'.

One story concerns a white cow which disappeared whenever it was let out by the farmer. One day the farmer follows the cow down to a furze bush at the bottom of the field. He hits the cow with a stick and resolves to sell it. A voice from the furze bush asks him not to do that until the cow has calved. Realising that it is the fairies who speak, he obeys and the cow gives great milk from then on. Not only that, but the following Samhain he is taken magically back to New York where he had previously worked, and helped to retrieve a large sum of money owed to him. In another story, the ghost of a local chieftain appears from a furze bush to a poor tenant farmer and gives him enough gold coins to pay his rent in full, before riding off on a white horse into a nearby lake. After the landlord's agent has accepted the money and given a receipt for it, the coins turn into gingerbread! In a third story a poor man is put

cutting furze for the day on a shilling's pay. At the first strike a shilling comes out of the bush, so the man is able to go home.

According to Lucas, in his work, 'Furze - a Survey of its History and Uses in Ireland', furze features in many Irish customs.[2] At Easter in parts of Ulster eggs were dyed yellow by boiling them in water with furze blossom. The eggs were rolled or thrown for sport and then eaten. In various parts of the country furze blossom was also used occasionally to dye clothes yellow while the young shoots were used for green. On May Day in many places furze blossom was brought into the house, or placed over the door or in the thatch, for luck and to 'bring in the summer'. A sprig was then often kept on the roof or under the rafter until the next year. In some places furze was placed around milk or butter at Maytime to protect it from the fairies. Furze was also occasionally used as a May bush instead of hawthorn. Indeed in parts of Clare furze seems to have been preferred to hawthorn for this purpose. Furze was also extensively used as fuel for May bonfires, being well suited for the purpose. In many places cattle were driven at Maytime through a gap in a fence filled with burning furze and grass. On St Stephen's Day in Ireland the Wren Boys went from door to door carrying a wren in a bush and singing a rhyme which usually began: 'The wren, the wren, the king of all birds, on Stephen's Day was caught in the furze!', but despite the rhyme holly was generally the preferred choice of bush.

Despite of the customs described a widespread tradition declares that it is unlucky to bring furze blossoms indoors.[3] Instances of this are found in Ireland, England, the Channel Islands and Cornwall. In Fifeshire in Scotland it was said that to give anyone a present of whin blossom would lead to quarrelling with them. In Wales gorse was believed to offer protection against the fairies.[4] In one case a woman in Anglesea surrounded her bed with a partition of gorse to keep the fairies away. In Ireland to wear a spray of blessed gorse or *aiteann mhuire* ensures that you will never stumble.[5] Furze was particularly prized as fodder for horses and in Offaly it was believed that a horse could never be startled if it was kept where it had a good view of furze bushes.[6] In Kerry it was believed that the man on the moon (*conuí na sguab*) carried a furze bush on his back.[7] The following phrase also comes from Kerry: *mac rí an t-aiteann, mac bodaigh an fraoch* (furze is the son of a king, heather the son of a lout). This is perhaps a version of the saying about finding gold under furze and famine under heather.[7] As furze is in blossom for most of the year, a well-known expression has it that 'when gorse is out of bloom, kissing's out of fashion'. In some parts of England this phrase led to the custom of a spray of gorse being inserted into the bridal bouquet.[8]

The spiny nature of furze did not go unnoticed in folklore either. According to Cormac's *Glossary* the Irish name *aiteann* is a combination of *aith* 'sharp' and *tenn* 'lacerating', and features the following verse where the author laments being torn by the furze growing around Turvey in North County Dublin:

> Not loved is a tree unworthy,
> Growing all about in Turvey,
> Its leaves together do me strike,
> No protection from its spikes.

Interestingly furze is here described as *fid* 'tree' or 'wood'.

LEGENDS AND MYTHOLOGY

In a story in the *Metrical Dindshenchus* furze is linked with the goddess of the land. In the story the goddess of sovereignty for Ireland and Scotland appears to the sons of Daire as a hideous hag with a 'scabby black crown with a crop of wens like a furzy hillside' (wens are a kind of skin tumour). After one of them offers to sleep with her she then becomes a beautiful maiden with 'three shafts of sunlight in each eye' and offers him the kingship of both lands.[9]

SEASONAL PLACING

The many uses of furze mean that in truth, it could reasonably be placed seasonally at any time of year, but its use as food, bedding and shelter for livestock in the winter make the autumn an appropriate time. The furze is associated with the Ogham letter *Gort* which means 'Field'.

THE USES OF FURZE

In Ireland the presence of furze on land was seen as adding to its value.[10] Lucas quotes the Civil Survey of 1654 which classified furzy land as profitable, and land with both furze and heath on it as part profitable. Furthermore, the presence of furze on waste ground raised its status to part profitable. A similar view of furzy land was held in ancient Ireland. In early Irish law furze was considered one of the *Losa fedo* or Bushes of the Wood. In a poem in the *Metrical Dindshenchus* a druid foretells that during a future king's reign the land of his kingdom will be fertile, declaring that 'there shall be an abundance of furze therein'. This attitude to furze can be put down to its varied uses. In many parts of Ireland furze was burnt in the spring or early summer to encourage the growth of new tender shoots which were readily eaten by livestock, with the ashes of the burnt furze fertilising the land. Later, in the autumn, furze would be cut both for bedding and fodder, particularly for cattle and horses.

The wood was used to make *camáin* or hurleys, and walking sticks. Hedges were made of furze and temporary shelters for livestock were constructed of it in fields away from the farm homestead. According to Lucas this last practice is universal throughout Ireland and probably ancient in origin.

Broom – Giolcach

Cytisus scoparius - Common broom
13th consonant of the Ogham Alphabet

The broom with its long, flexible, pointed branches had many practical uses and was also an important medical plant, often used to treat complaints of the blood. Its bright yellow blossoms at May time made it a symbol of female beauty, purity and maidenhood.

FOLK BELIEFS AND CUSTOMS

Broom's association with maidenhood, female beauty and love is reflected in many customs.[1] In England a bunch of green broom tied with coloured ribbons was carried by guests at country weddings. In the north-western and midland counties of England it was customary to leave a sprig of broom outside the bridegroom's door and a sprig of hawthorn outside that of the bride to be, as a compliment to both. In Brittany the go-between in arranging a wedding was called 'he of the staff of broom', while in Wales an illegal union was called a 'broomstick wedding'. Brooms in Wales were generally made out of broom or birch. In the Scottish Highlands on Bride's Eve a small white rod called 'Bride's Wand' was placed beside an image of the infant Bride (or St Brigid) made out of straw. The rod could be made of broom, birch, bramble or willow.

In common with other bushes that flower in May, it is a widespread belief that to bring broom blossom indoors at May time is unlucky. A Suffolk tradition states that: 'when you sweep the house with blossomed broom in May, you are sure to sweep the head of the house away'.[2] In Surrey it was believed that if a child was whipped with a branch of green broom it would never grow any more.[3] In Scotland the witch's broom was often made of a stalk of the broom with a tuft of leaves at the end, while in England broom

is also a witch's plant yet can be used as protection against them.[4] In Ireland a lone bush of broom was a suitable place for the fairies to adopt as a dwelling place.[5]

The broom also appears in several old English ballads.[6] In the 'Ballad of Broomfield Hill' a lady has a tryst with her lover among the flowering broom and fears that she will lose her maidenhood. To avoid this a witch advises her to strew the broom blossoms around the knight: 'Ye'll pull the bloom frae off the broom/Strew't at his head and feet/And aye the thicker that ye do strew/The sounder he will sleep'. In another English ballad 'Tam Lin' the maiden Janet has just rescued Tam Lin from the fairies when: 'Out then spak the Queen o Fairies/Out of a bush o broom/"Them that has gotten young Tam Lin/has gotten a stately groom".' Also, a thirteenth century English poem involves a woman consulting a being in the broom about how to keep her husband's love. The being answers her; 'When your tongue is still/you'll have your will'! Conversely, an old tradition has it that when Joseph and Mary were fleeing into Egypt, the Virgin cursed the plants of the broom because the crackling of their ripe pods as they touched them in passing risked drawing the attention of Herod's soldiers.[7] Perhaps here the broom is hostile to the Virgin because it is in seed, not in blossom.

The broom was adopted as the badge of Brittany. Legend has it that Geoffrey of Anjou picked a sprig of it and thrust it into his helmet before going into battle. The broom or *Planta Genista* thus became in time the badge of Henry II of England, giving its name to his royal line, the *Plantagenets*.[8] In Scotland the Forbes clan also adopted the broom as their badge, calling it *bealadh* or 'beautiful' in Scots Gaelic.[9] In a reference to broom's long, thin twigs the Welsh Poem the '*Cad Godeu*' or 'Battle of the Trees' states that 'The broom before the rage of war/in the ditch lie broken'.

LEGENDS AND MYTHOLOGY

In the Welsh tale 'How Culhwch won Olwen', the beautiful maiden Olwen's hair is described as being 'yellower than the broom', while in the tale 'Math son of Mathonwy' the lovely Blodeuedd is created magically from the flowers of oak, broom and meadowsweet.

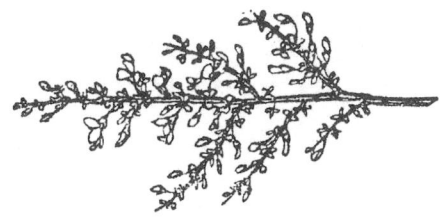

SEASONAL PLACING

For similar reasons to the furze, the broom can be placed seasonally in the autumn. Broom is associated with the Ogham letter *Gétal* which means 'Wounding'.

THE USES OF BROOM

As well as making brooms, basket work and fencing, broom was used in medicine as both a diuretic and cathartic throughout Europe.[9] It was used by the ancient Anglo-Saxons and by Welsh physicians in the Middle Ages. Henry VIII used to drink a water made from its flowers to cure his gout. The Cornish distinguished between a male broom or 'he-bannal' which made a diuretic drink for men, and a 'she-bannel' which made a similar drink for women. Broom held the place of modern disinfectant in ancient Ireland.[10] Premises were fumigated by burning the broom twigs in the centre of the affected area. Perhaps for similar reasons, Lenten fires in Belgium were made of broom and juniper, juniper being another bush burnt for fumigation purposes.[11] In early Irish law broom was classified as one of the *Losa fedo* or Bushes of the Wood.

Blackthorn – Draighean

Prunus spinosa - Blackthorn, Sloe
14th consonant of the Ogham Alphabet

 Str

The blackthorn, with its bitter black fruits, sharp thorns and tough wood is a symbol of fierceness and malevolence, but also of strength and protection. In contrast to this, however, its white blossoms are a symbol of female beauty.

FOLK BELIEFS AND CUSTOMS
In Ireland a blackthorn stick was regarded as providing protection against harm.[1] It was a good thing to carry at night to keep the fairies away, on account of their high regard for it. One story concerns a woman bothered by a shadow that appeared to her every night. On the advice of a wise woman she sprinkled holy water about and placed a blackthorn stick beside her bed and the shadow never appeared again. In another instance, a friar known for his ability to drive out evil spirits was supposedly able to wallop the devil out of a madman with a blackthorn. A twist on this power features in a story of a farmer who has a fairy cow which gives him great milk and a calf every year. One day the cow gets into a field of oats and the farmer, in a fit of fury, strikes it with a blackthorn stick. The cow bellows, gathers her calves around her and promptly leaves, never to be seen again. Another Irish story conveys the ambiguous nature of blackthorn as both helpful and harmful. A man who has had all his corn stolen falls asleep under a blackthorn bush and in his dream a voice tells him that the fairies have his corn and how to get it back. The farmer manages to retrieve his corn, but the fairies have their revenge, as the corn kills any livestock who eat it.

Given this ambiguous nature, blackthorn is often considered an unlucky tree.[2] In Scotland blackthorn is considered to be a 'crossed'

or unlucky wood, in contrast to the bramble which was seen as blessed. The blackthorn was not regarded as completely bad however, as an old saying makes clear: 'Better the bramble than the blackthorn/better the blackthorn than the devil'. In England blackthorn was also considered evil and it was believed that Christ's crown of thorns was made of blackthorn. In south Devon, villagers feared 'the black rod' when carried by local witches, as it was believed to cause miscarriages. In England the flowering of the blackthorn is believed to coincide with a spell of bad weather called 'the blackthorn winter' and in many places it was considered unlucky to take blackthorn blossom, among others, indoors. However, in Herefordshire, scorched blackthorn was mixed with mistletoe as a Christmas decoration to bring good luck.[3] According to Frazer, in Germany witches can be repelled on May Eve with a bundle of twigs of various plants, including blackthorn.[4]

In Ireland the blackthorn is said to be protected by fierce beings called 'lunantishees' who will punish anyone who tries to cut a stick on 11 May or 11 November (1 May and 1 November under the old calendar).[5] Perhaps the 'lunantishee' mentioned here is the same as the *Leannán Sídhe* or 'Fairy Lover', a female spirit who seeks the love of men. Any man she has under her power wastes away with love for her unless he can find someone else to take his place but in return she provides great poetic inspiration. Indeed, the blackthorn was used by the Gaelic poets as a symbol of female beauty: *Tá mo ghrá-sa mar bhláth na n-airne ar an draighneán donn* – 'My love is like the flower on the dark blackthorn', i.e., fair of skin with jet black hair.[6] In Wales love divination was practised with blackthorn. Pins made of blackthorn points were thrown into wells and if they sank the lover was believed to be insincere.[7]

LEGENDS AND MYTHOLOGY

The blackthorn features frequently in literature, though not always in a positive light. According to Cormac's *Glossary* the name *Draighean* comes from *Trog-Aon* or 'Wretched One', on account of its abundance of thorns. Suibhne Geilt (Mad Sweeney) in his exile in the woods is tormented by the thorns of hawthorn, briar and blackthorn. He complains that: 'the brown blackthorn bush/has nigh caused my death'. In Iubhdán's poem about different woods blackthorn is described as 'Hardy outlaw the blackthorn, wood no craftsman will burn/Although scanty, bird flocks cry out from its frame'. St Mochae was said to have been held in a spell for 150 years by the power of the song of a bird in a blackthorn bush.[8] The Welsh poem the '*Cad Godeu*' makes the enigmatic comment: 'The blackthorn full of spines – how the child delights in its fruit'. Perhaps this means that the sloe is not a fit fruit for adults but is only taken as a childish thrill due to its bitterness. In contrast, in the Life of Brigid, the saint blesses an alder tree, causing it to bear two-thirds apples and one-third 'sweet sloes' (*airni cumrai*). Either the sloes have been made sweet by a miracle, or this is a reference to some kind of early domesticated plum.

Given its tough, thorny nature it is not surprising that blackthorn appears in the context of war and combat.[9] In the story 'The Intoxication of the Ulaid', the druid Crom Deróil compares the advancing warriors to sloe bushes, saying that bushes would remain in silence unlike the warriors. In the *Lays of Fionn*, the story of Oscar's sword begins with it being won by Jove from his father at Sliabh Dosaigh of the 'brown sloe trees' (*droighean ruaidh*). The swords later passes through Queen Meadhbh's hands before ending up with Oscar. A story relates how the Mainí, the seven sons of Queen Meadhbh, hold a hostile force at bay at a ford by erecting a fence of briars and blackthorns, until such time as Queen Meadhbh comes to relieve them.

Blackthorn is also associated with fierce and warlike animals.[10] In the story 'The Wooing of Étaín', Midir challenges Echu to a game of *fidchell* (or chess), and among other things offers him 'fifty fiery boars .... and a blackthorn vat that can hold them all' if Echu wins the game. The story of 'The Pursuit of Diarmuid and Gráinne' includes a tale about Conn Céadchathach (Conn of the Hundred Battles) and his wife Sadhbh. Sadhbh eats her fill of sloes from a branch of blackthorn she finds hanging above her chariot. As a result of this she later bears a son called Cian who has a strange bulge across his forehead. Eventually the bulge is cut open and a worm leaps out, wrapping itself around one of Cian's spears. The worm grows enormous and fierce, with 100 heads, each one capable of swallowing a warrior. An attempt is made to burn it to death and it is driven away to a remote cave.

Perhaps because of its association with witches, the blackthorn often appears linked to women who are hostile and threatening.[11] In an incident in the *Metrical Dindshenchus* the seer Dallán is challenged by a woman to tell her what she has beneath her cloak. Dallán replies correctly that it is a branch of blackthorn covered with dark sloes. So that he will not satirise her for her insolence, the woman is then forced to give away her land to him. In ancient Ireland a woman who had no one to vouch for her had to clear her name by undergoing an ordeal involving rubbing her tongue on a red hot adze of bronze or melted lead, heated in a fire of blackthorn or rowan. A folk tale from Donegal explains how a dangerous stretch of sea just off the coast, called Béal an Bharra, came to be.

Béal an Bharra used to be land protected from the sea by three rods of blackthorn. If the three rods were ever cut, the houses and land would all be drowned. One day as a result of a disagreement, two of the local women resolved to stay up late in order to cut the rods. On their way to carry out the deed they met a third woman who agreed to help them, but the two women were hurrying so much she could not keep up with them. Before she caught up with them, the two woman had cut the rods, drowning the land and themselves. The third woman survived to tell what had happened. The story ends by stating that this is why the women of the locality can never be trusted again!

Also from Donegal comes a strange story about a place called Mín an Droighin (The Blackthorn Pasture).[12] A man in a cart is passing there when he stops to give a woman a lift. The woman is tall and wearing white clothes with a weary expression on her face. As soon as the woman gets into the cart the horses refuse to move, and the woman explains that it is her burden that is the cause. She goes on to say that she used to own a public house and would water down the spirits she served, and that she is burdened by that fact for ever more. She then leaps from the cart and the horses rear up and run non-stop until they have reached their destination. The origin of this story may be a play on the name of the warrior queen Maedhbh which in Irish means 'intoxication' and who may have been seen as a suitable character to associate with a place where blackthorns grow. In any case the overall evidence points to blackthorn being seen as a 'female' tree linked to warlike or fierce female spirits, perhaps derived ultimately from the war goddesses of pagan Ireland.

SEASONAL PLACING
Seasonally blackthorn can be placed in mid to late autumn when the sloes ripen. Blackthorn is associated with the Ogham letter *Straif* which means 'Sulphur'.

THE USES OF BLACKTHORN

Blackthorn was classified in early Irish law as one of the *Fodla fedo* or Lower Divisions of the Wood. The blackthorn was prized for its hard wood and shillelaghs were often made out of blackthorn.[13] Faction fighters at fairs and other public gatherings would often carry a blackthorn stick or ashplant with them as a weapon. In the early Irish tale 'The Destruction of Da Derga's Hostel', Da Derga is accompanied by three fifties of warriors, each carrying a great blackthorn club with a band of iron around it. Sloes were not completely useless either, as sloe gin was widely made. For example, in Maigh Cuilinn, County Galway the custom at Halloween was to drink sloe wine.[14]

Elder – Trom

Sambucus nigra - Common Elder

15th consonant of the Ogham Alphabet

3 October - 30 October
13th month of Ogham Tree Calendar

The elder or bore-tree, with its untidy appearance, unpleasant smell and dark berries, is regarded as a symbol of witchcraft and evil. However, its many medicinal uses, especially for rashes and inflammation of the skin, give it the reputation of a powerful and protecting tree as well.

Folk Beliefs and Customs

The elder is universally held to be an unlucky and malevolent tree.[1] In Ireland elder is considered to have a *crostáil* or 'bad temper or mischief' in it and it was believed that if someone were struck with an elder branch that after their death their hand would grow out of their grave. An old Irish saying states that there are three signs of the cursed and abandoned place; the elder, the nettle and the corncrake. Adamnán, the Abbot of Iona, created a law that women and children were not to be killed in war and any who broke this law were to be cursed. The curse was that they would face ruin and their heirs be elder, nettle and corncrake. In many countries it was believed that elder wood or flowers should never be brought into the house, and that it was dangerous to fall asleep under an elder as the smell of its leaves and flowers had a narcotic and poisonous effect. A widespread belief also considered it very unlucky to burn elder wood as that would bring death or the devil into the house. A story in the *Lays of Fionn* called 'The Headless Phantoms' illustrates this in an Irish context. Fionn and his men arrive at a house in the Yew Glen which has a welcoming fire. As soon as they enter, however, they are greeted by a grey churl who throws a log of elder wood onto the fire, choking it. The house is in fact inhabited by

Folklore of the Trees

phantoms seeking revenge, and Fionn and his men are immediately attacked.

Perhaps because of its association with witches, elder is considered hostile to children, especially infants.[2] In Ireland it is dangerous or foolhardy to make a cradle out of elder as the child would sicken and the fairies steal it. In England a cradle made out of elder also made the child sick, or else led to the child being pinched black and blue by the fairies. A story in the *Annals of the Four Masters* relates how a queen set a charm to exact revenge on the king's pregnant mistress by tying up a bundle of elder rods in a magic string with nine knots in it. The effect of the charm is to prolong the agonies of her childbirth. In Ireland it is also said to be wrong to strike a child or animal with elder as they would not grow from then on.

In many countries there are stories of the elder being inhabited by an elder spirit or mother spirit who protects the tree from harm.[3] In Denmark the *Hylde Moer* or Elder Mother should always be asked for permission before any wood is cut, otherwise any furniture made of the wood will be haunted by her. In England it was also believed that when cutting elder you should first ask permission of the Mother Elder. In Leicestershire the person would bow three times and say: 'Old woman, old woman, give me some of your wood, and when I am dead I'll give you some of mine.' In Northamptonshire it was said that a local witch could be uncovered by cutting a branch from an elder tree. If sap flowed freely from the cut, the witch would be the person with his or her arm bandaged to cover a new wound. It is not hard to see how the elder could be believed to be inhabited by a witch or hag. A mature elder has a hunched appearance, deeply gnarled bark and tangled twigs like crabbed fingers. No doubt these traditions of a witchlike Elder Mother also explain why elder is seen as particularly hostile to children.

In common with other trees possessing a malevolent reputation like hawthorn and aspen, a belief arose that elder was the tree upon which Christ was crucified.[4] A Scottish rhyme puts it like this: 'Bour tree, bour tree, crookit rung,/Never straight, and never strong/Ever bush and never tree/Since our Lord was nailed t'ye'. In Cornwall the reason cradles should not be made of elder is because it was believed to be the tree on which Jesus was crucified. In Suffolk lightning was believed never to strike an elder as the cross of Calvery was made of it. In Ireland it was believed that the elder tree once refused to shelter Christ but the ivy did so, hence the elder is the last tree to come into leaf, while the ivy is evergreen. A strong and widespread tradition also existed that elder was the tree upon which Judas hanged himself.

Despite (or perhaps because of) its malevolent reputation, elder was also believed to be a powerful tree to use against evil.[5] The elder was widely planted around houses to keep witches away. In Scotland the elder ranks second only to the rowan in its power to protect against witchcraft and evil spells, and crosses made of elder were fixed to stables and byres. In Ireland a wreath made of elder wrapped around a milk churn was used to protect milk from bad spirits. In the Isle of Man elder leaves were picked on May Eve and fixed to doors and windows to protect the house from witchcraft. In Suffolk it was believed that elder sticks kept in the pocket would prevent saddle sores when riding, and drovers and cattle men would carry an elder stick as a charm against evil. In Scotland hearse drivers had whip handles made of elder to avert evil.

Given its reputation, it is not surprising that the elder is a tree particularly preferred by the fairies.[6] In Scotland it was believed that if a baptised person applied the green juice of the inner bark of an elder to their eyelids and stood under a elder near a fairy hill on Halloween, he or she could see the fairy train go by. Similarly, in Denmark those who stood under an elder on Midsummer Eve would see the king of Fairyland and his retinue ride by. In the Isle of Man elder was thought of as a fairy tree and every house had its *tramman* (or elder in Manx) planted by the door. The fairies liked to play and swing out of the trees and if a branch or the tree itself was cut down they would grieve and desert the house. When the wind blew through the branches of an elder the Manx believed that it was the fairies riding on them. A similar belief must have existed in Ireland, as Iubhdan has this to say in his poem about various trees: 'Elder with its tough bark, truly wounds the most / burn it into charcoal, steed of the fairy host'.

Legends and Mythology

There seem to be no legends that involve the elder but it does appear in some folk tales. In one Irish folk tale a fairy piper waits under an elder tree for a priest to ask a dying man where the piper will go on the last day. The priest relays the message that the fairy piper will only go to heaven if he can find enough blood in his body with which to write his name. At that the piper stabs himself but only froth comes out, and in a fit of rage he declares he will do only harm from that day on.[7]

Some stories from Ireland and Gaelic Scotland hint that elder is a tree particularly hostile to women.[8] In an Irish folk tale a man looks over a cliff and sees fairies involved in preparing a meal. Beside them a big pot is boiling on a fire of elder twigs. The man is spotted and seized, beaten and scalded with boiling water from the pot before he is let go. Yet the following morning it is his wife who dies. In a tale from Scotland the heroine tricks a giant into thinking she is hidden in a goat's paunch which has been hung up, when in fact it is the giant's wife who is hiding there. The giant unknowingly beats his wife to death with elder wood clubs. Perhaps the reason for the enmity between the elder and women is that women were seen as particularly vulnerable to a feminine 'witch's' tree.

Seasonal Placing

Elder is associated with the Ogham letter *Ruis* which means 'Redness'. It can be seasonally placed in mid to late autumn when its dark purple berries ripen and brings to a close the seasonal cycle of the consonant letters.

The Uses of Elder

In early Irish law elder was classified as one of the *Fodla fedo* or Lower Divisions of the Wood. Although its timber is virtually useless, its medicinal properties and the use of its flowers and berries for making wine earned it a place.

Pine – Giúis

Pinus sylvestris - Scot's pine

1st vowel of the Ogham Alphabet

29 November - 26 December
2nd month of Ogham Tree
Calendar

The pine or fir is an evergreen tree with an invigorating scent from its resin, which also makes its wood burn with a bright, white flame. This makes it a symbol of renewal, rebirth, and eternal life.

FOLK BELIEF AND CUSTOMS

The associations of pine with birth and new life make it a natural tree to be involved in festivals welcoming the return of the sun and good weather.[1] Many such May Day and midsummer customs existed throughout Europe. In Swabia on 1 May a tall fir tree used to be set up in the centre of the village, where it was decked with ribbons and was the focus of dancing. In Saxony on May Eve or Whitsuntide the people went out into the woods to seek the May and brought young trees, especially firs and birches, to the village where they were set up before the doors of the houses or of the cattle stalls. Young men also set up such May trees before the chambers of their sweethearts. In Sweden in midsummer on St John's Eve young fir trees were raised at the doorway of the houses and elsewhere around the homestead. In Stockholm on this day a May pole made of a spruce pine was set up and decorated as the centre of festivities and dancing. In many parts of Germany on St John's Eve tall fir or pine trees were set up as May poles in a similar fashion. In Brittany the fire of St Peter in June called the *tan-tad* or 'fire of the dead' was lit with a pine candle by the oldest man in the area. A.T. Lucas in his article 'Bog Wood: A Study in Rural Economy', records an instance from County Cavan of bog fir being especially used for the midsummer fire.

In Silesia many villages welcomed summer by throwing an effigy of Death into water to symbolically drown it. After thus defeating Death the children celebrated the rebirth of life by cutting down a small fir tree, decorating it and carrying it from door to door singing songs and looking for money. In Eisenach on the fourth

Sunday in Lent a straw man representing Death was tied to a wheel, set alight and sent rolling down a hill. After this, a tall fir tree was cut and set up dressed in ribbons in the plain below. The birch was used in many similar summer time ceremonies and both trees were probably regarded as similar in nature as trees of birth. Indeed, the Icelandic rune poem for the rune *bjarkan* or 'birch' is glossed with the word *abies* – a Latin word for pine.

The fir tree also has well-known associations with Christmas time.[2] Nowadays this is chiefly due to the custom of setting up Christmas trees in the home, a custom which originated on the continent. Legend has it that the idea of the Christmas fir tree first came to Martin Luther. After walking one Christmas Eve under a clear winter sky lit by 1,000 stars, he set up for his children a tree with countless candles as an image of the starry heaven from whence Christ came. However, the first known record of a modern Christmas tree comes from Strasbourg in 1605 where fir trees were set up in parlours and decorated. Perhaps the Christmas tree was a more modern expression of an older link between the evergreen pine with its bright flaming wood and the birth of the new year and the new sun. In Ireland, A.T. Lucas records several instances in Counties Cork and Kerry of logs of bog pine being especially burnt on Christmas Eve to provide a good blazing fire. In Carbery the *Bloc Nollag* or Christmas Log was often made of pine, and the priest would have pine and palm in the church. In Maigh Cuilinn in Connemara pieces of dry pine wood would be used as candles at Christmas time 'on account of the fine light it gave off'.

The bright light and invigorating scent of burning pine was considered to have purifying powers against evil influences.[3] In some parts of Silesia people burnt pine resin all night between Christmas and the New Year in order that the pungent smoke might drive away witches and evil spirits. In Scotland on all Halloween torches of lighted fir splinters were carried around the cornfields to bless and fertilise them, the bearers travelling sunwise. In a Scottish folk tale three ghosts are banished by the nephew of one of them carrying seven lighted staves of pine into the room they have been haunting. The ghosts lost their strength immediately and disappeared saying: 'Were it not for the slender lances of pine, this would be to your hurt, young Donald Gorm'. A possible Irish example is found in a story involving a hunting challenge between the Fianna and Aongus of the Tuatha Dé Danann. The Fianna burn to ashes the enchanted pigs they have caught to prevent them from coming to life again. The wood used is not named but we are told that it lit up like a candle when put on the fire.

Because of its scarcity and possible extinction as a native tree in Ireland, there is not much Irish folklore associated with the pine except regarding the use of ancient bog pine wood. Folklore about pine survives in Britain, however.[4] In Scotland pine is known as *Clársach nan craobh* or 'The Harp of Trees' on account of the musical sound the wind makes through its long needle-like leaves. Scots pine is the official clan badge of the Grants and the McGregors.

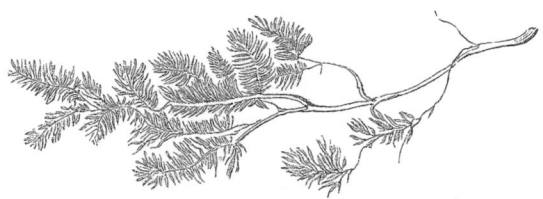

LEGENDS AND MYTHOLOGY

There is evidence that the pine and palm tree were seen as linked, both being associated with birth and fertility.[5] In the French Pyrenees shrines to the Celtic Jupiter have altars carved with solar signs accompanied by both conifer and palm tree symbols. A stone mother goddess at Caerwent holds what is either a palm branch or a conifer in front of her as either a symbol of victory or fertility. According to Robert Graves, the palm is a symbol of birth sacred in ancient Egypt, Babylonia, Phoenicia and Arabia. In Greek mythology the goddess Leto clasped a palm tree when she was about to give birth to the divine twins Apollo and Artemis. Similarly, the pine was worshipped by the Phrygians as a symbol of the god Attis who was reborn every spring. Attis was said to have been transformed into a fir tree by the goddess Cybele who loved him, when he lay dying from a wound dealt him by a boar sent by Zeus. The god Adonis was said to have been born under a fir tree. An ivy-twined, fir cone tipped branch was the sacred symbol of the goddess Artemis, waved in ceremonies sacred to her. Pine cones were regarded as symbols of fertility and at the festival of the Themophoria they were thrown into the sacred vaults of Demeter for the purpose of quickening the ground and the wombs of women. In later times, St Martin of Tours, despite converting the people to Christianity, was not allowed by them to harm a much venerated pine tree that stood near their former pagan temple. Conifers appear in carvings on altars at Glanum in Provence and at Toulouse.

Much of the folklore in Britain also points to an association of pine with birth.[6] The museum of Newcastle-on-Tyne houses a Romano-British altar dedicated to 'the mothers' which shows a triangle on its base with a fir cone enclosed. In the Orkneys mother and child are 'sained' or blessed soon after birth with a flaming fir candle whirled three times around the bed. In a Scottish folk tale the daughter of a smith relates a dream in which she sees a shoot of fir growing from the heart of the king and a shoot growing from her own heart, with the two shoots twining together. 'That is our babe son,' replies the king when he hears of the dream.

Perhaps because of its links with youthfulness and virility, pine also appears to be linked to warriors.[7] The great warrior Fionn had a pine forest where the Fianna would be sure to find hunting whenever they could not find enough elsewhere in Leinster. This forest was 'like a herb garden' to the Fianna. A popular phrase in Scottish folk tales goes like this: 'There was a king and a knight – as was and will be, and as grows the fir tree, some of them crooked and some of them straight'. At Rooscorr in Yorkshire a group of Iron Age warriors carved from pinewood was found, deposited as an offering to some god perhaps. They had eyes made out of quartz and a hole for a phallus, perhaps also of quartz.

Finally, pine's evergreen quality is used as a symbol of eternal love in the story of the doomed lovers Deirdre and Naoise. In one version of the story a pine tree grows out of each of their graves and the branches grow towards one another until they become entwined.[8]

SEASONAL PLACING

Seasonally the pine's association with birth and renewal make it a natural tree to place at the beginning of the year, whether it be at the winter solstice or Imbolc. Pine is associated with the Ogham letter *Ailm* which means 'Palm'.

THE USES OF PINE

It is not surprising that the bright flame of pine's resinous wood meant that it was widely used as a source of light.[9] In England torches were made of the young fir branches, whose resinous twigs burnt easily with a clear strong light. Because of this the name fir tree was said to derive from 'fire tree'. However, an English rhyme has this to say: 'birch and fir logs burn too fast/blaze up bright and do not last'. In Ireland pieces of Scots pine dug out of the bog were widely used as lighting, especially by the poor. A.T. Lucas, in his study of bog wood, gives a detailed account of the uses of bog pine in Ireland, and gives many examples of its wide use for providing domestic light, both as a torch or splinter and as a firewood which threw out good light. According to the Scottish folklorist Carmicheal bog pine was also used as a candle in the Highlands. It made good light but again did not last. In Brittany also, pine candles were used to light cottages in winter. In early Irish law pine was considered one of the seven *Airig fedo* or Nobles of the Wood, because in ancient Ireland pine resin was collected from the living tree and made into a pitch used for caulking boats and preserving wood.

Ash – Fuinseóg

Fraxinus excelsior - Common ash

16 May-12 June
8th month of Ogham Tree Calendar

2nd vowel of the Ogham Alphabet

The ash tree is noted for its strong and flexible timber, the delicacy of its leaves and new growth. It has associations with fertility and healing through its symbolic link with water. Indeed, the impressive site of a tall mature ash tree is a symbol of the well-being of the land itself.

FOLK BELIEFS AND CUSTOMS

Many superstitions surround the ash.[1] Folk tradition in Ireland has it that the ash will be the first tree to be hit by lightning while in England the saying was: 'Avoid an ash/it courts the flash'. In Ireland ash wood was burned to banish the devil and an ash staff protected against evil. In the Life of St Moling the saint confronts an evil spectre and drives him away successfully with his ashen staff. In Antrim ash sticks were believed to be a 'kindly' wood to drive cattle with, protecting them from harm. In Buchan in Aberdeen a herding stick of ash when thrown at cattle is sure not to strike a vital part. In Scotland, a sprig of ash placed under a milk pail would ensure that the goodness would not be stolen by fairies. Ash keys carried in the hand were a protection against witchcraft.

Despite its role in protecting against witches the ash was also used by them.[2] The ash is the favourite tree of witches for making ritual dolls into which to stick pins. In Zealand in Denmark the prehistoric remains of a woman believed to be a witch have been found with various ritual objects including aspen and ash twigs. A story about Beare Island in County Cork tells of two hags, one on the island and one on the mainland, having an argument by throwing hurling sticks or rods at one another. The ash, of course, is used to make hurleys.

Furze – Aiteann
Ulex gallii

Broom – Giolcach
Crytisus scoparius

Blackthorn – Draighean
Prunus spinosa

Elder – Trom
Sambucus nigra

The ash could also be used for cures.[3] W.B. Yeats, in *Fairy and Folk Tales of Ireland*, quotes an example of a 'fairy doctor', or local man known for the power to heal, who shunned hazel sticks but always carried an ash wand with him which he placed across his knees while saying his charms. In England it was believed that shrews stiffened the limbs of cattle when they ran over them. The cure was to stroke the cattle with an ash branch that had a shrew entombed in a hole bored into it. In England children with ruptures were passed through an ash split held open with wedges of oak. The ash was then bandaged up and as the split healed so the child was cured.

The ash tree is also associated with childbirth.[4] In many parts of the Highlands at the birth of a child, the nurse or midwife would put one end of a green stick of ash into the fire and collecting on a spoon the sap which oozed out the other end, administered this as the first drop of liquid to the new-born child. This was done to give the child the strength of the ash and to protect it from witches and goblins. In Norse myth the cooked fruit of the World tree, the ash Yggdrasill, ensured safe childbirth. In Devon and Somerset an old custom on 5 January or Old Christmas Eve was 'burning the ashen faggot' – a bundle of ashen sticks bound together and burnt on a bonfire to much celebration. The traditional reason for using ash in his way is that Our Lady kindled a fire with ash wood in order to wash her new-born son.

Like the hazel, an ancient belief exists that the ash protects against snakes.[5] The Roman naturalist Pliny says that 'So great are the virtues of this tree that no serpent will ever lie in the shadow thrown by it'. The folklorist Trevelyan states that in Wales the ash tree is said to have a spite against snakes and in Cornwall it was believed that a branch of ash would keep away snakes. A Cornish charm against the bite of an adder goes 'bradgty, bradgty, bradgty, under the ashing leaf' repeated three times. The word 'bradgty' or 'braggaty' is said to mean 'mottled like an adder'. The link of ash and hazel with snakes is probably through their association with water, as snakes are believed to inhabit dark, dank places.

Ash trees have a strong link with holy wells.[6] A.T. Lucas found that of 210 trees surveyed growing next to holy wells, 75 of them were ash trees, a figure surpassed only by hawthorn. Lucas believed that this frequency was for arbitrary reasons but the wealth of folklore about the ash and holy wells contradicts this. For example, St Patrick's Well at Kilcorkey in County Roscommon had a great old ash growing beside it called St Patrick's Walking Stick. As a baby, St Colman was found beside an ash tree near a well known for curing the blind and the lame. At St Kieran's well at Castlekeeran, County Meath in 1840 an ash tree was said to bleed and people flocked to the well for cures. In Outeragh a pilgrimage to St Brigid's Well held on 1 February began with walking around an old ash tree. Similarly, at Brideswell in County Roscommon on the last Sunday in July the pilgrimage involved walking around a single ash tree on a small mound. St Brigid herself is clearly linked to the ash. *The Life of Brigid* tells of the saint kneeling to pray at the church at Magh Taulach, and turning an ash beam, which supported the altar, into acacia wood which neither burned nor aged. A renowned giant ash also stood beside St Brigid's Cathedral in Kildare.

Sometimes the tree itself would provide the source of water.[7] One such was a huge ash at Collnamooneen in County Sligo called Crannavilla which had a hollow, like a bowl or font, cut into the trunk and a stone marked with a cross at its foot. Another tree at Borriskane in County Tipperary was called the 'Big Bell Tree' (from the Irish *Bile*). The water which lodged in a hollow of its branches was regarded as holy and anyone who used its branches for firewood would have their own house burnt down. A similar story concerned a man called Deeley who cut down some ash trees growing near the well at Corker in County Galway. The next day his lip was drawn down with water running from it, and this drooling continued for life. There is evidence from other cultures of the link of the ash tree with wells and water.[8] In Norse myth the world tree, the ash Yggdrasill, had a well at each of its three great roots, while in Greek myth the ash was sacred to Poseidon, god of the sea. There is also archaeological evidence of the association. In Britain around 21 ritual shafts dating from between 1600-1000 BC have been found, most containing ash wood, potsherds and human and cattle bones.

There are also many stories of sacred ash trees not near wells.[9] In the parish of Clenor in County Cork stands a sacred ash tree called Crannahulla (*Crann a' Shúile* or tree of the eye) which sprang up when a beautiful girl called Craebhnat plucked out her eye rather than marry the son of the king of Munster. Another ash sacred to St Craebhnat at Killura in County Cork was said to protect against drowning and emigrants carried chips or twigs of it away with them. A sacred ash tree known as *An Crann Comhaita* or the Tree of Power, was believed to be made miraculously bear apple blossoms by St Patrick to demonstrate his power to the prince of Munster. Sacred ash trees were also linked to funerals. In County Offaly near Kennelly church, every funeral cortège would stop for a few minutes to say a prayer and throw stones into a cairn at the foot of an ash tree. The same practice occurred in Bweeounagh in County Galway and in Palmerstown, County Dublin, while in Cong in County Mayo wooden crosses were left. A revealing Irish folk tale tells of a witch whose soul resides in an ash tree. When the heroine of the tale strikes the ash with an axe the tree screams and the witch hears it, losing her mind and sense (*meabhair agus ciall*). Thus, she rushes towards the tree leaving her clothes immodestly undone and the heroine is able to kill her by striking a vulnerable spot on her body. This compares with a legend about a well at Teelin in County Donegal which was blessed by three holy women called *Ciall* (Sense), *Tuisge* (Understanding) and *Náire* (Modesty). Perhaps qualities such as these were associated with the power of holy wells and by extension with ash trees.

LEGENDS AND MYTHOLOGY

The warrior queen Maedhbh seems to be especially linked to the ash. In the *Táin* it states that every spot where she planted her horsewhip was from then on called *Bile Maedhbh*, or the Sacred Tree of Maedhbh and horsewhips were usually made of ash. Iubhdan in his poem about different timbers says: 'horsewhip in horseman's hands' about the ash. A tree by a sacred or holy well is generally also called *Bile Maedhbh*, again suggesting the ash.[10] Maedhbh was originally a goddess of sovereignty so this links the ash to kingship. The king Cormac Connloinges was placed under *geasa* or taboo not to repair his chariot with a yoke of ash.[11] The '*Cad Godeu*' has this to say about the ash: 'The ash was exalted most/before the sovereign power'. A goddess called Onniona was worshipped by the Gauls in ash groves.[12]

The ash seems to appear in three very important carvings from Celtic Gaul which depict a bull and three cranes in a leafy tree, and the god Esus striking at the tree with an axe. Miranda Greene, the Celtic scholar, believes that the tree depicted is a willow, but the ash is a more likely option. In the first place the leaves depicted in the carving appear to be pinnate in form, that is the leaflets emerge in pairs from the same place on the leafstalk. Ash leaves do this but those of willow do not. In addition, the thick tree trunk depicted in the Esus carving looks a lot more like ash than willow. The ash is also a better candidate for mythological reasons. The Roman poet Lucan in his famous poem Pharsalia mentions Esus as being propitiated with human sacrifices, who had been stabbed and then hung in trees to bleed to death. He then describes a grove of the druids at Marsalia in which grew yew, alder, cypress and ash, which was the scene of bloody human sacrifices. There may be a parallel here with the Norse god Odin who ritually hung himself from the ash tree Yggdrasill for nine days and nights in order to gain occult knowledge. Certainly the ash has a warlike aspect as it was a favourite wood for making spears. Suibhne Geilt speaks of the ash tree as 'Thou baleful one, hand weapon of a warrior'. Perhaps this explains the link with cranes, seen in Irish mythology as harbingers of war and misfortune. Greene also speculates that the tree depicted is the Tree of Life that is regularly cut down and yet springs up again. This also could describe the ash as it can regenerate very quickly and was widely coppiced like willow and hazel.

Three of the five great trees of Ireland were ash trees. *Bile Uisnigh* stood at the historic centre of Uisneach; *Bile Tortan* stood at Ardbreccan in County Meath, roughly at the centre of a triangle formed by the three great centres of Tara, Tlaghtga and Tailltiu (Teltown) and the third *Craobh Daithi* stood in the barony of Farbill in County Westmeath, roughly halfway between the other two. It is surely no coincidence that two of the trees should stand near to each of the two great centres of Ireland, while the third stood roughly halfway between them. This is a triplification of the idea of a great ash tree standing at the centre of the land, as a sign of the protection by the goddess of the land of her territory and its fertility. There is an obvious parallel in Norse myth with the World Tree, the ash

Yggdrasill, which as the timeless Guardian Tree stood at the axis and centre of the cosmos, its roots reaching down to the lowest world and its branches reaching up over heaven. The five trees were said to have been planted by Fintan Mac Bóchna from the berries of a magical branch he received from a mythological being called Trefuilngid Tre-Eochair, and they remained hidden from view until the birth of the famous king Conn Céadchathach. The trees stood until the time of the king Aed Sláin who was murdered in 600 AD when they were felled by the satire of poets.

The most celebrated of all the trees was *Bile Tortan*. In a 21-stanza poem in the *Metrical Dindshenchus* its virtues are praised and its loss mourned. The mighty tree was 50 cubits thick and 300 cubits high, and stretched out so far that all the men of Tortu could safely gather under it from the pelting of the storms. The tree waged a constant battle with the wind, which tossed its green, leafy branches and in the storms of winter the sound of the wind and snow through the tree was fierce as they tore bundles of twigs from it. Eventually despite its great strength, the tree's colour faded and it decayed and was brought down. When it fell the plain of Tortu lost two-thirds of its prosperity and Meath became deserted as its people were without protection or shelter. The poem, however, makes the claim that one day a new tree will shoot up again from the roots of the old. The tree is obviously a symbol of the heroic golden age of Gaelic Ireland and is a potent symbol of the protection of the goddess of sovereignty. It is significant that when the battle of Maigh Tuiread is over, it is the Morrigan and not the Dagda who declares: 'Peace up to the skies, the skies down to earth, the earth under the skies, strength to everyone'. This is as succinct a description of the role of the ash as a sacred Guardian Tree as it is possible to make.

TREE OF TORTAN

Ultán   The tree of Tortan is no more
        Its edges battered by raging storms.
        Rival crowns gather in common pain
        Grieving long after they part again.

Mochuma   Tree of Tortan, proud its display

	Mid roaring winds forever a-sway.
	Firm it stood here from its green youth
	Until its death, so barren of growth.

Mochúa	The men of Tortan are forlorn
Clúana	For that unique tree they mourn.
Dolcain	The sight before them valued most
	Over all things that have been lost.

Cróin	Tribe of Tortan, in a great mass
Galma	Under the outstanding tree so vast.
	From the rainstorms they were spared
	Until the day it was old and bare.

Colum	Though it is now sapless wood
Cille	A great age on earth it stood.
	The King who once raised up its frame
	Has brought it back down again.

Ultán	Fifty cubits its girth so strong
Tige Túa	Rearing over the forest throng
	And three hundred, a perfect number
	The full height of its great timber.

Mochuma	Three ramparts of Ireland, you see
	Are shorn of their security
	Tree of Rossa, Tree of Mugna wide,
	Tortan's Tree strong on every side.

Mochua	Tree of Tortan, deep its roar
	Through the peril of fierce storms.
	From it torn great swarms of litter
	By the winds of nights in winter.

Ultán	Residing over great Tortan's Plain
Ua	When the fine sons of Mil did reign
Conchubair	Until it fell when its strength waned

In the reign of the sons of Aed Slaine.

Cróin	The wind did cause the tree to fail
Galma	Only the hard heart could bear the tale.
	Three times fifty Conaille were killed
	When at their fair the tree was felled.

Sinche Ó	Though you, O bent over old crone
Chillín	Take firewood from it for your home
Íchtair	Once many a fair youth was blest
Thire	Under its bright branches to rest.

Ultán	When winter loosed her snowy locks
Tige Túa	She loosed fair sticks in circling flocks
	Deathly horrid her gleeful scorn
	At the felling of the Tree of Tortan

Cróin	As all the eye can see must fall
Galma	So they joined in unending war.
	The wind never once did stay her hand
	'Til the tree's pride was at an end.

Mochua	All things fade and lose their worth
	Death comes to every thing on earth.
	They are red earth, but withered clay
	All who gathered about the tree.

Ultán	The plain of Tortan is a kingless land
	Since the fair tree no longer stands.
	Two thirds of its wealth now gone
	Since the great tree was brought down.

Torannán	Vain pride of Adam, the first man
Tulcha	Destroyed the sons of the noble clans.
	The same fate is for us in store
	Now their mighty tree is no more.

Colum Cille	Fair Ochann and Tlachta are wastelands Without Ailell of the warrior bands Son of Nathu, just ruler of Meath Law giver and great champion tree.
Mochua	I Mochua, with Cróin do plead Please do not grieve excessively. From the bare stump so grey in hue Many a tree might spring anew.
Colum Cille	On a particular summer's day I was in the wood of bushy leaves. In a burst of rain I was kept dry Under the Tree of Tortan's eaves.
Mochuma	I have no comfort, though winds shake The fertile woods in cheerful play. Alone a ghostly woman takes Wood from the Tree of Tortan today.
Ultán	Though the wind made sport against it While it was young, it could not break it. But it brings all old things to earth: So the Tree of Tortan met its death.

SEASONAL PLACING

The ash tree's connection with water, fertility and growth place it seasonally in late spring or early summer when its delicate foliage first appears. The ash is associated with the Ogham letter *Onn* which itself is the Old Irish word for ash.

THE USES OF ASH

In early Irish law the ash was classified as one of the seven *Airig fedo* or Nobles of the Wood. As well as making hurleys and spears, ash had a wide variety of uses including building, making fences, furniture and boat building. Ash bark could be used for tanning and the dried leaves were sometimes used as fodder for livestock.

Elm – Leamhán

Ulmus glabra - Wych Elm
3rd vowel of the Ogam Alphabet

The elm, with its rich foliage and sap, is associated with fertility, and the ability of its timber to remain submerged in water without rotting makes it a symbol of durability.

FOLK BELIEFS AND CUSTOMS

Wych elm protects against harm and a sprig of it is needed in a churn before the milk will come.[1] In Scotland a twig of wych elm placed in the churn ensured that the fairies could not take the butter. The elm is also associated with fertility.[2] In Sweden a guardian tree existed around every farm, and pregnant women would clasp it to ensure an easy delivery. The trees were either lime, ash or elm. An old Irish cure for a man rendered impotent by charms was to write the man's name on a wand of elm and to strike him with it. An association between the elm and churches appears in other countries.[3] In Lichfield in England at the Feast of the Ascension the clergy and choir of the cathedral carry elm boughs as they go around 'beating the bounds', stopping at various points where wells formerly stood. On their return they place the elm boughs around the church font. In Brittany in the village of Locmaria on Belle Île stands a church called Notre Dame de Bois Tord (Our Lady of the Twisted Wood). The story goes that a splendid elm stood outside the church until Dutch sailors cut it down for a mast. As soon as they had done so, however, the wood became twisted and useless.

LEGENDS AND MYTHOLOGY

The elm tree appears in several stories involving Irish saints and holy men as a nourishing and protecting tree, often in connection

with holy wells. Whitley Stokes' *Lives of the Saints* tells the story of St Ruadhán of Lorrha. The saint had an elm at his monastery which used to drip a sweet tasting fluid in which everyone would find the flavour he or she desired. The monks were displeased with this and entreated Findian, who was in charge of religious affairs in Ireland, to put a stop to it. On Findian's request St Ruadhán made a sign of the cross over the tree and the dripping immediately stopped. However, Ruadhán then blessed the nearby well so that the water in it turned into the same sweet liquid. At this, Findian turned the well back to water and instructed Ruadhán to conform with his will, and Ruadhán then agreed.

Several stories from the life of St Patrick also involve elm trees.[4] In one instance St Patrick came to a place called Nairniu on the Roscommon-Mayo border and met Iarnascus, a holy man, and his son Locharnach under an elm tree there. Patrick founded a monastery at the spot and made Iarnascus abbot. On another occasion Patrick went to a well called Mucno at Drumtemple in County Roscommon and found a holy man, Secundinus, alone under an elm with rich foliage (*sub ulmo frondoso*). Patrick also erected a church on the spot. The most interesting reference, however, concerns a hollow elm which stood at Clonmacnoise. In one story about it a leper in St Patrick's retinue went to Clonmacnoise, and finding the elm, sat into the hollow. The leper asked a man passing by if he was a believer and when the man answered yes, the leper instructed him to pull out a bundle of rushes beside the tree. When the man did so a spring appeared which is today known as the well of Kieran. The leper then died and was buried beside the well. In another story about the tree, Patrick's servant Muinis arrived at the spot as night fell. He put relics into the hollow of the elm and it closed over them. Muinis was upset at this but Patrick told him that a 'son of life' was coming who would require them (meaning St Kieran). In another version of this tale it is a leper called Comlach who hid the relics, and on finding the next morning that the tree had closed over them, attempted to cut the tree open with an axe. However, as the chips flew off they stuck to the tree again, making his labours in vain. Again Patrick told him that the relics would be needed by another who would come later. The elm is also associated with St Colmcille, as a poem attributed to the saint praises 'the sound of the wind against the elms' as dear to him.[5]

The elm also appears in a protecting role in several ancient references.[6] In ancient Gaul a tribe existed known as the Lemovices or 'People of the Elm'. In a story in classical myth which echoes the ash's role as a guardian tree, the hero Aeneas saw a mighty elm standing at the entrance to the underworld Avernus. Overall, the stories about the elm hint at a role for it as a symbol of the protection and fertility of the goddess of the land.

Seasonal Placing

The characteristically rich sap and foliage of the elm place it seasonally at the time of greatest growth in late spring or early summer. The elm is associated with the Ogham letter *Úr* which means 'Moist'.

The Uses of Elm

The resistance of elm timber to water made it a valuable wood with many uses.[7] Over the centuries elm has been used for laying piles under bridges and buildings in damp locations, for shipbuilding, and for making water troughs and many items of furniture. The first water pipes were made of elm, and its resistance to damp made it a favourite wood for making coffins. In medieval times wych elm was a favourite wood for longbows, on account of its flexibility. Branches of wych elm were also formerly used as divining rods. Of the several species of elm in existence, the wych elm is the only one which is native to Ireland, and it was classified as one of the *Aithig fedo* or Commoners of the Wood in early Irish law.

Aspen – Crann Creathach

Populus tremula - common aspen
4th vowel of the Ogam alphabet

Also 1st supplementary vowel of the Ogham Alphabet

The aspen, with its flattened leaves that constantly rustle in the slightest breeze, is believed to be a sign of the approach of death and the nearness of the otherworld. The aspen's constantly whispering and rustling leaves tie it symbolically to the ear and sense of hearing, and are reminiscent of the sound of waves on the shore. The aspen also shares its associations of death and the otherworld with waves and the sea.

FOLK BELIEFS AND CUSTOMS

The aspen is traditionally considered an unlucky tree associated with death and misfortune.[1] In common with other trees with a sinister reputation like hawthorn, blackthorn or elder, the idea grew up that aspen was involved in Christ's crucifixion. In Scotland, the people of the island of Uist used to say that the 'hateful' aspen was banned three times – once because it held its head up haughtily as Christ was being led to Calvery, when all the other trees of the forest were bowed; twice because Christ was crucified on a cross of aspen wood, and the third for a reason not known. The aspen ever after trembles with guilt even in the stillest air. So hated is it that clods, stones and other missiles are thrown at it and its wood is never used for farming or fishing implements.

Every St Michael's Eve in Scotland a cake was baked on a fire in honour of the saint, and because of its status as a 'crossed' or unlucky wood, on no account was aspen wood to be used for the fire. However, this does not mean that aspen wood does not burn well. Iubhdan in his poem about various timbers has this to say:

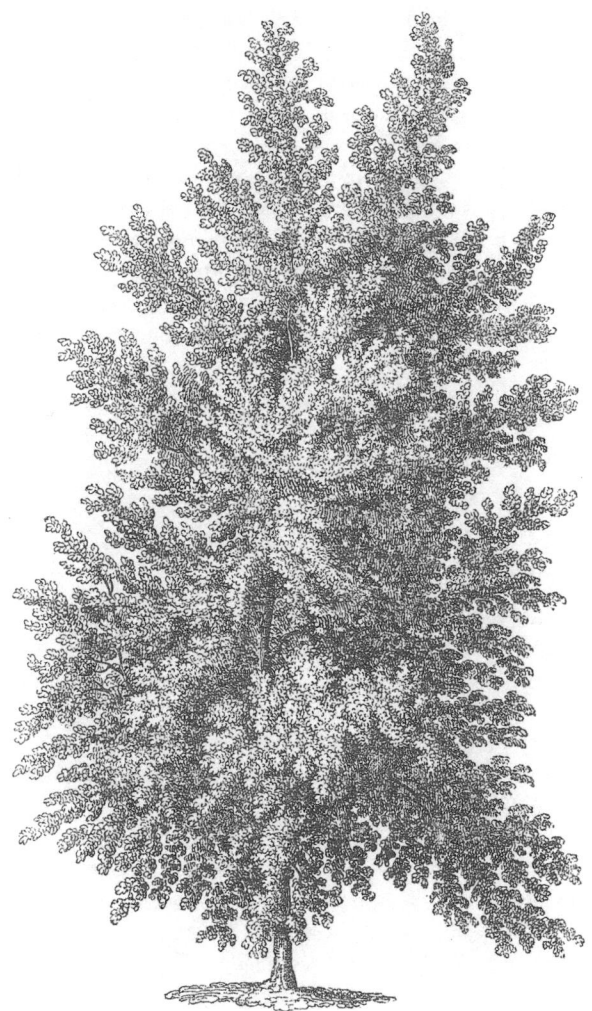

'Lay down a good staff, aspen racing without stop/ burn it late or early, tree with the shaking top'.

Despite its malevolent reputation the aspen could be used to cure illness.[2] In Lincolnshire the shivering of the aspen meant that it could be used to cure the ague. Sufferers were told to nail a piece of their hair on an aspen and recite: 'Aspen-tree, aspen-tree I prithee shake and shiver for me' Poplar could be used in a similar way to cure fever. In Scotland whooping cough could be cured by drinking mare's milk from a spoon made of aspen. Furthermore, aspen could even be used to expel evil. In an Irish folk tale a beggar with 'special knowledge' suggests freeing an old woman from possession by the devil by burning three bits from an aspen growing in Norway under her nose. In the end, however, his advice is not taken as the woman's faith is enough to cure her. In Irish folk tales Norway or *Lochlainn* stands for the mysterious otherworld over the sea.

LEGENDS AND MYTHOLOGY

In Cormac's *Glossary* is contained a passage which graphically portrays the horror with which aspen was regarded in ancient Ireland. The passage describes the *Fé* or wand of aspen which was used for measuring bodies and graves and 'was always in the cemeteries of the heathen'. It was regarded as a horror for anyone to take it into his hand; and everything that was odious to them they marked on it in Ogham. Anything abhorrent was struck with it with the cry *'fé fris'* or 'a *fé* to it'! The wand was considered to be so repulsive, we are told, because 'it was of the aspen which the wand used to be made'.

The aspen also appears in Irish tales as a metaphor for approaching death.[3] When Oscar, son of Oisín of the Fianna, is trembling on his last legs, he is described as 'like leaves in a strong wind, or like an aspen tree that is falling'. Oisín, in a lament about his old age, describes himself as like 'an aspen, my leaves gone from me'. In one version of the tale 'The Fate of the Children of Uisneach' Deirdre became so overcome with emotion when she first met Naoise that her colour came and went as quickly 'as the aspen by the stream', perhaps as some kind of premonition of their doomed fate. In Mad Sweeney's poem about his existence among the trees of the forest, the trembling and racing leaves of the aspen are to him a sign of impending plunder and loss: '*dar liom is í an chreach*', 'methinks it is the foray'.

The aspen is also associated with witches and witchcraft.[4] In a Scottish Lay about the Fianna a hag called 'The Yellow Muileartach' comes to challenge the Fianna on the tops of the wave from Lochlainn. She is described as having upon her head 'gnarled brushwood/like the clawed old wood of the aspen root'. In Zealand in Denmark the remains of a cremated Bronze Age woman were found with a large box holding various animal bones and twigs of ash and aspen. The woman was believed to have been a witch.

The aspen is a kind of poplar and poplars too have a tradition of being sorrowful. In classical myth poplars weep golden tears because they are sisters of Phaeton who misguided the horses of the sun and were burnt up. The willow also has a reputation as a tree of sorrow which probably originated in psalm 137, traditionally translated as: 'By the rivers of Babylon we sat down and wept when we remembered Zion. There on the willow trees we hung up our harps.' However, biblical scholars have recently stressed that the trees in question were not willows, but poplars.[5]

SEASONAL PLACING

Aspen's link with death and the otherworld place it seasonally in autumn at the death of the year. Aspen is associated with the Ogham letter names *Édad* and *Ébad*.

THE USES OF ASPEN

In early Irish law aspen was classified as one of the *Fodla fedo* or Lower Divisions of the Wood. However, its timber is very soft and does not appear to have been used very much.

Yew – Iúr

Taxus baccata - Yew
Taxus baccata 'fastigiata' - Irish yew
5th vowel of the Ogham Alphabet

1 November-28 November
1st month of Ogham Tree
Calendar

The yew, with its poisonous dark evergreen leaves, tough wood and long life, is a symbol of death, eternity and the afterlife. Its excellent timber meant that it was considered one of the most important trees to man.

FOLK BELIEFS AND CUSTOMS

Yew trees are best known for their association with graveyards where they are widely found, often close beside churches.[1] Gerald of Wales in his *History and Topography of Ireland* remarks that: 'yews with their bitter sap are more frequently to be found in Ireland than in any other place I have visited; but you will see them principally in old cemeteries and sacred places where they were planted in ancient times by the hands of holy men to give them what ornament and beauty they could'. In ancient Ireland yew was planted to mark the boundaries of a church and was associated with the word *fid-nemed* or 'sacred grove'. At least seventeen townlands in Ireland are known by names that mean 'church of the yew'. An entry in the Annals of the Four Masters for the year 1077 notes the burning of the monastic site of Gleann Uiseann (Killeshin, County Wicklow) along with its yews. In the year 1149 the Annals mention the destruction by lightning at Clonmacnoise of a sacred yew tree planted by St Kieran, and again in 1162 the burning of the monastery at Iubhar Chinntrechta (Newry) together with the yew tree planted by St Patrick himself. St Ailbhe founded a monastery at Imleach Iubhair ('the lakeside at a yew tree') now Emly in County Tipperary. This location may have been a pre-Christian sanctuary. At St Colmcille's monastic site in Derry was a 'Yew of the Saints'

especially beloved by him where he used to chant the hours with his other saints and 'ten hundred angels ... , above our heads, side close to side'. At Glendalough in County Wicklow there once stood in the cemetery a yew tree said to have been planted by St Kevin. In Scotland the island of Iona, site of the famous monastic settlement, is believed to have got its name from 'yew place'.

Inevitably myths grew up around the association with graveyards.[2] In medieval England it was believed the reason yews were planted in churchyards was because they absorbed the bad humours and odours of the decaying corpses. Sitting or sleeping under the shade of a yew was said to be fatal on account of the poisonous vapours it was supposed to give off. In Brittany it was believed that the yew in churchyards spread a root to the mouth of each corpse. Another widely held belief was that yews were planted to provide wood for archers' bows. On the other hand, Gerald of Wales refers to an incident in Finglas, County Dublin, where archers cut down yew and ash trees around a churchyard for fuel and were smitten by a 'singular and sudden pestilence' for their impiety so that most of them perished. Perhaps because of the combination of death and sanctity, a widespread tradition held either that Christ was crucified on a yew tree or that the cross of Calvary was made of yew. In ancient Ireland yew was also made into croziers and shrines for books.

The yew was also considered a good tree to provide protection against harm.[3] In several parts of England, such as Wiltshire and Dorset, yews were planted near houses to provide shelter and protection, both practical and magical. In Ireland yew was widely used as palm on Palm Sunday, and after the ceremonies the branches were placed in houses and cattle byres to bring good luck. In the Scottish Highlands the yew was used for making bows and was also considered good for warding off witches, safeguarding milk and divining events.

LEGENDS AND MYTHOLOGY

An example of divination with yew is found in the story of Midhir and Étain. Unable to find the missing Étain, the High King Eochaid is helpless until the druid Dallán writes Oghams on four rods of yew, and through this and his enchantments he locates Étain with Midhir at Brí Leith. Another version of this tale states that it is Codal of the Withered Breast who writes the Ogham.[4] Similarly, yew wands marked with runes have been found in Frisia. Three magical billets of yew appear in an Irish folk tale 'The Lad of the Ferule', which if put under a cauldron from Lochlainn together with three fairy stones, would produce, ready boiled in the cauldron, any kind of food one desired. A story about Loch an Iúir (Lake of the Yew) in Donegal tells of an enchanted tree which grew on the island in the lake. A man who went there to get ribs for his currach was forced to return and leave the wood back at the foot of the tree, as great waves sprang up over the island. The instant he did so the lake became calm again.[5]

A well-known story tells of the yew tree which grew out of the grave of the doomed lover Baile Mac Buain. After their tragic deaths, Baile and his lover Aillinn are buried side by side. An apple tree grew out of Aillin's grave, while a yew tree grew out of his, and the trees were later cut down to make writing tablets. The tablets are brought to the High King in Tara, and as he held each one in his hands, they sprang together, entwining about one another like woodbine on a branch. The tablets could not be parted and were kept from then on in the treasury at Tara.[6] The yew is also associated with spirits of a more sinister nature. In the story of 'The Phantoms of Yew Valley', Fionn and his men are attacked by the phantoms in revenge for the death of their sister at Fionn's hand. Elsewhere we are told that on Halloween in the Yew Glen Fionn prophesied the end of the Fianna, though whether this is the same place is not clear.[7]

The yew is noted for the great age to which it can live. In 'The Settling of the Manor of Tara', the semi-mythical being Fintan Mac Bóchna proves his great age by recounting how he outlived a yew tree. He remembers planting a yew berry in his garden, watching it grow until it could shelter 100 men under its foliage and protect him from wind, rain, cold and heat. Eventually the tree shed its foliage and died, and Fintan then cut from its timber seven churns, pitchers, vats and various other containers. When these containers eventually fell apart from old age and use he re-made some new containers from the useable wood and they too in their turn decayed from old age. In Iubhdan's poem about various woods the yew is 'Senior of eternal woods, yew of the learned feast/ make with it now brown vats of the best'. The Fianna had a vat made of yew that could hold enough beer in it for 600 men.[8]

The yew tree's place at sacred sites meant it was associated with the laws of sanctuary.[9] An example of this is the case of Mael Mordha of Leinster who sought refuge in a yew tree after the battle of Gleann Mama in 999. The best known example, however, is in the tale *Suibhne Geilt* or 'Mad Sweeney'. Sweeney is driven mad by the shouts of the battle at Magh Rath and flees the battlefield to find shelter in the yew tree of Gleann Earcain. Throughout his wanderings as a madman Sweeney shelters mostly in yew trees, especially in Gleann Bolcáin described as the 'valley of yews'. Gleann Bolcáin was said to be the place where madmen would reside after their frenzy was over and was described as very beautiful and peaceful. Later he shelters in a yew by a well at Ros Comain and again in a yew by the church at Druim Iarainn where he speaks to a cleric of his unhappiness. At one point he settles again in Gleann Earcain and recovers his reason until a hag comes and reminds him of his frenzy so he takes flight once more with the hag pursuing him. The hag is perhaps a version of the hag of battle, which was said to hang over the battlefield shrieking and exulting in the slaughter.

Paradoxically as well as being a tree of sanctuary, the yew tree is associated with war.[10] Yew was a favourite wood for making bows and spears. The world's oldest known artifact of wood was a yew spear 150,000 years old found in Clacton in England and neolithic longbows have been found in Somerset. Part of the compensation paid to Lugh by the sons of Tuirill for the death of his father included the Spear of Assal, a spear made of ridgy red gold. The spear would kill anyone whose blood it shed and never missed its target so long as the word 'yew' was said when throwing it. If the word 'again-yew' was said the spear instantly returned to its leather sheath. In a poem about Fionn's foray to Tara, Diarmuid Ó Duibhne is described as having as an emblem 'a branch of the curly topped smooth yew'. In the '*Cad Godeu*', the yew is described as 'to the fore at the seat of war'. The Roman poet Lucan speaks of an infamous sacred grove at Marsalia in which the yew, among others, was worshipped. The grove was the site of bloody human sacrifices.

The yew is also particularly associated with war-like females.[11] In the tale 'The Pursuit of Emer', Cúchulainn goes to the female warrior Scathach in Scotland to learn skill in arms and when he arrives at her house she is training her two sons Cuar and Cett under a great yew tree. A story about the goddess Áine tells of how she got revenge on a king of Ireland, Oilioll Olum, for killing her brother. By enchantment, she created a great yew tree beside the river Maigh in Limerick and put a little man in it playing sweet music on a harp. Oilioll's son was passing with his stepbrother when both heard the music and quarrelled about who should have the little harper and the tree. Unable to agree they brought the matter before Oilioll who decided in favour of his own son. The bad feeling caused by this led to Oilioll and his seven sons being killed at the battle of Magh Mucruimhe. Thus Áine got her revenge. Áine was believed to be the same being as the war goddess, the Morrigan. The *Book of Invasions* states that Eochu, son of Oilill Finn, slew the king of Cermna, Clair and Cliu at a place called 'Áine of the Yew Shields'. An old Irish poem describes a witch called Camóg (Crooked one) who was blind in one eye and could knock down a yew tree by tying a magic thread around it.

The association of yew with the themes of churchyards, sanctuary and war links it with the goddess of the land who both protected her own, living and dead, and waged war on their enemies. The goddess was often thought of as the land of Ireland itself, which protected and sheltered the honoured dead.[12] In several poems about the Fianna, Ireland is referred to in this way as a land of yew trees. In a poem called the 'Adventures of the Men from Sorcha', the men who are fighting a battle overseas describe their homeland as 'yew-clad Ireland'. Again in the poem 'Battle of Gabhair' which describes the graves of the Fianna, there is a mention of 'beautiful Ireland of the yew trees'. Another poem about the warrior Goll's tomb again refers to 'yew clad Ireland'. Similarly, on the continent a whole series of ancient Celtic tribes were named after the yew. There were the Eburones between the Main and Rhine, Eburovices at Évreux, an Eburobriga in Yonne, Eburmagus in Aude, Eburodunum in Switzerland and the same in Hautes Alpes.

Naturally in the light of this, the yew tree is also associated with kingship.[13] A legend about the Munster king Conall Cerc tells of how a swineherd saw a vision of a yew tree on top of the rock of Cashel with angels descending to an oratory in front of it. A druid to the local chieftain Aodh explained that this meant that the kingship of Munster would be sited at Cashel and that the first person to light a fire under the yew tree would be the king. Aodh travelled there first thing the next morning only to find that Conall Corc had arrived in the meantime, and quite unaware of the prophecy, lit a fire under the yew. Aodh submits to his authority and Conall becomes king. The famous king Cormac Mac Airt was protected as a young boy from the crush of a welcoming crowd by being placed in a vessel of yew covered with a purple cloth. In an Irish folk tale involving the hero Bioultach a king sends a messenger to him carrying a branch of yew to seek the release of his two captured sons. In a story about the famous king Niall of the Nine Hostages, the young prince is identified as his father's heir by being the one to carry the anvil out of a burning forge. One of the other brothers, however, comes out carrying a bundle of kindling with a stick of yew in it. For this he was pronounced sterile and thus gave rise to the saying 'a stick of yew in a bundle of kindling' meaning to be sterile.

The most celebrated yew in Irish mythology was the Eo Rossa or Yew of Ross which stood at Old Leighlin in County Carlow, close to the seat of the kings of Leinster. Like the great ash *Bile Tortan*, its existence first came to light on the night that the famous king Conn Céadchathach was born.[14] The tree stood until it was uprooted by the prayers of St Laserian, who wanted its wood for building a church. Its timber was distributed among other saints, including St Moling who used it to roof his oratory. Eo Rossa is the subject of an extraordinary poem in the *Metrical Dindshenchus* which praises it as an almost sacred object. The poem describes the tree among other things as a 'straight strong tree a stout strong god', 'Banba's renown' and 'spell of knowledge'. Banba is a poetic name for Ireland deriving from a land goddess of that name.

YEW OF ROSSA
Yew of Rossa,
Royal wheel,
Regent's rule,
Wave's sound,
Best of beings,
Straight, strong tree,
Stout, strong god,
Door of heaven,
Building's strength,
Crew's captain,
Man of pure words,
Plenteous bounty,

Trinity's might,
Measure of matter,
Mother's good,
Mary's son,
Fruitful sea,
Beauty's honour,
Mind's master,
Diadem of angels,
Cry of life,
Banba's renown,
Vigour of victory
Decision's basis,
Doom's decision,
Fuel of sages,
Noblest tree,
Fame of Leinster,
Gentlest bush,
Champion's cover,
Vitality's Vigour,
Spell of knowledge,
Yew of Rossa.

SEASONAL PLACING

The yew tree, being associated with death and eternity, is appropriately placed seasonally at Samhain or Halloween, the Feast of the Dead and the death of the old year. This completes the small seasonal cycle of the vowels and also provides a fitting end to the sequence of the original twenty letters. The yew is associated with the Ogham letter *Idad* which is a variation of its Irish name.

THE USES OF YEW

Due to the value of its wood in making household containers, spears, bows and various other uses like building, yew was classified as one of the *Airig fedo* or Nobles of the Wood in early Irish law.

Spindle – Feoras

Euonymus europaeus - Spindle

2nd supplementary vowel of the Ogham Alphabet

The spindle's bright, colourful berries tie it symbolically it to the eye and sense of sight. The pink and gold colour of the berries can make an arresting show and provide a suitable link with the sun.

LEGENDS AND MYTHOLOGY

There appears to be little folklore about the spindle in Ireland. However, the *Metrical Dindshenchus* contains a curious story linking the spindle with a place called *Hirarus*.[1] The name itself is a play on the Irish name for spindle *feorus* or *herus*. According to the story, Cairpre Lifechair was being followed everywhere by the four birds of Aongus, who called to him incessantly and gave him no peace. Seeking a solution, Cairpre consulted his druid Bicne, who asked him from which quarter did the birds come. Cairpre replied that they came 'from the east and the bright sunrise'. After trying unsuccessfully every kind of tree, the druid sang a spell over the spindle tree, which rose up over the woods of Erin and detained the birds in its branches, preventing them from bothering Cairpre further. Thus the name Hirarus or *Hér herus* meaning the 'high spindle'. The story ends with the following poem:

> Up aloft the tree did soar
> Wafting timeless scent so pure
> And at once caught every bird
> Silencing their songs for sure.

It is interesting to note the link in the story between spindle and birds with solar associations.

FOLKLORE OF THE TREES

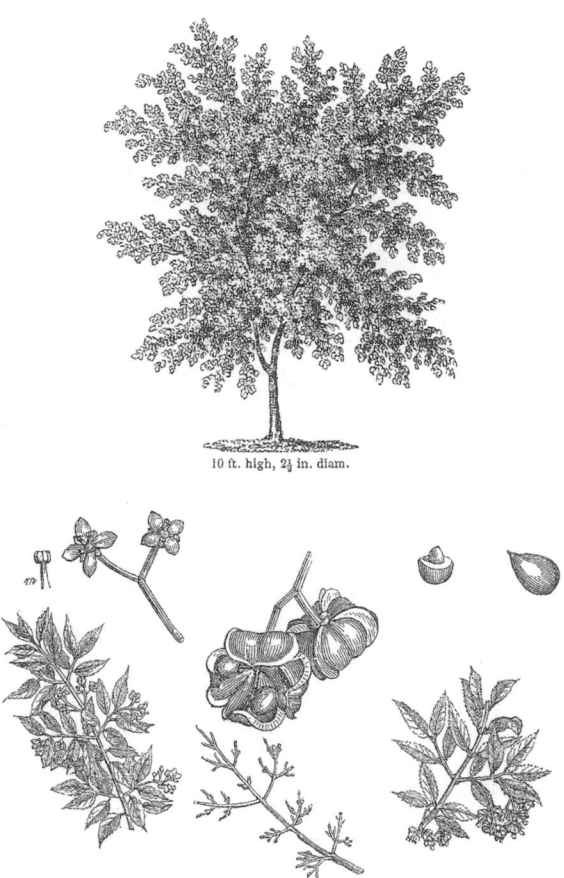

10 ft. high, 2½ in. diam.

THE USES OF SPINDLE

In early Irish law spindle was considered one of the *Fodla fedo* or Lower Divisions of the Wood. Spindle wood is hard and tough and was used in many countries for making items such as skewers, toothpicks, pegs and spindles – hence the name. Spindle was probably also coppiced in Ireland for its wood.[2] Spindle is associated with the Ogham letter name *Ór* meaning gold.

Juniper – Aiteal

Juniperus communis - Common juniper
3rd supplementary vowel of the Ogham alphabet

The juniper when left to mature grows into a small tree, often with a bent, elbow-shaped trunk. Its aromatic leaves and wood (especially when burnt) tie it symbolically to the nose and sense of smell, which also provide a link to the wind and air.

FOLK BELIEFS AND CUSTOMS

Juniper was considered to have protective powers.[1] In Scotland juniper placed before cattle or put in their tails was a counter charm against witches. It was considered a protection by sea and land, and no house in which it was would take fire. The juniper had to be pulled in a certain manner. It had to be held by the roots, with its branches made into four bundles and taken between the five fingers, whilst the incantation was repeated: 'I will pluck the bounteous yew*/through the five bent ribs of Christ/In the name of the Father, the Son and Holy Ghost/Against drowning, danger, and confusion' (*Mountain yew is the name given for juniper in Scotland). Carmicheal quotes a more extensive version of this charm:

> I will pluck the gracious yew
> through the one rib of Jesus
> In name of Father and Son and Spirit of Wisdom
> against distress, against misfortune, against fatigue.
>
> I will pluck the gracious yew
> through the three fair ribs of Jesus
> In name of Father and Son and Spirit of grace
> against hardness, against pain, aggainst anguish of breast.

I will pluck the gracious yew
through the nine fair ribs of Jesus.
In name of Father and Son and Spirit of grace,
against drowning, against danger, against fear.

In the Scottish Highlands rods of juniper and rowan were put up over the lintel of the door on the first day of the quarter and at Beltane and Hallowmass to ward off witches. In Wales it was believed that anyone who cut down a juniper would die within the year. For this reason, aged junipers were often let die a natural death.

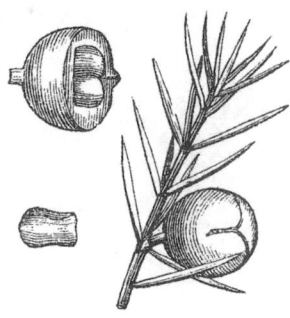

LEGENDS AND MYTHOLOGY

According to Italian legend a juniper tree sheltered the infant Jesus on his flight into Egypt and thus saved his life, while the Old Testament states that a juniper canopied Elijah in his flight from queen Jezebel.[2]

THE USES OF JUNIPER

Juniper wood and berries were widely burnt to purify the air and drive away evil.[3] In French hospitals it was customary to burn juniper berries and rosemary to purify the air and prevent infection. Similarly, in England juniper wood and berries were burnt in sickrooms to purify the air and refresh the patient. It was believed that burning juniper deterred witches and that the smoke drove away serpents and destroyed disease. In Central Europe to prepare for Mayday, houses were cleansed and fumigated on the last three days of April with juniper berries and rue. In the Belgian Ardennes bonfires were lit on the first Sunday in Lent, usually with juniper and broom. On New Year's Day in the Scottish Highlands the doors and windows of the house of byres and stables were stopped up, and branches of juniper which had been brought in the previous night were set alight. Once the pungent smoke had filled the house and the inhabitants could bear it no longer, the windows were opened to blow the fumes away. This was done to drive out evil and disease. In Scotland cattle were 'sained' at Shrovetide by burning juniper before them. In early Irish law juniper was classified as one of the *Fodla fedo* or Lower Divisions of the Wood. Juniper is associated with the Ogham letter *Uillenn* which means 'Elbow'.

Arbutus – Caithne

Arbutus unedo - Arbutus or Strawberry tree

A rbutus or strawberry tree is noted for its white bell-like blossoms and orange or red strawberry-like fruits, which both appear on the tree at the same time. It is one of Ireland's rarest trees, being found only in a few locations in the west of the country, mainly around Killarney in County Kerry.

FOLK BELIEFS AND CUSTOMS

The Irish word for arbutus, *caithne*, appears in placenames throughout the west and south of Ireland, indicating that the tree was once more widespread and better known than it is now.[1] As well as placenames in Kerry like Ard na Caithne (height of the arbutus) or Smerwick on the Dingle Peninsula and the River Owenacahina or Abhainn na Caithne, arbutus appears in the name Derrynacaheny or Daire na Caithe (oakwood of the arbutus) in County Clare. In the Irish form, *cuinche*, arbutus appears in placenames like Cappoquin - Ceapach Cuinche (field of arbutus) in County Waterford and Quinsheen Island or Oileán Cuinchín (Arbutus Island) in Clew Bay, County Mayo.

LEGENDS AND MYTHOLOGY

Arbutus appears in the story 'The pursuit of Diarmuid and Gráinne', when the Tuatha Dé Danann brought crimson nuts, arbutus berries and unspecified fragrant berries with them as food from the Land of Promise. As they passed through the Cantred of Ó Fiachrach one of the berries fell and grew into the Quicken tree of Dubhros.[2]

THE USES OF ARBUTUS

The fruit of Arbutus is indeed edible but it is insipid and to some people indigestible. However, baskets of it were apparently on sale

Pine – Giúis
Pinus sylvestris

Ash – Fuinseóg
Fraximus excelsior

Elm – Leamhán
Ulmus glabra

Aspen – Crann creathach
Populus tremula

in Killarney in the nineteenth century.[3] Arbutus wood was used in Ireland for making charcoal and later for making small pieces of decorative inlay, as the wood is a rich reddish brown when polished. Arbutus was classified as one of the *Fodla fedo* or Lower Divisions of the Wood in early Irish law.

Ogham – the Gaelic Tree Alphabet

Reference has been made throughout to the Ogham alphabet and to the tradition that each of its letters are named after trees. Let us turn our attention now to that tradition, so central to the folklore of Irish trees, and examine the assertion that Ogham is indeed a 'tree alphabet'. In particular it is necessary to explain the link between each species of tree and its Ogham letter in greater detail.

The Ogham alphabet is the first form of writing ever used in the Irish language and was probably invented some time between the second and fourth centuries AD. Several hundred Ogham inscriptions are still found today throughout Ireland, and in places of Irish settlement in Scotland, Wales, the Isle of Man and Cornwall. The alphabet looks nothing like our own, being a series of strokes or notches arranged at right angles along the edge or *druim* of a stone or piece of wood. The following diagram shows the twenty letters of the original alphabet. The order of the letters in the diagram begins with B in the bottom left hand corner, and reading the four lines from the bottom up, ends with I in the top right hand corner.

The form of the letters indicate that Ogham was obviously meant for short inscriptions or messages rather than as a fully fledged literary vehicle. The reasons for Ogham's invention are not entirely clear but given the time of its invention and the structure of the alphabet it is undoubtedly the product of relations between the Irish and the Romans or Romano-British. While the order of the letters shows that Ogham was inspired by the Latin alphabet, it is not a mere copy or cipher of Latin but a true alphabet in its own right.

Apart from its striking appearance the most noteworthy aspect of Ogham is the fact that each letter was given a name as an *aide-memoire* and that tradition holds that each letter is named after a different native Irish tree. The most recent scholarship on the subject by Damian McManus has cast doubt on this tradition of Ogham as a 'tree alphabet' by pointing out (correctly) that only half the letter names are actually those of trees;[1] but this does not necessarily invalidate the tradition. I believe that it can be shown that the order of the Ogham alphabet is indeed based on a seasonally arranged sequence of trees, modified by the classifications of Latin grammar. In other words, the order of the letters is arranged firstly on the basis of letter names signifying trees placed in a seasonal order; and only secondly on the basis of grammar or phonetics.

To modern minds trees might seem an obscure choice but it must be remembered that trees were a very important part of life in ancient times, not just in Ireland but indeed universally. Trees had considerable economic, nutritional, symbolic or ritual significance, and there were few areas of life that were not bound up in some way with their use. In early Ireland, as we have seen, trees were important enough to be individually ranked or classified in order of importance, and heavy penalties could be incurred from damaging or interfering with them. Given also that most inscriptions were probably on wood anyway, they would also have suggested themselves as a natural choice. Looked at in this light, it is not difficult to see how they would present themselves as suitable candidates for ordering the letters. In addition to this, the terminology of Ogham is itself replete with references to trees, quite apart from the letter names. Thus the letters are known as *feda* or singularly as *fid* which means 'wood' or 'tree'. The term *feda* can also be used exclusively to mean the vowels, with the consonants distinguished from them by being called *táebomnai* or 'side of a tree-trunk'. This no doubt refers to the fact that they are inscribed to the side of the *druim* or ridge of the piece of wood or stone being used. Yet another arboreal term is the word *flesc* or twig, which refers to a single score of a letter.

We also read in the beginning of the collection of medieval manuscripts concerning Ogham called *Auraicept na nEces*, or the *Scholar's Primer*, that Ogham is read as a tree is climbed, starting at the bottom 'treading on the root of the tree first' and working one's way up from there. Finally, another arboreal term used to describe a letter is *nin* (as in the letter name) which literally means 'branch fork'. This probably explains the expression '*Beith-Luis-Nin*' as another name for the alphabet as meaning literally 'Beith-Luis letters'. The expression Beith-Luis-Nin arose as another name for Ogham on the model of the name of our own alphabet, the 'Alpha-Beta'. In other words, the first two letters were used as a shorthand to describer the whole alphabet. But because the word *nin* meant both a letter in the general sense and the name of the fifth letter in particular, it was added on to make the phrase 'Beith Luis Nin'. This expression is the reason why some commentators have the impression that the order of the first five set of letters is 'BLNFS' instead of the proper 'BLFSN'. There is no evidence to suggest that this was ever the case.

Before discussing the letter names it is worth examining the compelling notion that Ogham and its link with trees may even have given the Irish their name in their own language. The Irish and Welsh at the time of Ogham's invention spoke very similar languages and they naturally borrowed words from one another. A striking feature of this is the fact that the Irish borrowed the word *gwyddel* from the Welsh to describe themselves. Most Irish people today are totally unaware that the name *Gael* or *Gaedhil* stems from a Welsh source. So what does *gwyddel* mean? Most scholars believe that it comes either from *gwydd* meaning 'wild' or *gwydd* meaning 'wood/forest'. A *gwyddel* then is either a wild man or a man from the woods, neither of which is very complimentary. But if *gwyddel* is simply a derogatory word for a wild woodsman, why did the Irish adopt it with such enthusiasm? From the sixth century on, Irish genealogists and historians promoted the term to such an extent that *Érainn*, the original name for the Irish, almost became extinct.[2]

The answer lies in looking at the meanings of other words in

Welsh that derive from *gwydd*. Among them are *gwyddon* 'scholar/scientist' and *gwyddoniaeth* 'science/knowledge'. Most interesting of all, however, is *gwyddor* 'rudiment/element', or more specifically, 'alphabet' (the alphabet in Welsh is called *Yr Wyddor*). This last meaning is identical to that of the related Irish word *fid* which also means both 'wood' and 'letter'. *Gwydd* in Welsh thus seems to combine the meanings of the Irish words *fios* (wisdom or knowledge) and *fid*. In other words, far from *gwyddel* meaning a wild man of the woods, it in fact means something like 'one who has knowledge of tree-letters' and is a reference to the use of the tree alphabet Ogham by the Irish. This must have been taken by them as a compliment to their learning and the name *gwyddeleg* adopted to describe the standardised Irish of the scholars, which was informed by the rules of grammar. *Auraicept na nEces* or the *Scholar's Primer*, is quite explicit that *gaedelg* (or *gwyddeleg*) is the 'selected language' of the scholars and that its invention coincided with the invention of the *Beithluisnin* or Ogham.

It should also be noted that the Welsh of the time do not seem to have regarded the Irish as wild woodsmen. The proof of this can be seen in the depiction of the Irish in noted Welsh tales like 'Branwen, daughter of Llyr', where the Irish appear as people much like the Welsh themselves. This is not far from the truth, as Wales was still essentially a Celtic society with only an overlying veneer of Roman influence. Also, a fact that a combination many Welsh tales have borrowed extensively from Irish sources is another testament to the cultural mixing mentioned earlier. Indeed, some of the Welsh Ogham inscriptions consist of names that are Welsh or mixed Irish-Welsh in character. This indicates that the Irish in Wales settled down peacefully with their Welsh/British neighbours after the initial conflicts were over. It is true that the British churchman Gildas in his *Excidio* attacks the Irish but he is rarely positive about his fellow British either.

The *Scholar's Primer* gives us two etymologies for the name Ogham. It states that Ogham is named after the god Ogma and that Ogham derives from *óg-uaim* or 'perfect alliteration'. However, these two explanations have been rejected by the scholars as linguistically impossible. In particular, Ogma cannot be made turn into Ogham, despite their similarity in sound. McManus rejects alternative explanations like Greek *ogmos* 'furrow' and the Greek letter name *Agma* for similar reasons. The Celtic scholar James Carney, in his work 'The Invention of the Ogham Cipher', suggested a 'half etymology', equating the first syllable with the word *og* meaning the point of a weapon, and suggesting that Ogham might mean something like 'point-seam'. McManus favours this explanation, especially as the early use of the word makes it clear that Ogham referred to the inscribed or written script only, with *Beithluisnin* the actual name of the alphabet. The problem with this, as McManus admits, is that the second syllable of 'Ogham' in its various forms 'um/am/om', does not occur in Irish so that it is hard to explain how such a word would arise without being borrowed from outside.

I believe it is therefore possible that Ogham travelled into Irish from Wales alongside *gwyddel*, and that it derives from the Welsh word *gogam* meaning 'crooked/slanting' in a reference to Ogham's unique characteristic of being written at an angle to the *droim*, instead of on a flat surface like other alphabets. Words in Welsh, like Irish, change their initial letter in different settings, and words beginning with an initial 'G' lose it. Thus we have the Welsh word *igam-ogam* meaning 'zigzag', and *gwyddor* or 'alphabet' becomes *Yr wyddor* or 'the alphabet'. It follows from this that 'the slanting alphabet' reads *Yr wyddor ogam*, which could be easily shortened by the Welsh over time to *Yr ogam* as a name for the strange Irish writing. As the Irish did not have a name for the script itself, it would have been natural for them to borrow the term. The case for *gogam* being linked to *gwyddel* is further strengthened by the existence of words that combine both *gogam* and *gwydd*. Thus we have *gogwydd*, an inclination or declension, *gogwyddo*, to incline or slope, and most interesting of all, *gogwyddor* meaning a principle or pattern. Nothing could demonstrate more clearly how much Wales has contributed to the history of Ogham than that it should have provided a name for the script itself, as well as for those who used it.

Regarding Ogham letters and the letter names, McManus has proved beyond doubt that of the original twenty letter names only eight are actually those of trees. But that is not the end of the matter. Surely all the terminology described above cannot be excluded from consideration. If the letters are described in terms of trees, it surely lends weight to the argument that the letter names and their order are also to be connected to trees. The other factor to be considered is the sheer strength of the tradition in the manuscripts that the letter names are those of trees.

Although McManus can give convincing explanations in most cases for what the other twelve names mean, we are still left with the problem of why those particular names were chosen and they are a very mixed lot indeed. Firstly few of the kinds of names we might expect to find are present. There are no animals or birds, and the only element of nature to be found (like sun, mountain, water, etc) is *luis* (flame). There are also no letter names relating directly to human activities or concerns like harvest, season, hunting, ploughing, etc; except perhaps for *gort* (field). Instead what we have is a collection of names that are either oblique like *uath* (fear) or curiously nondescript like *cert* (bush). In fact, the only definite category of letter name is that of trees, with the other letter names seemingly being chosen at random.

This apparent dilemma can be resolved if we consider that even if it were the intention of the inventor to create an alphabet with every letter having the name of a tree, it would not in fact be possible to do so. The range of native Irish trees and large shrubs is simply too limited to allow scope to create a proper alphabet using their proper names only. This is because the names of the trees themselves do not oblige by each beginning with a different letter of the alphabet. Thus for instance three important trees *coll*, *cuilend* and *caerthainn* (hazel, holly and rowan) all begin with the letter 'C'. It would be a poor tree alphabet which left out two of these trees on the basis that their initial letter was already used. The obvious response to this problem is to abandon the principle that every letter name must be the actual name of a tree, and to seek suitable alternative 'poetic' names based on some distinctive characteristic of the tree in question. For instance, the letter name *luis* or 'flame' describes the rowan tree on the basis that its berries, its most notable feature, are flame red and are thought of in folklore as having similar magical properties to fire. Most of the other letter names can be similarly explained. Failing that, the fallback position would be to choose a generic name like 'bush' or 'branch' (as in *cert* and *nin* – see below). This is what the invention of Ogham appears to have done, as all the letters not directly named after trees can be shown to fall into either of these two categories.

The first descriptions of Ogham appear in medieval manuscripts such as *Auraicept na nEces* or the *Scholar's Primer* and it is here that we first learn the name of the letters. Each letter is accompanied by a gloss or brief explanation stating what tree it is linked to and giving an explanation why. Unfortunately these glosses are often confused about which tree goes with which letter; and the explanations given can not to be trusted. Each letter name is also accompanied by several *briatharogaim* or word-oghams. The word-oghams are short, two word, poetic descriptions of each letter name which have traditionally been associated with the alphabet. They derive from the Old Irish period, considerably earlier than the manuscript tradition which records them, and were composed at a time when the tradition was much clearer than the medieval period of the glossators. As such they are our most valuable source of information on the letter names. They come down to us in three lists, B*riatharogaim Morainn mic Moín, Briatharogaim Maic ind Óc* and *Briatharogaim Con Culainn* (or *Cú Chulainn)*. All three lists are shown together here in the following diagram (A, B and C respectively), along with translations in English. The translations are mostly McManus' but in some cases, my own alternative is used.

The dubious nature of the medieval glosses means that to have any hope of reconstructing the original tree list it is necessary to look only at the letter names and word-oghams; measuring them against the likely candidates on the basis of the trees' most important characteristics. The characteristics are based on the uses of the trees (e.g., timber or fruit), some distinctive aspect of their appearance (e.g., blossoms), or on their symbolic association with certain times of the year (e.g., the yew tree and the death of the year). It is reasonable to take as a starting point the trees mentioned by the glossators, and fortunately in most cases one of these trees emerges as the clear candidate. It is also the case that sometimes none of the trees or shrubs mentioned can be made to suit. However, when this is the case, an obvious candidate can be found to fit either the letter name or word-oghams or both.

The original twenty letter names fall into three categories: those letter names which are those of trees – *Beith, Fern, Sail, Dair, Coll, Onn, Edad* and *Idad* (the last two are artificial variations of the tree name); those letter names which are 'poetic' alternative names based on some important characteristic of the tree in question – *Luis, Uath, Tinne, Gort, Gétal, Straiph, Ruis, Ailm, Úr*; and those letter names which are poetic alternatives based on a general 'arboureal' theme – *Nin, Cert* and *Muin*.

WORD-OGHAM LISTS			
OGHAM LETTER	**LIST A**	**List B**	**List C**
Beith	Féochas foltchaín	Glaisem cnis	Maise malach
Luis	Lí súla	Carae cethrae	Lúth cethrae
Fern	Airenach fían	Comét lachta	Dín cridi
Sail	Lí ambí	Lúth bech	Tosach mela
Nin	Costud Síde	Bág ban	Bág maise
Huath	Condál cúan	Bánad gnúise	Ansam aidche
Dair	Ardam dosae	Grés soír	Slechtam soíre
Tinne	Trian roith	Smuir gúaile	Trian n-airm
Coll	Caíniu fedaib; Ithcar, cnocar, caincar fid	Carae blóesc	Milsem fedo
Qert	Clithar baiscill	Bríg anduini	Dígu fethail
Muin	Tressam fedmae; Ardam maisse	Árusc n-airlig	Conar gotha
Gort	Milsiu férai; Glaisem gelta	Ined erc	Sásad ile
NGétal	Lúth lego	Étiud midach	Tosach n-échto
STRaif	Tressam rúamnai; Aire srábae; Aire adhon draigin	Mórad rún	Saigid nél
Ruis	Tindem rucci; Ruamna rucci/ruisg	Rúamnae drech	Bruth fergae
Ailm	Ardam íachta	Tosach frecrai	Tosach garmae
Onn	Congnaid; congnamaid ech	Fétham soíre	Lúth fían

OGHAM LETTER	List A	List B	List C
Ur	Úaraib adbaib; Gruidem; guirem dál	Sílad cland	Forbbaid ambí
Edad	Érgnaid/áerchaid fid	Commaín carat	Bráthair bethi
Idad	Sinem fedo	Caínem sen; Áildem aís	Lúth lobair
Ébad	Snámhchaín feda	Cosc lobair; Aca fid	Caínem éco
Ór	Sruithem aicde	Lí crotha	
Uillen	Túthmar fid	Cubat oll	
Pín	Milsem fedo	Amram mlais	
CHoll	Lúad sáethaig	Mol galraig	

ENGLISH TRANSLATION

OGHAM LETTER	List A	List B	List C
Beith	Withered foot with fine hair	Greyest skin	Beauty of eyebrow
Luis	Lustre of eye	Friend of cattle	Sustenance of cattle
Fern	Vanguard of warriors	Milk container	Protection of the heart
Sail	Pallor of a lifeless one	Sustenance of bees	Beginning of honey
Nin	Otherworld sustenance	Boast of women	Boast of beauty
Huath	Assembly of hounds	Blanching of faces	Most difficult at night
Dair	Most exalted of trees	Work of a craftsman	Most carved of craftmanship
Tinne	Third part of a wheel	Marrow of charcoal	Third part of a weapon
Coll	Fairest tree; Edible nutty, fairest tree	Friend of nutshells	Sweetest tree
Qert	Shelter of the wounded	Power of the weak	Dregs of clothing
Muin	Strongest in action; Most noble goodliness	Proverb of slaughter	Path of the voice
Gort	Sweetest grass; Greenest pastures	Suitable place for cows	Satisfaction of all

OGHAM LETTER	List A	List B	List C
NGétal	Sustenance of a leech	Raiment/Strength of physicians	Beginning of slaying
STRaif	Strongest reddening dye Chief of Streams; Dam of a river Dam/Hedge of blackthorn	Increase of secrets	Seeking of clouds/ Arrow of the clouds
Ruis	Most intense blushing; Hue of the eye	Reddening of faces	Glow of anger
Ailm	Loudest groan	Beginning of an answer	Beginning of calling
Onn	Wounder/Helper of horses	Smoothest of craftmanship	Sustenance of warriors
Ur	In cold dwellings; Most devoted sharing	Propagation/Dripping of plants	Shroud of a life less one
Edad	Discerning/Satirising tree	Exchange of friends	Brother of birch
Idad	Oldest tree	Fairest of the ancients/ Most beautiful in age	Sustenance of a leper
Ébad	Fair swimming letter	Prevention of a leper; Water letter(?)	Fairest fish
Ór	Most venerable	Splendour of form	
Ullen	Fragrant tree	Great elbow/cubit	
Pín	Sweetest tree	Most wonderful taste	
CHoll	Groan of the sick	Groan of the ill	

It should be noted that the word-oghams usually refer to the letter name only when the letter name is that of a tree or a poetic alternative; but when the letter name is a general 'arboureal' one like *nin, cert* or *muin*, the A and B lists refer to the relevant tree only and not the letter name; no doubt because the letter name itself gives no clue to the tree concerned. Tradition C gives word-oghams for Cert and Muin which I believe are based on a misunderstanding of the letter names. The other guide to linking a particular tree to each letter is the seasonal placing of the letter and proposed tree in the whole sequence of letters. At this stage it is enough to say that the fifteen consonants form one seasonal cycle, starting with midwinter, and moving around to late autumn and the start of winter again. The vowels form a short, separate year round cycle of their own. The *forfeda* or supplementary letters also form a pattern. Indeed far from being an arbitrary sequence as has usually been thought, they in fact form a very distinct pattern of their own.

Having presented the arguments for a tree alphabet it necessary to look at each letter in detail:

Beithe: This is the Irish name for birch so there is no dispute as to the meaning of this name. Seasonally, the birch can be associated with the re-birth of the year, at either the winter solstice or *Imbolc*.

Luis: McManus gives two possible meanings for this name: *luis/loise* - 'flame, radiance' or *lus* - 'plant, herb, vegetable'. However, the former appears to be correct, as the letter name refers to the rowan with its flame red berries. Seasonally the rowan can be placed at the festival of the goddess Brigid, or *Imbolc*, the beginning of spring (2 February). This is the time of the first born calves and the new milk, when it might be expected that livestock would need special protection. The goddess Brigid also had a strong link with fire or flames, a link that was carried into the folklore of the Christian saint who succeeded her.

Fern: Fern is the Irish name for the alder so this letter name is clear. Seasonally the springtime is when the alder's catkins are out, and when the red sap for which alder is noted can be seen in the opening buds. Alder catkins (as well as its bark) are also noted for their use to make dyes.

Sail: Again this is the Irish name for willow so the letter name is not in doubt. Seasonally the willow's catkins are an important source of nectar for bees in the springtime and one of the tree's most distinctive features. The willow is noted for its ability to root and grow quickly which would also place it symbolically in springtime, the season of growth.

OGHAM – THE GAELIC TREE ALPHABET

Nin: McManus considers this letter name probably means 'branch-fork' which fits it well into the third category of general names. The question remains, however, as to what tree is in fact linked to *nin*. The letter name itself does not help as it is too vague, so we must rely on the word-oghams. The first word-ogham is *costud side* which the medieval glossators and Dr McManus consider to mean 'establishing of peace'. However, the word *costud* in fact means 'staple supply, consuming, tasting, enjoying' and *side* means 'otherworld being', or fairy. A better reading of the word-ogham would then be 'staple enjoyment or supply of the otherworld'. This refers to nectar or honey (the otherworld foods) and indicates that we are looking for a tree noted for its show of blossom. The other word-oghams fit well with this. *Bág ban* ('boast of women') and *bág maise* ('boast of beauty') could also be taken to refer to the beauty of blossoms. The description appears to refer to the gean, or wild cherry, the native tree with the most spectacular show of flowers of any. The cherry flowers in late spring or early summer, at the correct place in the seasonal letter sequence.

(h)Uath: The word *uath* means fear or awe, and the glossators all equate *uath* with the whitethorn (or hawthorn) which suits the letter name. The word *uath*, with its connotations of respect and awe, succinctly sums up the traditional attitude to the tree. The whitethorn is correctly placed seasonally as it has always been associated with the festival of Bealtaine, a time of great otherworldly power; and the start of summer on account of it flowering at this time.

Dair: This letter name is the Irish name for the oak tree. Seasonally the oak is correctly placed at around the time of midsummer, with which it is connected by tradition.

Tinne: The letter name *tinne* means 'bar of metel or iron' and the word-oghams support this. The glossators all associate *tinne* with the holly tree. This makes sense as holly is noted for the toughness and density of its timber, giving it 'ironlike' qualities. The word-oghams can also be taken to refer to holly. 'One of three parts of a wheel' fits well with the fact that holly timber, being so strong, was used to make shafts for chariot wheels. 'One of three parts of a weapon' could also mean holly, as its wood could well have been used to make handles for knives, and possibly swords. These uses of holly place it seasonally around the festival of Lughnasa, the time when contests such as chariot races and feats of arms were held. Holly, of course, is more usually associated with midwinter and the Christmas season, but the evidence of the word-oghams, plus the fact that there is evidence linking holly mythologically with the god Lugh, make this placing a plausible one.

Coll: Coll is the Irish for hazel so there is no dispute as to this letter name. The word-oghams describe the hazel's characteristics at mid-autumn in the seasonal cycle, the time when hazel nuts are ripe.

Cert: McManus believes that this letter name means 'bush', and this fits well with the third category of letter name. The tree mentioned by the glossators in connection with Cert is the apple. The first word-ogham *clithar baiscill* is explained as 'shelter of a lunatic or doe' equating *baiscill* with *baois ceall* or 'foolish minded', on the basis that the lunatic and doe are both foolish minded creatures. Both of these appear to be rather contrived explanations of the meaning of the word *baiscill*. A simpler and more direct explanation is that *baiscill* derives from the word *bascadh*, meaning to severely wound or injure. *Bascall* (in its non-genitive form) is therefore a severely wounded or injured person. *Clithar baiscill* then reads as 'shelter of the wounded/injured' and is a reference to the supposed healing and regenerative powers of the apple.

The second word-ogham *bríg anduini* ('power/life of the weak/mediocre person') is taken to be a reference to rags, but I believe it refers to the same strength giving and healing properties traditionally associated with the apple. Seasonally the apple is correctly placed in the autumn beside its natural partner, the hazel.

Muin: This is the most controversial letter name of all with no less than four different explanations for it. *Muin* is described variously as meaning 'neck/upper part of the back', 'wile/deceit', 'love/esteem' and 'brake/thicket'. The word *muin* (or *muine* in the case of 'brake/thicket') actually does have all these meanings, so it is not surprising that confusion should have occurred even as early as the time the word-oghams were invented. At first sight 'neck' and 'love' seem the best candidates. There is no doubt that the C list word-ogham *conar gotha* ('path of the voice') is based on the meaning 'neck'. But as McManus pointed out in the case of the letter name *cert*, the C list can be wrong and appears so on this occasion. An alternative word-ogham for the A list *ardam maise* (most noble goodliness') supports the love/esteem meaning but I also believe that this is based on a misunderstanding of *muin*. The meanings 'neck', 'love' and 'wile' cannot be related convincingly to the main word-oghams of the A and B lists. These are *tressam fedmae* ('strongest in action') and *árusc n-airlig* ('proverb of slaughter'). McManus considers that 'strongest in action' fits well with 'neck/upper part of the back' and this is plausible but it does not fit with 'proverb of slaughter'. 'Wile/deceit' on the other hand could be made to fit 'proverb of slaughter' but I don't see any real connection with 'strongest in action'. 'Love/esteem' does not fit either of them. The two word-oghams *tressam fedmae* and *árusc n-airlig* seem close in spirit, both having a warlike feel, so they possibly refer to the same thing. As they do not both convincingly fit any of the meanings, 'neck', 'deceit' or 'love', the likelihood is that they refer to the characteristics of the tree in question rather than the letter name. This would make *muin* a general arboureal letter name, like *nin* or *cert*, and I therefore believe the meaning 'brake or thicket' is the most likely one.

However, we still do not know which trees are referred to by the word-oghams 'strongest in action' and 'proverb of slaughter'. The glossators mention no trees in connection with *muin* so they can give us no help. One glossator mentions 'vine' probably on the basis that its name in Irish *finemain* sounds something like *muin*, but it has little else to recommend it. The most plausible explanation for such violent sounding expressions is that they refer to a tree known for its purgative properties. 'Proverb of slaughter' could as also be translated as 'proverb of misery/rottenness' – an accurate description of the act of purging. Slaughtering one's enemies can also be taken to be a symbolic purging.

The specific tree meant is most likely to be the buckthorn, a tree known for the purgative properties of its bark and berries and used since ancient times in medicine, as its Latin name *Rhamnus Cathartica* testifies. It was widely used in Ireland and valued as an important medicinal plant up to recent times.[3] Seasonally buckthorn is correctly placed, as its fruits ripen in autumn at around the same time as the apple and other fruits.

Gort: This is the Irish word for field and all the word-oghams support this interpretation. What we are looking for then is a tree associated with fields and the fertility and abundance of the land. The glossators mention honeysuckle and ivy. Honeysuckle is not a tree and is in any case inappropriate seasonally, being a summer plant, so it can be discounted. The Irish for honeysuckle, *edlenn*, is very close to that of ivy, *edeand*, so the chances are that it is a confusion with ivy. Ivy would seem to be a better candidate, given that it is evergreen and can become quite woody, but it is not really associated with abundance and can hardly be described as a plant of the open fields. The furze or whin seems to be the most appropriate 'tree'. It is true that furze is not a true tree, but a fully grown bush can reach six foot high and across, large enough to included in a 'tree' list.

The furze fits the requirements well. According to Lucas in his study of the uses of furze,[4] furze was traditionally seen not as a weed but as adding to the value of land. The presence of furze gave otherwise barren land some value, and on good land was considered as a boon. This was because of its many uses, such as fodder and bedding for livestock, as hedging, and as a shelter in the open field. Lucas quotes the earliest known reference to the use of furze as fodder and bedding, which speaks of the fact that 'in the extremest violence of winter tempests it affords ... both food and shelter'. This, and the fact that it was cut for both fodder and bedding in the autumn, give good reasons why it should have an autumnal placing in the list. Furthermore, furze, being evergreen, is capable of blossoming all year round, and one of the two species of furze in Ireland, the western furze, actually does come into bloom in the autumn. Finally, it is worth noting that the Irish word for furze (*aiteann*) is not very different than that for ivy, *edeand*. Is it possible that later scholars, half-hearing *aiteann*, took it to be (for them), the more plausible, wintry, *edeand*?

Gétal: McManus argues that the letter name *gétal* means 'wounding' or 'act of wounding', related to the Welsh *gwanu* 'to pierce, stab', and the word-oghams support his interpretation. The glossators mention the broom or reed (*gilcach*), the bog-myrtle and the fern in connection with *gétal*. Fern is only mentioned by one source and it may be that it is a confusion with bog-myrtle as their Irish names are very similar (*raith* and *rait* respectively). Neither the bog-myrtle nor fern have any obvious connection with wounding, and as neither have any important medical uses they can be safely discounted. It is likely they became connected with the letter name because they were used for bedding in the same way that reeds were. That leaves us with the broom or the reed. The glossators state that *gilcach* is associated with the letter name on account of its healing powers. Broom fits this description rather the reed, as it is an ancient medicinal plant used to cure many different ailments. As well as being used as a diuretic and a cathartic, broom is also known for the effect it has on the nervous and circulatory system. Small doses slow the heart for a time before increasing the pulse and heartbeat, while large doses have a narcotic effect, lowering blood pressure and slowing the heartbeat. It is possible that broom could have been given to wounded patients who had lost a lot of blood, in order to give them extra strength, or help them heal through sleeping, depending on the dose. As well as its medical uses, the sharp tips of broom branches and their ability to prick or stab can be taken as an connection to the letter name. At around six foot tall when full grown, broom is also large enough to be considered a 'tree'. Broom, as its name suggests, was cut to make brooms and its pliable branches have many other uses, such as making baskets and wicker fences. According to Lucas in his study of furze, broom and furze were seen as similar and broom was put to many of the same uses as furze. It is likely then, that the letter names *gort* and *gétal* and their associated 'trees', can be taken as a pair.

Straif: All the word-oghams point to the letter name meaning 'sulphur'. Most of the glossators mention the blackthorn in relation to *straif*. 'Sulphur' is a suitable poetic name for the tree as there are several properties of the blackthorn which can be likened to sulphur. The most obvious is the blackness of the blackthorn's branches and thorns (hence its name). Sulphur is well known for the blackening or tarnishing effect it has on silver. Another is the bitterness of its fruits which parallel the fiery, burning sulphur, or brimstone. The blackthorn is also known mythologically as a fierce and warlike tree, so it fits well with the harsh reputation of brimstone. Seasonally the blackthorn is also well placed as its fruits are ripe in late autumn and early winter.

Ruis: There is no doubt that this letter name means red or redness, or more exactly, redness of face or blushing. The glossators mention the rowan, dog rose and elder in connection with this letter name. The rowan is no doubt cited because of its red berries and the same reasoning applies to the inclusion of dog rose (mentioned only once) on account of its red rose hips. The strong emphasis in the word-oghams on redness of face, however, means that we can safely discount them as neither tree has any obvious link with red faces. The elder, on the other hand, has a clear connection. Since ancient times elder flowers have been used as a cure for spots and blemishes, and the berries when green have been used as a salve for scalds and burns. Furthermore, in ancient Ireland ripe elderberries were used as a kind of rouge, giving a red colour to the cheeks. The elder's berries are ripe in late autumn, placing it in the appropriate place seasonally.

The consonant series has now covered the whole seasonal year, and a new smaller cycle begins with the vowels.

Ailm: One of the glossators states that this name derives from Latin *palma* or palm, and this is probably correct for two reasons. The first is that early Irish had no 'P' sound, so that the initial 'P' would have been dropped in the transition into the language, producing the word *ailm*. The second is that the glossators associate *ailm* with the pine tree, and both trees are close mythologically speaking, making *ailm* a suitable alternative name for the pine. In Classical tradition the palm tree was seen as a tree of rebirth and fertility, and there is evidence to show that the pine was seen in a similar light in Ireland and Northern Europe generally. In Ireland the burning of splints or logs of pine-wood was a custom particularly associated with Christmas or midwinter. The bright flame from the resin in the wood was probably originally a symbol of the re-birth of the new year. There is, in fact, some evidence that *ailm* was used as a name for the pine. The scholar Fergus Kelly, in his survey of the trees listed in early irish laws, quotes a line from an old Irish poem where a hermit says 'Beautiful are the pines which make music for me'.[5] The word used for 'pines' is *ailmi* and Kelly considers the pine to fit the context better than any other, as the pine is noted for the musical sound of the wind through its branches. The word-oghams all refer to the sound of the letter, which is unusual and could show that the letter name was regarded as needing no explanation. As stated above, the pine is symbolically associated with midwinter, and as such begins a new seasonal cycle for the vowels.

Onn: This letter is associated by the glossators with the furze or heather but there can be no doubt that the ash is the tree that is meant. *Onn* is the ancient Irish word for the ash tree (cf. Welsh *Onnen*) and the word-oghams all refer quite clearly to it. *Onn* was replaced later in the language by *uinnius* and the connection to the letter name was lost as a result. The ash tree is associated with birth, growth and fertility, so it is appropriately placed seasonally in late spring or early summer, when its foliage is at its most lush.

Úr: The glossators and McManus take this letter name to be the word *úr/úír* 'clay/earth' but an alternative based on the word *úr* meaning 'moist/fresh' better explains the word-oghams. '*Úaraibh adbaib*' ('in cold dwellings') is taken to refer to graves, but a simpler explanation is that it refers to the damp frequently found in 'cold dwellings'. Similarly *sílead cland* ('propagation of plants') could be better read as a reference to moisture, as plants will not germinate in dry earth. It is also possible that the word-ogham should read '*sílead cland*' or 'dripping of plants'. The third word-ogham *forbbaid ambí* ('shroud of a lifeless one') is admittedly more suited to a meaning based on clay or earth but it could be that this word-ogham is based on the 'clay/earth' meaning through a misunderstanding of the letter name. It is also possible that the shroud referred to in the word-ogham is the cold, moist clamminess believed to cover a dead person. In any case, the first two word-oghams better fit a meaning based on 'moist'.

The only tree or shrub mentioned by the glossators is heather, which has nothing to recommend it. Most of the glossators do not mention any tree. The most likely candidate is the only major tree not linked to any of the other letter names, namely the elm. After the alder, the elm is the native timber tree most noted for its ability to withstand moist or watery conditions. The elm is also an important mythological tree, noted for the richness of its foliage and sap. A strongly growing, sap-filled tree is even today still known in Irish as a *crann úr*. Mythologically speaking, the elm is presented as a provider of nourishment or fertility, and this would explain the meaning of the alternative A list word-ogham *guirem dál*. This has been taken to mean variously 'most pious', 'most prompt' or 'most painful of meetings'. It should instead read 'most pious sharing' or 'most pious giving' and this would fit in well with the character of the elm as it is portrayed in folklore. Seasonally the time of the greatest growth of foliage is the early summer around Maytime, so this would be a suitable time to place the elm. It is also the correct place in the seasonal cycle of letters after *onn*.

Edad: McManus considers this to be an artificially altered word, designed to form a pair with the last letter *idad*. This is probably true but this is not to say that the word is a complete invention. The glossators mention the aspen and the juniper in relation to this letter, and while the juniper has nothing to recommend it, the word-oghams point clearly to the aspen. In fact the old name for aspen is *idhadh* or *idhat* (later *fiodhadh*) and this is very close to *edad* (it is also very close to the old name for the cherry *idaith,* a fact which probably caused a lot of confusion). The likelihood is that the letter name is a deliberately altered version of *idhadh*, both to fit in with *idad* and to provide a letter name beginning with 'E'. McManus and other scholars cannot follow the word-oghams on this occasion, but an understanding of the aspen resolves the problems. *Érgnid fid* ('most discerning tree') refers to the aspen's reputation since ancient times for sensitivity. The aspen has unusually flattened leaf stalks, causing its leaves to flutter in the slightest breeze, giving rise to the expression 'to tremble like an aspen' (and to the later Irish name *crithach*). The aspen was believed to tremble because it was aware of the otherworld, and was thus also aware of the approach of death or misfortune. The glossators mention it as a 'stick of woe' and this is a reference to its use in measuring corpses and graves, a use no doubt dictated by its unlucky associations. An alternative reading of this word-ogham *aerchaid fid* ('satirising or destroying wood') is likely to be explained by this. The B word-ogham *commaín carat* ('exchange of friends') most probably refers to the constant whispering of the aspen's leaves being like the lowered, intimate talk of friends. The C word-ogham *bráthair bethi* ('brother of birch') is explained by the fact that aspen is found in many of the same habitats as birch, such as rocky mountain sides and the edge of forests. The two trees are also not dissimilar in appearance. Symbolically, the aspen can be associated with autumn and the dying of the year, placing it in the next position in the seasonal cycle.

Idad: This is the last of the original twenty letters and despite being similar to the early Irish word for both the cherry and the aspen (*idadh* or *idaith*), appears to be an artificial variation of the Irish word for yew, *ibar*. The word-oghams all point to the yew and the glossators mention the tree. The yew tree's association with death places it seasonally at the festival of Samhain, the time of death and make it the natural choice to end the alphabet.

It is necessary at this point to look at the native trees and shrubs not included in the tree list. It is possible to see reasons why they were not chosen. The two most obvious trees omitted are the whitebeam and the juniper. The Irish name for whitebeam is *findcholl* or 'whitehazel' due to the supposed similarity of its leaves to hazel, and for having conspicuous white undersides. The vernacular Irish names for the juniper include *iubhar craigi, iubhar beinne* and *iubhar talamh*, or 'rock yew', 'mountain yew' and 'ground yew'. The name *aiteal* is a modern borrowing from Scotland but Fergus Kelly does suggest *crann fir* as another possible name. These names suggest that the whitebeam and juniper may have been left out to avoid confusion with the hazel and yew respectively.

Of the other trees, spindle and arbutus, though striking in appearance, have little practical value or place in folklore to justify their presence in the tree list. Alder buckthorn is too close to buckthorn to merit a separate letter. The bird cherry is very rare in Ireland and seems to have such a low profile that Fergus Kelly was unable to find an Irish name for it. That leaves the large shrubs. The most obvious are dogwood, guelder rose and bog myrtle, and there seem to be no compelling reasons why they should be considered as likely to be included, as again they have a limited practical value and place in folklore. Another shrub, wild privet, is very rare and of no practical use. As the *Beithluisnin* is supposed to be a tree alphabet, there no reason to suppose small shrubs like heather and dog rose, or climbing plants like ivy and honeysuckle, are included in the list. As we have seen, there are no letters names or word-oghams which compel us to accept a link to plants like these, despite their being mentioned by some glossators.

THE ORDER OF THE LETTERS:

The order of the alphabet is based, on the seasonal order of the trees linked to each name and letter. The consonants form a cycle of fifteen letters and the vowels another one of only five. The first *aicme* (or group of five letters) stretches from midwinter to April or May; the second from May to September/October and the onset of winter. The third *aicme* is placed in late autumn or winter. Each of the vowels in the fourth *aicme* cover a different part of the year, A being midwinter, O and U around Bealtaine or Maytime, E in autumn, and I in winter or the festival of Samhain. The alphabet begins with B for the birch, the tree of beginnings and renewal, and ends with I for the yew, the tree of death and the afterlife. The first *aicme* seems linked to the second by the fact that the last letter of the first (*nin*), and the first letter of the second (*hÚath*) are both connected to trees noted for their blossoms, albeit with contrasting images. Similarly the last letter of the second *aicme* *(cert)* and the first letter of the third *(muin)* are both contrasting trees noted for their health giving properties, the apple of *cert* and the 'stink-apple' of *muin*.

In terms of grammar, the alphabet is partly based on the Roman classification of letters as *semivocales, mutae* and *vocals*.[6] The letters within the alphabet are also phonetically paired where possible. The phonetic pairs are paralleled by an obvious pairing of the trees concerned.

F and S: Alder and willow, both trees noted for growing near water.
D and T: Oak and holly, both 'warrior' trees, noted for the hardness of their timber.
C and Q: Hazel and apple, both 'otherworld' fruits noted for their nourishment.
G and NG: Furze and broom, similar in uses and appearance.
O and U: Ash and elm, both trees linked to water, and having associations with fertility.
E and I: Aspen and yew, both trees linked to misfortune and death.

The letters STR and R probably also form a pairing as the blackthorn and elder are quite similar, both having dark fruits and hostile mythological associations. This suggests that the original sound of *straif* may have been something like 'SR'. This principle of pairing trees as well as letters is probably the reason why opportunities to name other letters directly after trees were not taken. For example, the chances to name T after the elder *trom*, and L after the elm *lem*, were passed over. It would have been quite inappropriate to pair the oak *dair* with the elder, as the two trees have nothing in common. Instead, holly was the obvious partner for the oak, so a suitable poetic name beginning with T had to be found. Similarly, a tree needed to be paired with the ash and the elm was the obvious choice. The availability of the suitable poetic name *úr* for U clinched the matter. To sum up, the chance to name more letters directly after trees was sacrificed to the desire to achieve some phonetic order and the trees involved were given poetic alternatives instead.

However, the one principle of the alphabet which could not be sacrificed was the seasonal order of the trees, and all other considerations had to take second place to that.

THE FORFEDA OR SUPPLEMENTARY LETTERS

The five supplementary letters form a category, *aicme*, all to themselves, being of a later date and having, as we shall see, a completely different order than the original twenty. Like the original twenty letters each letter has its own name. Their names and values in order are: *Ébad* (É), *Ór* (Ó), *Uilen* (UI), *Pín/Iphín* (P) and *Emancholl* (CH). The letters were created soon enough after the original twenty to appear in the later orthodox inscriptions, so the likelihood is that they were created only a century or two after the original twenty. The *Scholar's Primer* states clearly that the supplementary letters were for the purpose of bringing Greek and Latin words into Irish. The letters themselves show a greater classical influence, with the names *Ór* and *Pín* being borrowed from Latin, and with the shape of some of the letters echoing their Latin or Greek counterparts. However, in practice there does not seem to have been a great need of extra letters for whatever new words were being borrowed into Irish, and the letters never found much favour with Oghamists.

Below is how the letters are presented in the *Auraicept*:

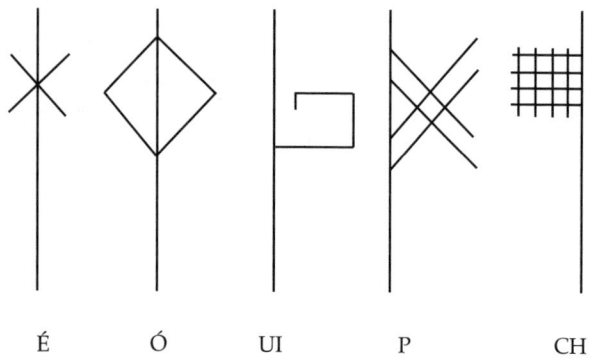

OGHAM — THE GAELIC TREE ALPHABET

Like the original twenty letters, the supplementary letters are accompanied by word-oghams and are linked by tradition to different trees. The letter names and word-oghams do not on the whole present any great difficulties, nor do the associations with various trees.

Ébad: This letter originally had the sound É but was later changed to the diphthong EA and the name is a variation on the letter name Edad. The word-oghams refer to the fact the sound of the letter É or ÉO is the same as the Irish word for salmon. The glossators mention the honeysuckle and aspen in connection with *Ébad*, but as the name is undoubtedly a variation on *Edad* the aspen is the obvious choice. There are also good grounds for connecting the aspen to the letter name, as we shall later see.

Ór: This letter originally had the sound Ó, but was later changed to the diphthong OI. There is no doubt this letter name means gold as it is similar to the Latin and the word-oghams support that interpretation. The glossators mention ivy and the spindle tree. Once again, ivy has nothing to recommend it but the spindle fits as it is noted for the bright orange-red colour of the flesh of its fruits, which are surrounded by pink shells called 'arils'. A spindle in autumn laden down with fruits is a striking sight, with its orange-red (or 'gold') flesh showing through the shells.

Uilen: McManus considers this letter sound to be modelled on Latin Y, or the diphthong UI. The letter name means 'elbow' or 'angle'. The B list word-ogham *cubat oll* ('great bend') confirms this. The A list word-ogham *'tuthmar fid'* means 'most fragrant tree'. It is worth noting that the word-ogham itself relates the letter name to a tree, even though the letter name is not actually that of a tree. The glossators mention honeysuckle and juniper (*crann fir'*). The honeysuckle is fragrant but it is not a tree and does not have any obvious connection to the letter name. Its choice is perhaps partly dictated by the similarity of its Irish name *edlenn* with *Uilen*. The juniper is fragrant when its wood is burnt and can be called a tree, so it would appear the better choice. Juniper also fits the letter name 'elbow'.

Fergus Kelly identifies the juniper with the tree *crann fir* in the medieval tree list *Bretha Comaithchesa* (Laws of Neighbourhood) on the basis of its description.[7] The fact that it appears here to describe a fragrant tree, which juniper is, lends further weight to his conclusion. He is however, unable to explain the origin of the word *fir* in *crann fir*. This is the same as the word *fiar* meaning 'twisted, diagonal-wise, awry, bent'. The juniper is noted for its twisted and bent trunk when it grows in an upright and spreading form, so *crann fiar* or *fir* meaning 'twisted tree' would be a good description for it. This characteristic of juniper suits the name *Uilen* or elbow/angle well. The name *crann fir* appears only in the *Bretha Comaithchesa*, a single poem, and in connection with the letter name *Uilen*. Is it possible that the name *crann fir* was coined especially by the creator of the supplementary letters to get around the confusion of the juniper with the yew? It could then have survived in tradition as a scholarly name for the juniper, to be used in the medieval tree list and virtually nowhere else.

Pín: The original sound of this letter was P but later scholars changed the sound to IO as part of the process of making diphthongs out of all five supplementary letters, changing the letter name to I*phín*/I*fín* in the process. This letter name is considered by McManus to derive from the Latin *Pínus* or 'pine' but a better explanation would be that it is an adaptation of the Latin word *Spina* or 'spine' as the glossators all connect the name to the derived Irish word *spin* or *spinan*. *Spinan* is the accepted Irish word for the gooseberry and literally means 'spiny one' which the gooseberry bush is. The word-oghams also point to the gooseberry. *Milsem fedo* ('sweetest tree') and *amram mlais* ('most wonderful taste') are both good descriptions of the gooseberry. The chief objection to the gooseberry is that it not a native bush (though it could have been introduced quite early). However, as it represents the letter P which is itself an import, its use may have been deliberate. The gooseberry is native to Britain and it could have been that it was thought appropriate to use to represent a 'British' letter. Fergus Kelly is reluctant to connect *spíonán* with gooseberry when it appears in the *Bretha Comaithchesa* list on the grounds of its not being native but he admits that there is no obvious alternative.[8] The anomaly of a non-native bush being included in the list can be explained if it gained its place on the strength of its link to an ogham letter. In any case, as we shall see, there are other good grounds for believing that *pín* is linked to the gooseberry.

Emancholl: This letter means simply 'twin of hazel' or 'twin of C'. The tree associated with *emancholl* is of course the hazel.

At first sight the order of the supplementary letters appears to be purely arbitrary. They are certainly not arranged in any seasonal order since three of the trees – aspen, spindle and hazel – are linked to autumn, gooseberry is linked to summer, and juniper does not have any clear seasonal link at all. More than that, the choice of trees appears to be rather strained as hazel and aspen are repeated from the original list, spindle is a relatively obscure choice and gooseberry can hardly be called a large shrub, let alone a tree. First appearances would seem to suggest that the choice of tree or shrub was made purely for the sake of providing some continuity with the original alphabet without any symbolic intent, and perhaps even in ignorance of the seasonal order of the original twenty letters.

The word-oghams for *uilen* and *pín* provide the clue to proving this is not so. They contain the information that *uilen* is the most fragrant tree and *pín* the sweetest tasting. Following this through by looking at the characteristics of all the trees reveals that each of them can be linked to one of the senses:

Ebad/Aspen:	A tree noted for the constant whispering sound of its leaves
Ór/Spindle:	A tree noted for the bright sight of its display of fruits in the autumn
Uilen/Juniper:	A tree noted for the aromatic smell of its leaves and wood when burnt
Pín/Gooseberry:	A 'tree' noted for the sweet taste of its berries
Emancholl/Hazel:	A tree noted for the nourishment and nutritious value of its nuts.

What we have then is a scheme based roughly on the five senses, with physical strength as the fifth sense, rather than touch; or more accurately, a scheme based on the five organs of those senses; the ears, eyes, nose, mouth and heart. The heart is often compared to a nut in folklore (as in the expression *a chnó mo chroíse* – 'O nut of my heart') and so would be a fitting symbol of the bodily strength achieved from eating the nourishing hazelnut. This explains the order of the letters, starting at the organs closest to the top of the head, the ears, and working down the body to the heart. This also explains the repetition of the aspen and hazel, as they are the obvious choices to express sound and nourishing strength respectively. Far from being an arbitrary collection of trees and letter names as might be first thought, the supplementary letters therefore actually form an ingenious scheme of their own.

This scheme also offers us an explanation for the shape of the supplementary letters. The letter shapes (with the exception of the last one) are representations of the relevant sense organs. This is the logical extension of the original twenty letters which clearly represent fingers. Hence:

EA: The symbol for *ebad*, instead of being seen as an 'X' shape, really represents a pair of ears, or singly (as seen from each side of the *droim*) as > and <.

OI: Similarly, the symbol for *Ór*, instead of being seen as a lozenge, is really a pair of eyes, or singly, seen from the side, as < and >.

UI: Following the same pattern, the symbol for *uilen* is a representation of a nose or nostril.

P: The obvious follow on is that the symbol for *pín* represents a mouth, but at first sight, this does not seem so. However, the letter could literally represent a pursed mouth sucking on a berry.

CH: Rather than trying to represent a heart the creator, perhaps wisely, chose to invent a letter based purely on the letter name, i.e., the letter C twinned or doubled over on itself.

That there is, however, enough imagery built into the letter names,

OGHAM – THE GAELIC TREE ALPHABET

LETTER NAME	MEANING OF NAME	MEDIEVAL TREE	ORIGINAL TREE
Beithe	Birch	Birch	Birch
Luis	Flame	Rowan	Rowan
Fern	Alder	Alder	Alder
Sail	Willow	Willow	Willow
Nin	Branch-Fork	Ash	Cherry
hÚath	Fear	Hawthorn	Hawthorn
Dair	Oak	Oak	Oak
Tinne	Iron Bar	Holly	Holly
Coll	Hazel	Hazel	Hazel
Cert	Bush	Apple	Apple
Muin	Thicket	Vine	Buckthorn
Gort	Field	Ivy	Furze
Gétal	Wounding	Broom/Reed	Broom
Straif	Sulphur	Blackthorn	Blackthorn
Ruis	Red	Elder	Elder
Ailm	Palm	Pine	Pine
Onn	Ash	Furze	Ash
Úr	Moist/Fresh	Heather	Elm
Edad	Aspen	Aspen	Aspen
Idad	Yew	Yew	Yew
Ebad	Aspen	Aspen	Aspen/wave
Ór	Gold	Spindle	Spindle/sun
Uilen	Elbow	Honeysuckle	Juniper/wind
Pín	Spine	Gooseberry	Gooseberry/moon
Emancholl	Twin-hazel	Hazel	Hazel/earth

trees and word-oghams to suggest that a full explanation has not yet been provided. A closer look demonstrates this is so, and that each of the letters can be symbolically linked to each of the five elements known to the ancient Celts. Briefly then:

Hearing and the aspen are linked to the sea or the waves;
Sight and the spindle are linked to the sun;
Smell and the juniper are linked to the sky or the wind;
Taste and the gooseberry are linked to the moon;
Strength and the hazel are linked to the earth.

The sound of the letter *ebad* is the same as the word for salmon and the word-oghams speak of a 'fair swimming' and 'water' letter, which ties in with the sea. Mythologically the sea was often regarded as hostile, and the roar of the waves was seen as foretelling the death of kings. This fits the aspen with its similar unlucky associations as a harbringer of death and its link to hearing. The letter name *ór* meaning gold and the choice of spindle with its pink and gold fruit, which are the colours of sunrise and sunset, provides the link to the sun. The sun is also often portrayed as a great eye in folklore. Juniper was burnt as its fragrant, antiseptic smell was thought to clear the atmosphere of bad humours and protect against the evil spirits of the air and wind. The gooseberry with its round transparent fruits could be said to resemble the moon and it has a medical connection to it as well. An infusion of the leaves taken before the monthly period was considered a useful tonic for young girls,[9] and Culpeper considered it 'excellent good to stay the longings of women with child'. Perhaps ideas like this gave rise to the notion found in English folklore that babies are left under gooseberry bushes! Finally, hazelnuts could be said to contain more of the goodness and fertility of the earth than most fruits.

But we are not finished there. Each of the elements can be linked through folklore and mythology to each of the five directions. The sea and aspen correspond to the 'black north', the most hostile, warlike direction. The sun and spindle correspond to the south of light and growth. Wind and juniper correspond to the west, a direction associated with death, magic and wisdom. Traditionally the fairies or spirits of the air and wind were considered the most hostile and magically powerful. Moon and gooseberry correspond to the east, the direction of growth and fertility. Finally, the earth and hazel correspond to the centre, the place of sovereignty, wisdom and authority. The attributes of the directions are laid out most comprehensively in the story 'The Settling of the Manor of Tara'. The order of the directions as set out in the letters is the exact reverse of the normal order used in Irish, *Thoir/Thiar/ Theas/Thuaidh* or East/West/South/North and forms a cross, a symbol found frequently in folklore.

Finally, the directions can be linked to the seasonal festivals: North to *Samhain*, the festival of the dead; South to *Bealtaine*, the festival celebrating the sun's return; West to *Lughnasa*, the start of autumn and the onset of the death of the year; and East to *Imbolc*, the start of spring, the return of fertility, and the appearance of newborn animals. The centre can be linked to the festival of Tara supposed to be held every three years to make laws and reaffirm authority. Thus we have a seasonal framework for the supplementary letters to complement the original seasonal cycle. The reality is that far from being the jumble of letters and trees which at first sight they may appear, the supplementary letters actually form an ingenious scheme of their own which is extraordinarily rich in symbolism.

In conclusion, the folklore of trees is central to understanding the meaning of each letter and the order of the Ogham alphabet. We have explored that folklore and mythology in great detail and confirmed the wealth of evidence for the associations of each tree. To modern eyes basing the order of an alphabet on the seasonal attributes of trees might seem rather esoteric but to the creators of Ogham, trees were a central part of their lives, important to their environment, livelihood, beliefs and learning. Contrary then, to the belief of most modern scholars, tradition is correct when it states that Ogham is an alphabet based on 'the trees of the forest'.

An Ogham Tree Calendar

Robert Graves in his book *The White Goddess* was the first to suggest that the ancient Celts measured time by the use of a lunar tree calendar of thirteen months. Unfortunately, there is no evidence that this was the case. Graves was not wholly off the mark with his suggestion, however. He deserves credit for being the first in modern times to realise the Ogham alphabet was based on a seasonal cycle of trees. He was also correct in saying that the Celts used a Lunar calendar. What Graves in fact did was to marry these two facts in a creative way. Even if his efforts owe more to poetic licence than historical precedent, the result is something that the Celts would not have found alien in spirit.

However, the list of trees and shrubs that Graves used is incorrect, so his calendar cannot be taken as definitive. It is worthwhile, therefore, seeing what shape a suitable tree calendar would take. Graves' idea of thirteen months of 28 days plus one day has the advantage of simplicity, but the calendar should start at *Samhain*, the recognised beginning of the Celtic year. Each month should also be linked to its nearest equivalent in the Gaulish calendar of Coligny, as this is the only complete surviving Celtic calendar that exists. The names of the Coligny Calendar months are quite obscure and there is some controversy over what they mean. In particular, there is a division over which month begins the calendar year. There is agreement that the year as set out in the calendar consists of two halves, one half beginning with the month Samonios and the other with the month Giamonios. However, some scholars maintain that Samonios corresponds with the beginning of summer and Giamonios with the beginning of winter, while others maintain the exact opposite.[1] To put it another way, one argument holds that Samonios means simply 'summer' (Irish *Samhradh*, Welsh *Haf*); while the other holds that it means 'summer's end' and is analogous with the Irish *Samhain*. It appears that the case for Samonios

An Ogham Tree Calendar

	Month	Tree	Date	Gaulish Equiv.
‡	*Idad*	Yew	1 Nov - 28 Nov.	Antaranos
┼	*Ailm*	Pine	29 Nov. - 26 Dec.	Giamonios
├	*Beith*	Birch	27 Dec. - 23 Jan.	Simivisonnos
├=	*Luis*	Rowan	24 Jan. - 20 Feb.	Equos
├≡	*Fern*	Alder	21 Feb. - 20 Mar.	Elembivios
├≣	*Sail*	Willow	21 Mar. 17 April	Edrinios
┤	*Huath*	Hawthorn	18 April - 15 May	Cantlos
┼	*Onn*	Ash	16 May - 12 June	Samonios
┤	*Dair*	Oak	13 June - 10 July	Dumannios
≡┤	*Tinne*	Holly	11 July - 7 Aug.	Rivros
≣┤	*Coll*	Hazel	8 Aug. - 4 Sept.	Anagantios
≣┤	*Cert*	Apple	5 Sept. - 2 Oct.	Ogronios
≢	*Ruis*	Elder	3 Oct. - 30 Oct.	Cutios

Bile Buadha	Tree of power	31 October (Samhain Eve)	No letter

   I   A   B   L   F   S   H

   O   D   T   C   Q   R

corresponding to the beginning of summer is the stronger one. There is no basis in Celtic tradition for a month called 'winter's end', which we are required to believe is the meaning of Giamonios if Samonios corresponds to *Samhain*. It is more plausible to believe that Giamonios simply means 'winter ' (Irish *Geimhreadh*, Welsh *Gaeaf*). In particular, the name for May in old Irish and Welsh was *Cétamuin* and *Cyntefin* respectively, both of which mean 'first of summer'.[2] There is also the fact that 'summer's end' or *Gorffennaf* in Welsh refers to July, not November.

The choice and order of trees should also be made to harmonise as closely as possible with their role in folklore; and the order of the Ogham alphabet be followed as much as possible. Bearing all these factors in mind I have compiled the scheme as set out below. The calendar involves the important trees from each of the first three Ogham *aicmi* of consonants placed in letter order, with the important trees from the fourth *aicme* of vowels inserted at the first and second halves of the year. Nevertheless, the choice of the last Ogham letter *idad*, (the yew) to begin the calendar does need explaining. The ancient Celts counted days as beginning with sunset not sunrise, and their year began with the onset of winter. It seemed appropriate, therefore, to begin the calendar with the yew given its strong seasonal link with November. Also, the fact that it is the last letter does not seem so strange if we consider that it symbolically represents the entry into the otherworld season of darkness when the cycle of life ceases for a time. Finally, a feature of the calendar is that each month also forms a contrasting pair with its opposite seasonal number.

Before going into the calendar in detail it is important to explain its value. A tree calendar is obviously not needed today for the purposes of time-keeping. But for those of us who love our native trees it provides a simple way of bringing them into our everyday lives and of connecting with their folklore and symbolism in a meaningful way. For this reason I have arranged each month in the form of a meditation on the link between our own lives and nature's seasons as typified by each of the trees. Let us now examine each month in detail and what is associated with the tree and time of year it represents.

Yew – Idad

1-28 November

At first sight the yew may appear to be gloomy and depressing with its dark leaves. However, at this time of year the yew wears its crop of pink-red berries, a sign of hope. These lighten what otherwise may appear to be a forbidding tree. Allow yourself to find rest in the yew's dark appearance. The yew represents the goddess of the land in her dark aspect, who protects both the living and the dead. Now is the time to think of loved ones that have passed away, the family, ancestors and heritage. In Irish tradition it is Samhain, the time when the other world and the world of spirits is closest. In the Christian calendar it is the Feasts of All Souls and All Saints. It is not a time to be gloomy but to celebrate the spiritual things of life. It is a time of rest, reflection and meditation. The yew is associated with death and the afterlife but it is also traditionally a tree associated with sanctuary for those fleeing a hostile world. It is no accident that the yew stood beside the church as well as the graveyard. The yew is a symbol of stability, of certainty, a tree that stays green when most other trees are bare. This is a time to huddle around the fire just as the high kings of Ulster did in their great hall of Eamhain Mhacha, which was supported by pillars of yew. Imagine the dark red wooden beams gleaming richly in the firelight. This is the time to emphasise inner spiritual strength and renewal, and to seek nourishment for the soul, to step back from the rush of every day life to renew a sense of peace. *Idad* corresponds best to the Gaulish month Antaranos which means 'inter-month'. It was the intercalary month which was inserted on occasion to keep the calendar aligned with the solar year. As such, it stood outside of ordinary time.

Pine – Ailm

29 November - 26 December

The pine is an evergreen and at first sight it looks dark like the yew. But move closer and listen to the musical sound of the wind through its branches. In Scotland the pine was *Clairseach nan Craobh,* the Harp of Trees, on account of the music of its branches. Step up to the pine and breathe in deeply. Its sap smells invigoratingly of freshness and new life. Let the pine infuse you with its promise of renewal. This is the month of the winter solstice when the darkness reaches its limit and the days begin at last to lengthen once more. In the Christian tradition, of course, it is Christmas with its message of hope and celebration. The pine was traditionally used for the Christmas tree which stood in every home. Its fresh scent, green leaves and colourful decorations brought hope at the darkest time of year. The Christmas or Yule log was traditionally of pine, as its bright flame cheered, dispelling the gloom and protecting against evil. Pine splinters were also used as candles in winter for this reason. This is the time when we celebrate with family and friends the renewal of hope, and rejoice and give thanks for what we have. It is a time for the giving and receiving of gifts and for a spirit of generosity and goodwill to all. The pine is a symbol of the promise of imminent new birth and life, and anticipates the spring. Now is a good time to put the past behind you, to look ahead and plan for a new beginning. It is a time of optimism and restored belief, a time to look on the bright side of things. *Ailm* corresponds to the Gaulish month Giamonios which means 'winter month'.

Birch – Beith

27 December - 23 January

At this time of year the birch glimmers through the gloom of winter, its pale white trunk mirroring the snow beneath. It is a graceful sight with its sweeping, elegant branches gleaming dark red in the setting sun. The birch, with its bright bark, symbolises new life, the awakening at last of the new year and the return of the young sun with its promise of spring. It is a symbol of purity, love and youthfulness. This is a time of celebration and of new beginnings, a time to bring new things into being. This is the time when the New Year is celebrated and traditionally resolutions are made to change our ways and 'turn over a new leaf'. In Ireland 6 January is *Nollaig na Mban* or 'Women's' Christmas', when women could traditionally relax amongst themselves after their exertions over the holiday period. This month also anticipates the festival of St Brigid which comes on 1 February. Birch twigs were used in the St Brigid's Eve celebrations as 'Bride's wand' and were placed in a cradle to welcome Brigid coming into the house. Birch was traditionally used to make cradles due to its association with birth, and because its purity was especially effective at keeping away the fairies who might want to steal the child. Birch made very good besoms or brooms so good at sweeping and cleaning away the must and dust. Now is a good time to start new things, to act on our resolutions and reorder our lives. In particular, many people decide to lead healthier and purer lifestyles, and take steps to renew their energies and youthfulness. It is also a good time to look at the relationships in our lives (or the lack of them), and decide to improve things if necessary. *Beith* corresponds with the Gaulish month Simivisonnos which appears to mean 'spring month'.

Rowan – Luis

24 January - 20 February

The rowan now appears poised between winter and the arrival of spring. Perhaps there are still a few bright red berries left on the tree after the winter. But notice also that its buds are beginning to swell with the first stirrings of spring. The rowan is a tree of energy and protection because its flame red berries symbolise fire. Another name for it is the quicken or quickbeam as it was traditionally believed to be a tree that encouraged life to 'quicken'. This is the month when spring at last arrives and the first shoots of life appear. Snowdrops open their delicate white flowers, promising that other flowers will soon follow. In Irish tradition it is the Feast of Saint Brigid and the Festival of Imbolc, a time of nurturing and gentle encouragement. This is a time when young farm animals are born and when new things need nourishment and protection. Traditionally rowan was used to protect animals by tying it to their tails or manes. Rowan was also used to protect the first milk of the year, by putting it around the pail, or putting a sprig into the churn to keep the goodness from being lost. It is a time when energies need to be stimulated. At this time of year many of us feel washed out after the long winter. It is a time when we need to look after ourselves and rebuild our reserves. Perhaps we are beginning to flag in some of our previous resolutions. Be patient and do not expect too much too soon. This is a time to nurture our efforts and rejoice in every hopeful sign. Spring is here and soon things will change for the better. *Luis* corresponds to the Gaulish month Equos which means 'Horse Month'. In Gaelic Scotland roughly the same period of time was known as *Gearran* or 'Gelding Month'. The Roman festival of Equiria was celebrated with horseracing on the second last day of February and on 14 March.

An Ogham Tree Calendar

Alder – Fern

21 February - 20 March

The alder looks its most distinctive now, when it produces its green and yellow catkins and its purple buds are swelling with sap. The alder's orange-red sap is rising up now throughout the tree, reinvigorating it from root to branch tip. Alder is a tree of strength and battle, connected through its red sap with blood and war. Now is the time just before the spring equinox when growth has begun but the nights are still longer than the days and the weather is frequently cold and harsh. Nevertheless, the breakthrough into full leaf is about to happen. Bright yellow daffodils and other bulbs are in flower now, proclaiming the arrival of spring. St Patrick's Day falls in this month, when Irish people everywhere celebrate their heritage and the symbol of the festival, the shamrock, has sprouted rich and green. The alder was traditionally used to make shields and the Red Branch Knights of Ulster got their name from the reddish alder shields they carried. The alder was also used to make containers to hold liquids, especially milk. Thus it is also a tree of protection from harm. This is a time when new things need courage and strength to take their first steps in the world, to leave the shelter of the womb or nest and face the world and its sometimes harsh winds. Young birds and animals are now too big to be protected at every moment but too small to be secure on their own. Despite being vulnerable they must be stretched and challenged and this process, though difficult, is exhilarating and exciting as well as risky. It is therefore an appropriate time to test the waters and try out some ideas in the real world. *Fern* corresponds to the Gaulish month Elembivios whose meaning is obscure. MacNeill suggests 'Many Fences Month', the time when fences are repaired after the winter.

Willow – Sail

21 March - 17 April

The willow is wearing its yellow catkins now, which make a cheerful sight with bees humming around them, grateful for a source of honey at this early time. Its supple branches are breaking into bright green leaf. This is the time of the spring equinox, when at last the days become longer than the nights. By now growth is well underway and though things are still young and green, they are stronger and more confident. In many parts of Europe willow was often worn on Palm Sunday instead of palm, which is itself a symbol of rebirth. In the Christian tradition the Resurrection of Jesus Christ is celebrated around this time at the festival of Easter. Throughout Europe it was believed that the sun danced for joy when it rose on Easter morning. Easter eggs are decorated in celebration and in many places the game of egg rolling down a hill is played. This is a time to rejoice in the youthfulness of spring, in everything being fresh and new. There may still be harsh weather,but the growth in warmth and life is unstoppable. The willow is a tree of growth and fertility noted for growing beside rivers and water. It was traditionally used for protecting milk with a sprig tied around the churn to prevent the fairies from stealing the goodness from the butter. Willow's flexible branches gave it many uses, from baskets to fences. This is a time to look at new ways, try out new things, be flexible in adapting to an ever-changing world. In other words, to 'bend like the willow'. *Sail* corresponds to the Gaulish month Edrinios whose meaning is obscure. According to Duval it may mean 'fire-month'.

Hawthorn – Huath

18 April - 15 May

The hawthorn is a tree of power, creativity and fertility. At this time it is covered in bright white blossoms, heralding the return of the sun. Now is the time when growth is in full swing, spring turns to summer and winter has been banished. The light half of the year has begun. It is the time of the Celtic festival of Bealtaine, the second most important festival of the year to the Celts and the start of summer. The May bush (usually a hawthorn) is at the centre of attention, covered with many different types of flowers and with coloured streamers and cloths. Traditionally flowers, especially yellow ones, were gathered and placed on the bush, and on the doors and windows of the home. Later, on the night of May Eve, bonfires would be lit in the vicinity of the bush and the festivities would begin. Hawthorn is also associated with holy wells and the first water drawn from a well on May morning was regarded as particularly potent. The lone thorn or fairy bush was to be approached with care as the fairies are especially active at this time. Enjoy this period but remember that Maytime is unpredictable and capricious. A sudden frost can temper the good times. Maytime is like puberty, a time of great excitement, and the first steps in life and love. It is the movement from childhood into the adult world. This is a time to take a leap, enjoy new experiences and take some risks. But be careful that rash and foolish decisions do not bring consequences that are later regretted. Just remember that bright and intoxicating as the flowers of the whitethorns are, they are also surrounded by thorns. Everything is new and to be enjoyed, bold steps are to be taken and real life experiences to be had but be aware that some caution is needed. *Huath* corresponds to the Gaulish month Cantlos which means 'Song Month', when the arrival of summer is celebrated.

Ash – Onn

16 May - 12 June

The ash tree is at its most beautiful now. It is covered in bright green foliage and is growing quickly, its delicate leaves tossing in the breeze. Yet it stands tall and its strong branches spread out wide. Feel its strength and self confidence as it presides over the land at its time of greatest fertility. Summer is now well underway and the meadows and hedgerows are swathed in flowers. Growth is at its greenest and most lush, but the first excitement has passed and things are calmer and more confident under the strong summer sun. The danger of May frosts is gone. The ash represents the land goddess in all her summer glory. Three of the Five Great Trees of Ireland were ash trees, standing in the centre of Ireland as guardians and protectors of its prosperity and good fortune. Ash was used to make spears and horsewhips and for the throne of kings. This represents its role as protecting and supporting the rightful king in his 'marriage to the land'. Ash trees were also traditionally associated with holy wells and their fertility and curing powers. The ash is the Tree of Life that is cut down but springs up again anew. No other tree can spring up again so quickly and yet provide good, strong timber. This time is like young adulthood, a time of greater experience and maturity but when things are still new and fresh. Now is the time to spread your wings and live life to the full. This is a good time to be positive and look forward; for gaining experience for whatever responsibilities may lie ahead, while still exploring life and having fun. *Onn* corresponds to the Gaulish month Samonios which means 'summer month'.

Oak – Dair

13 June - 10 July

The oak now stands proudly covered in mature dark green leaves, often with a second growth of red new shoots providing a contrast. Its massive trunk is strong and imposing, encased in its coat of deeply ridged bark. The oak is lord of the forest, champion and protector of everything within it, especially animals like the deer and wild boar. Growth has now reached its full extent and the land rejoices in high summer. Plants and crops strengthen under the hot summer sun as the breakneck growth of the last few months slows down and consolidates. The land is now a darker green, not quite as fresh as before, but stronger and firmer. The festival of midsummer falls in this month, when the days reach their greatest length and slowly begin to shorten again. Midsummer, or St John's Eve as it was traditionally known in Ireland, was when bonfires were lit upon the hilltops or near holy wells and the summer was celebrated with music and dancing. In many places the midsummer fires were traditionally made of oak wood. The oak represents the rightful king's rule under which the land will bloom. It stands as the bringer of strength and stability, ensuring that the land moves towards the harvest safely. Now is the time to establish things on a firm basis, to make your mark. This is a time of action and solid achievement, a time to be positive and self confident. It was a tradition to burn any unwanted object in the midsummer bonfire with a sense of occasion. For example, old rosary beads and other sacred objects could be thrown on the fire to be disposed of without any disrespect. Now is the time to make new patterns in life and to discard any old ways that once had a place, but are now holding you back. *Dair* corresponds to the Gaulish month Dumannios whose meaning is obscure. MacNeill suggests 'Building Month' when good weather permits building to take place. Duval suggests 'Smoke Month'.

Holly – Tinne

11 July - 7 August

The holly flowers at this time, and although they are small and insignificant, these flowers will become the bright red berries of winter. Its leaves are dark and prickly but they remain fresh and shiny looking now when many things look decidedly dull. The land stands poised between summer and autumn. The sun is hot and drought is a possibility. The earth is often dry, hard and dusty and the time of lushness is now but a memory. Any growth that is weak or has shallow roots is by now beginning to wilt. Traditionally in Ireland July was known as 'Hungry July' when food had to be made last until the start of the harvest. But the Celtic festival of Lughnasa also falls in this month when the harvest does at last arrive. The first of the crops to be harvested were used to make a celebratory meal and the occasion was marked by festive gatherings on hilltops and by rivers. In ancient Ireland it was an occasion for games and sports, fairs and competitions. Holly is a tree renowned for its tough wood used for making spears and chariots; so it is a tree of strength and championship, appropriate for this time. Now is the time to stay the course, to find the extra energy and commitment to bring things to fruition. This is the time when projects that are underway sometimes need to be reviewed and amended in the light of experience. Anything carried out with a lack of commitment will face difficulties. But if we remain strong and confident we can relish the challenges and competition we face and successfully achieve our goals. *Tinne* corresponds to the Gaulish month Rivros which means 'Great Feast Month', i.e., the Feast of Lunasa, which was known to be celebrated in Gaul at Lyons.

Hazel – Coll

8 August - 4 September

The hazel is covered with green hazelnuts now, symbolising the first fruits of the harvest. Soon they will be a rich reddish brown and ready to be eaten. The land is turning golden as crops ripen in the sun and the harvest season gets underway. The 'Pattern' or 'Patron' day in honour of the local saint was widely observed throughout Ireland, with the time around Lúnasa being especially favoured. This involved a gathering at the local shrine of the saint, usually a holy well, and the reciting of prayers. The water of the well was often used for bathing or drinking by pilgrims in the hope of a cure. The hazel is a tree of wisdom and poetry and nine hazel trees surrounded the Well of Segais at the source of Ireland's great rivers. The trees dropped their nuts into the water and these fed the Salmon of Wisdom which in turn gave the hero Fionn Mac Cumhaill his great powers of foresight. Now is the time to think of the achievements you have under your belt, and of the level of responsibility at work and in your personal life you have reached. It is a time to remember that life can be complicated and that sometimes there are no easy answers. Often it is wrong to judge events and people too quickly and rely solely on appearances. This is a good time to develop qualities of wisdom and good judgement so that your achievements can be kept on course. It is a time to begin the process of developing self awareness and to seek a deeper meaning to life. This is also a time to take a break from the stresses of life and enjoy yourself when the weather is fine, and many people traditionally take their holidays now. Think of the wise Salmon lazing in the warm waters of the pool. *Coll* corresponds to the Gaulish month Anagantios which means 'Harvest Month'.

Apple – Cert

5 September - 2 October

The apples are filling out on the trees and getting a golden colour as they ripen. Soon they will be ready to be picked. The sun is still warm but at this time of year the nights are beginning to turn cold. There is a touch of melancholy in the air as autumn begins to take hold. The holiday period is over now for many people and the world of work is recommencing. The autumn equinox falls in this month when the nights will become longer than the days. The end of the grain harvest was usually celebrated around this time with a 'harvest home' meal for the labourers. The apple is a tree of healing and renewal. Apples in the otherworld are always golden coloured and taste of honey. They have great restorative powers. King Arthur was brought to Avalon, the Island of Apples, to recover from his wounds. Mannanán Mac Lir, the Irish god of the sea, lived at Eamhain Abhlach, the Place of Apples (the Gaelic Avalon). He had a branch from which hung nine gold red apples. The music they made as they struck each other was so sweet it restored life to the sick. This is a good time to pause and take stock of life and the value of what you have achieved. Often in life we suffer setbacks or things do not go as well as we hoped. This is a good time to 'lick your wounds' and reflect upon the lessons to be learned from any lack of success or disappointment. But it is not a time to be gloomy or negative. Enjoy the sunshine, which is still warm and look at the leaves of the trees as they begin to turn. The first fruits of the harvest are available now to restore energies and give new hope to your efforts. *Cert* corresponds to the Gaulish month Ogronios which means 'Cool Month', the time when cold weather once again arrives.

Elder – Ruis

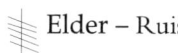

3 October - 30 October

The elder is a tree of witchcraft and magic. At this time of year its branches are heavy with bunches of rich, deep purple berries. They make a powerful red wine. Now autumn is well advanced, and the trees are a tapestry of red, orange, gold and brown. The evenings grow darker as the mysterious time of Samhain approaches. The harvest must be finished by then, with all crops and fruit gathered in for the winter. Samhain or Halloween is the time when ghosts and fairies are most active, and magic and witchcraft are at their most potent. Traditionally the festival was marked by games and storytelling around the fire and various kinds of fortune telling. Today children still call from door to door dressed up in costume looking for their 'Trick or treat'. The elder is an otherworldly tree especially loved as a home by the fairies and by witches. However, it is at the same time a very good tree to plant near the home to provide protection against them. With the otherworldly festival of Samhain now drawing near, the inner world of dreams and creativity can be helpful as it is particularly strong. This is a time when the experiences of our lives can be put to use to produce inner personal growth. It is a good time to confront your 'shadow side' – the issues that you are uncomfortable with and the side of you that is underdeveloped. Perhaps you need to develop qualities of greater assertiveness and strength. Perhaps you need to get in touch more with your feminine side. The wisdom of the elder tree opens a window onto the otherworld, a place where we can safely meet those parts of ourselves we normally do not look too closely at. *Ruis* corresponds to the Gaulish month Cutios whose meaning is obscure.

Tree of Power – Bile Buadha

31 October (Samhain Eve)

The *Bile Buadha* or Tree of Power appears in many Irish legends as the archetypal otherworldly tree of magic, power and fertility. Some stories tell of a great and stately tree, silver and gold in colour, standing at the centre of a fertile green before a royal fort. Often beautiful birds with multi-coloured plumage sing from its branches. One tale tells of three trees of purple glass, full of birds singing sweetly and unceasingly. This is the high point of the Celtic Year – the festival of Samhain or Halloween, when the old year ends and the new one begins. As such this day stands outside of ordinary time and is not a part of any month. The barrier between this world and the next is at its weakest tonight and is easily pierced. Numerous tales tell of adventures to the otherworld by the great heroes of Celtic myth and of appearances in this world of unearthly creatures; not all of them are friendly. Nevertheless, this is a time of celebration as the harvest has been gathered in and is now complete. Traditionally it was the start of the great feast of Tara when all rivalries were laid aside and peace reigned throughout the land. This is a time to set aside the cares and conventions of ordinary life and enjoy the fun. And so another year ends and another is about to begin.

Yew – Iúr
Taxus baccata

Spindle – Feoras
Euonymus europaeus

Juniper – Aiteal
Juniperus communis

Arbutus (Strawberry Tree) – Caithne
Arbutus unedo

The Months as Contrasting Pairs

A feature of the calendar is that it is also a series of contrasting pairs; and it adds an extra and stimulating dimension to contrast a particular tree with its opposite number. According to legend, the seasons of the otherworld were the opposite to our own; our winter was their summer and so on. The tree month that stands at roughly the opposite time of year to our own can therefore be taken to be the 'otherworld' month at that time and so is worthy of consideration. The contrasting pairs are as follows:

Yew/Ash: Two trees representing the land goddess, one in her winter aspect; the other in her image as the summer goddess of growth and greenery, presiding over the fertile land. Both are trees with a warlike aspect, used for making spears.

Pine/Oak: Two trees representing the sky god, one an evergreen representing the new sun just as it is born; the other the symbol of the high mature sun and the splendour of summer. Both good timber trees with many uses and prized for their strength.

Birch/Holly: Two trees representing a purifying aspect. The birch was used to flog out evil, while the holly was used at New Year to beat out the bad blood. The birch also represents the more gentle purity of birth and renewal; while the holly represents the purifying and ennobling aspect of physical maturity through championship, sport and games.

Rowan/Hazel: Two trees with powerful protecting abilities. The rowan is a tree that encourages new growth, nurturing and strengthening young things. The hazel is a tree of wisdom and the nurturing of physical strength, representing the fruits of the harvest.

Alder,Willow/Apple: The alder and willow mirror different aspects of the apple. The alder is a tree of war and death, contrasting the healing power of the apple. The willow is a protective tree of new growth and fertility, complementing the apple's restorative powers.

Hawthorn/Elder: Two trees bound up with magic power, charms and sorcery. The hawthorn is a tree of charms and spells, a masculine tree linked to the sun. The elder is a dark, feminine, witch's tree possessing great healing powers. Both trees also have a malevolent aspect to them.

It is important to remember not to take too rigid an approach to the calendar. If there is one thing the Celts hated (and still do!), it is rigid and inflexible boundaries. Therefore, do not feel obliged to end all thoughts of a particular tree the moment its month is over. It is in fact more in the spirit of things to allow the months to flow into each other in your mind. The months of the lunar calendar of the ancient Celts themselves had no fixed position in relation to the solar year. Of course, it is also perfectly acceptable to think of a particular tree at any time of the year if you wish to connect with its imagery and natural beauty. All of the trees have something to offer, no matter the season.

Postscript: the Universal Inspiration of Trees

We have seen, how trees are intertwined with every aspect of human experience. Trees surround us all the time in our daily lives, even in urban areas. They shelter and protect us from bad weather and enhance the air we breathe. They provide a roof over our heads and help to feed and clothe us. They appear in our dreams, they mark our places of importance, they guard our sacred sites. So it is no surprise that it is not only in Ireland or Europe but all over the world that we find examples of tree folklore as an integral part of everyday life. Indeed, one of the most fascinating things about the folklore of trees is how similar themes are found in every culture on earth.

One universal theme that emerges is the tree as the abode of gods and spirits.[1] In Europe we have seen how these ideas linger, with trees such as the oak, but this phenomenon is by no means confined to Europe alone. So to take one example, in India the coconut tree and its fruit are esteemed as sacred to Sri, the goddess of prosperity. Similarly in west Africa large silk cotton trees are believed to be inhabited by the god of the forest, Huntin, and are honoured with girdles of palm leaves and the sacrifice of fowl. The Dieri tribe of central Australia believe that certain sacred trees contain the souls of their ancestors and are on no account to be cut down, and much the same attitude prevails among the Miao Kia people of southern China, where every village is guarded by a sacred tree believed to be inhabited by the soul of their first ancestor. A natural extension of this is the idea that trees themselves have souls or spirits. In Africa the peoples of the Congo region traditionally believed that all things could be divided into two categories: people living and dead, gods and unborn children are all *muntu*. Animals, stones and everything else are *kintu*. Trees are classified as *muntu*, however, because like people, they have roots and a head, and the word of the ancestors lives within them.

Another universal theme is that of the tree as the link between earth and sky, this world and the next. Voodoo ceremonies revolve around the *Poteau-mitan,* a post in the centre of the temple which links the worlds of heaven and earth and represents the tree of life. The Oglala Sioux of Dakota saw the world as a sacred hoop with a flowering tree at its centre. To the Mayans the silk cotton was the sacred world tree which supported the heavens and stood at the centre of the earth. The tree's roots, trunk and foliage represented the underworld, world and heaven. It was represented as a leafy cross and symbolised life itself.[2] The shamans of the Central Asian Buryat and Altai climb a birch tree as part of their initiation ceremonies, symbolising the route they must take to ascend to heaven.

Needless to say, trees have also been used universally in spells and charms, to ensure fertility, to repel evil and affect cures. For example, we find that among the Mundaris in Assam every village has its sacred grove, whose deities are held responsible for the fertility of the crops and so are honoured at all the agricultural festivals. With a preoccupation shared right around the globe, pregnant women in certain tribes in the Congo make garments for themselves out of the bark of a particular sacred tree, in the belief that it will deliver them from the dangers of child bearing.

However, it is not necessary to hold such traditional beliefs to appreciate trees. Even when they are not regarded as sacred, trees have provided inspiration as metaphors and objects of beauty. Trees are often mentioned in the bible, for example, and Jesus frequently used them in his parables. For instance, in Matthew's gospel Jesus compared the message of the kingdom of Heaven to a mustard seed: 'It is the smallest of all seeds but when it grows up, it is the biggest of all plants. It becomes a tree, so that birds come and make their nests in its branches'. In Buddhism the bodhi tree has become famous as a symbol of wisdom, as it was under such a tree that Buddha first had his awakening. Finally of course, trees have provided inspiration for countless poets and artists down the ages. It will do to quote just one example from Shakespeare, where old age is compared to a tree in autumn: 'That time of year thou mayst in me behold/When yellow leaves, or none, or few, do hang/Upon those boughs which shake against the cold/Bare ruined choirs, where late the sweet birds sang'.

But even if we are not great religious leaders or artists, at a fundamental level it is possible for us all to connect with trees. For trees are not just objects of beauty or utility, but fellow living beings that breathe and grow and struggle to survive and recreate, just as we do ourselves. This is the real source, the heart of our fascination with trees and it will last as long as both we and they do.

References

ASPECTS OF TREE FOLKLORE
1. T. Crisp, *Dream Dictionary* (London, 1990), p. 314.
2. J.E. Milner, *The Tree Book* (Collins & Brown 1992), p. 42 ; Ibid., pp. 80-84.
3. Geoffrey Grigson, *The Englishman's Flora* (Oxford 1996) (1958), p. 145.
4. J.E. Milner, op. cit., pp. 80– 84
5. A.T. Lucas, 'The Sacred Trees of Ireland', *Journal of the Cork Historical and Archaeological Society* 68 (1963), p. 25.
6. Ibid., p. 20.
7. Ibid., p. 40-42.
8. Miranda Greene, *Dictionary of Celtic Myth and Legend* (Thames & Hudson 1992), p. 213, Ibid., p. 108.
9. A.T. Lucas, op. cit., p. 27.
10. Roy Vickery, *A Dictionary of Plant Lore* (Oxford 1995), p. 167, p. 169, p. 334.
11. D. and L. Flanagan *Irish Place Names* (Gill & McMillan 1994)
12. A.T. Lucas, op. cit., p. 48.
13. Gerard Murphy, *Early Irish Lyrics* (Dublin 1998), pp. 110-19; Fergus Kelly, 'The Old Irish Tree List', *Celtica* Vol XI, (1976).

BIRCH
1. I. Opie & M. Tatem (eds), *A Dictionary of Superstitions* (Oxford 1989), p. 25; T. Gwynn Jones, *Welsh Folklore and Custom* (Methuen & Co. 1930), p. 199; D.A. Mackenzie, *Scottish Folklore and Folk Life* (Blackie & Sons 1935), pp. 191-2; A. Carmichael, *Carmina Gadelica* Vol I (Edinburgh 1900), p. 168; J.W. Campbell, *Witchcraft & Second Sight in the Scottish Highlands* (MacLehose & Sons 1902), p. 248; R. Elliott, *Runes* (Manchester 1989), p. 65; A. Carmichael, op. cit., Vol 6 (Edinburgh 1971), p. 12.

2. Lady A. Gregory *Complete Irish Mythology* (Slaney Press 1994) (1902), p. 430; S. Tóibín, *Troscán na mBánta* (Oifig an tSoláthar 1967), p. 91; T. Gwynn Jones, op. cit., p. 187; A. Rees & B. Rees, *Celtic Heritage*, (Thames & Hudson 1961), p. 287.
3. T. Gwynn Jones, op. cit., p. 154; T.Owen, *Welsh Folk Customs* (Cardiff 1959), p. 102; Roy Vickery, op. cit., p. 235; R. Elliott, op. cit., p. 65; Milner op. cit., p. 21.
4. R. Lamont Brown, *A Book of Superstitions* (David & Charles 1970), p. 53; I. Opie & M. Tatem (eds) ,op. cit., p. 244; A. Carmichael, op. cit. Vol 2, (Edinburgh 1928), p. 253; Campbell, op. cit. (1902), pp. 118 - 119.
5. Standish O Grady, *Silva Gadelica* (Williams & Norgate 1892), p. 29.
6. Peter Beresford Ellis, *The Druids* (Constable 1994), p. 137, Ibid, 176; Geoffrey Grigson, *The Cherry Tree* (London 1959), pp. 134-5.
7. A. Ross, *The Pagan Celts* (Batsford 1986), p. 33; J. Gantz, *Early Irish Myths and Sagas* (Penguin 1981), p. 206.
8. Daithi Ó hÓgáin, *Myth, Legend & Romance- An Encyclopaedia of the Irish Folk Tradition* (Prentice Hall Press 1991), p. 84.

ROWAN

1. A. Carmichael, op. cit., Vol 2 (Edinburgh 1928), p. 246; R. Lamont Brown, op. cit. , pp. 50,51; M. McNeill, *The Silver Bough* (McLellan 1957), pp. 78-79; Roy Vickery, op. cit., pp. 320-1; Daithi Ó hÓgáin, op. cit. (1991), p. 178; A.Carmichael, op. cit. Vol 6 (Edinburgh 1971), p. 25; T. Gwynn Jones, op. cit., p. 29; J. E. Milner, op. cit., p. 65; E. Neeson, *A History of Irish Forestry* (Lilliput Press 1991), p. 23; Jeremiah Curtin, *Hero Tales of Ireland* (Macmillan Press 1894), p. 43; S. Tóibín, op. cit., p. 27; F. Thompson, *The Supernatural Highlands* (Hale & Co. 1976), p. 169; S. O'Sullivan, *Legends from Ireland* (London 1977), p. 84.
2. Roy Vickery, op. cit., pp. 319-321; S.Ó hEochaidh, *Síscéalta ó Tír Chonaill* (Dublin 1977) p. 85; E. Nelson, *Trees of Ireland* (Dublin 1993), pp. 181,182; M. Killup, *The Folklore of the Isle of Man* (B.T. Batsford 1975), p. 172.
3. A. Carmichael, op. cit., Vol 6 (Edinburgh 1971) pp.92; Ibid, Vol 1, pp. 194,201; Campbell, op. cit. (1902), p. 246; J.E. Milner, op.

cit., p. 65.
4. E. Neeson, op. cit., p. 22.
5. E. O' Curry, *Manners and Customs of the Ancient Irish* (Williams & Norgate 1873), p. 216.
6. W.G. Wood Martin, *Traces of the Elder Faiths of Ireland* (London 1902), p. 156
7. Eily Kilgannon, *Folk tales of the Yeats' Country* (Mercier Press 1989), pp. 20-21.

ALDER

1. W.G. Wood Martin, op. cit., p. 156.
2. E. Nelson, op. cit., p. 49.
3. Robert Graves, *The White Goddess*, (London 1961) (1948), p. 191.
4. J. Gregorson Campbell, *Superstitions of the Highlands and Islands* (MacLehose & Sons 1900), pp. 87, 89.
5. Diarmuid McManus, *The Middle Kingdom* (London 1959), p. 53.
6. W. G. Wood Martin, op. cit., p. 157.
7. Daithi Ó hÓgáin, op. cit. (1991), p. 413; Geoffrey Grigson, op. cit. (1959), p. 148.
8. J.A. McCullough, *The Religion of the Ancient Celts* (Edinburgh 1911), p. 202; Miranda Greene, op. cit. (1992), pp. 62, 219.

WILLOW

1. J.E. Milner, op. cit., p. 69; S. Ó Cróinín, *Seanchas ó Cairbre* (Dublin 1985), p. 491; S.Ó Duillearga, *Leabhair Shéain Uí Chonaill* (Dublin 1948), p. 360; P.S. Dinneen, *Foclóir Gaedhilge agus Béarla* (Irish Texts Society 1927), p. 931; Roy Vickery, op. cit., p. 335; Douglas Hyde, *The Lad of the Ferule/The King of Norway's Sons* (Irish Texts Society 1899), p. 65.
2. Roy Vickery, op. cit., pp. 334-5; A. Carmichael, op. cit., Vol 1 (Edinburgh 1928), p.168; Ibid, Vol 2, p.119.
3. Carmichael, op. cit., Vol 2, p. 278.
4. W.G. Wood Martin, op. cit., p. 157.
5. I. Opie & M. Tatem (eds), op. cit., p. 412.
6. E. Nelson, op. cit., p. 215.
7. Miranda Greene, op. cit. (1992), pp. 94, 207.

CHERRY

1. C.E. Smith, *Trees shown to the children* (Edinburgh & London), p. 103; I. Opie & M. Tatem (eds), op. cit., p. 112; Roy Vickery, op. cit., p. 142.
2. Geoffrey Grigson, op. cit., (1959), p. 127.
3. Roy Vickery, op. cit., p. 398.
4. Grigson, op. cit., (1959), p. 321.
5. A. Rees & B. Rees, op. cit., pp. 287-8; P.S. Dinneen, op. cit., p. 277.
6. Fergus Kelly, op. cit., pp. 115-6.
7. J. Gantz, op. cit. (1981), p. 120.
8. Raynor, *Legends of the Kings of Ireland* (Mercier Press 1988) pp. 90-2; Daithi Ó hÓgáin, op. cit., (1991), p. 294; Daithi Ó hÓgáin, *Fionn Mac Cumhaill* (Gill & MacMillan 1988) pp. 93,95; P. De Barra, *Agallamh na Seanóirí* (Foilseacháin Náisiúnta Teo. 1984), pp. 57-8.
9. Ó hÓgáin, op. cit. (1991), pp. 161-163.
10. J.G. Frazer, *The Golden Bough* (London 1922), p. 336.

HAWTHORN

1. Wood Martin, op. cit. p156; Ó Duillearga, op. cit., p. 312; Patrick Logan, *The Old Gods – the Facts about the Irish Fairies* (Belfast 1981), p. 125; W.B. Yeats, *Fairy and Folk Tales of Ireland* (Colin Smythe 1973), pp. 383-4, pp. 307-8.
2. Vickery, op. cit., pp. 166-9.
3. Ó Cróinín, op. cit., p. 491; Ó Duilearga, op. cit., p. 372.
4. P. Breathnach, *Maigh Cuilin* (Indreabhán 1986), p. 28.
5. Lamont Brown, op. cit., p. 51; Ó hÓgáin, op. cit., (1991), p. 29; Logan op. cit., (1981), p. 123; McCullough, op. cit., p. 203; Gwynn Jones, op. cit., p. 175; Aubrey Burl, *Rites of the Gods* (Dent & sons 1981), p. 189; M.C.Randolph, 'Early Irish Satire & the Hawthorn Tree' *Collectanea* (1943), pp. 365-6.
6. Kevin Danaher *The Year in Ireland* (Mercier Press 1972), pp. 89-96; Vickery, op. cit., pp. 169-170; Owen, op. cit., p. 99; Opie and Tatem, op. cit., p. 245; K.Hawkes, *Cornish Sayings, Superstitions and Remedies* (Penzance 1973), pp. 14-15.
7. Lucas, op. cit., (1963), pp. 40-42; J. & C. Bord, *Sacred Waters* (Granada Publishing 1985), p. 62; Máire Mac Neill, *The Festival*

of Lughnasa (Oxford 1962), p. 602; Patrick Logan, *The Holy Wells of Ireland* (Colin Smythe, 1980), pp. 89-96.
8. Lucas, op. cit., (1963), p. 26, p. 36; Patrick Logan, op. cit, p. 93.
9. O'Curry, op. cit., p. 217.
10. T.W. Rolleston, *Myths & Legends of the Celtic Race* (London 1985), p. 354.
11. Frazer, op. cit., p. 76.
12. Randolph, op. cit., pp. 365-6.
13. Daragh Smyth, *A Guide to Irish Mythology* (Dublin 1988), p. 70.

OAK

1. Carmichael, op. cit., Vol. 2, p. 332; Frazer, op. cit., p. 618, 620; Carmichael, op. cit., Vol. 1, p. 201; Ibid, Vol. 4, (1941), p. 102; Owen, op. cit., p. 97.
2. J.W. Campbell, *Popular Tales of the West Highlands* (Hounslow Press 1983), p. 469.
3. Owen, op. cit., p. 96.
4. Opie & Tatum, op. cit., p. 291; McCullough, op. cit., p. 199; E. Gwynn, *The Metrical Dindshenchus* Part 3 (Dublin 1913), p. 281.
5. Greene, op. cit., p. 194; Ibid, p. 32; T.D. Kendrick, *The Druids* (London 1927), pp. 124-5.
6. Ó hÓgáin, op. cit. (1991), p. 168.
7. Berresford Ellis, *Dictionary of Celtic Mythology* (London 1992), p. 173; Logan, op. cit., (1980), p. 91.
8. Dinneen, op. cit., p. 303; *Y Geriadur Mawr*; Gregory, op. cit., (1902), pp. 88-90, p. 39; G. Keating, *History of Ireland* (Dublin 1809), p. 31.
9. Whitley Stokes, *The Bodleian Dinnshenchus* (London 1892), p. 67.
10. Grigson, op. cit., (1959), p. 323.
11. Barry Raftery, *Pagan Celtic Ireland* (Thames & Hudson 1994), p. 78.
12. D. Hyde, *The Stone of Truth & other Irish Folktales* (Irish Academic Press 1979), pp. 29-30; E. McNeill, *Duanaire Finn* (Irish Texts Society 1908), pp. 130-131, p. 195; Ó hÓgáin, op. cit., (1988), pp. 203-4; Jeremiah Curtin, *Myths & Folktales of Ireland* (New York 1890), pp. 204 –6, p. 181, p. 223; Carmichael, op. cit., Vol 4, p. 12; Whitley Stokes, op. cit., (1892), p. 48; J. Gantz, *The*

Mabinogion (Penguin Books 1976), p. 115; Hyde, op. cit., 1899, p. 135.
13. Frazer, op. cit., pp. 159-161.
14. Burl, op. cit., p. 168.

HOLLY

1. M. Grieve, *A Modern Herbal* (Jonathon Cape Ltd. 1931), p. 405.
2. Gwynn Jones, op. cit., p. 181; Danaher, op. cit., (1972), pp. 243-250; Owen, op. cit., pp. 39-41; Lamont Brown, op. cit., p. 52; Christine Hole, *A Dictionary of British Folk Customs*, (Paladin 1984), p. 38; A.A. MacGregor, *The Peat Fire Flame* (Moray Press 1937), p. 4; Gregorson Campbell,op. cit., p. 20.
3. Grieve, op. cit., p. 405; McNeill op. cit., (1957), p. 84; Mackenzie, op. cit., p. 274; Grigson, op. cit., (1958), p. 116; Opie and Tatum, op. cit., p. 200; Lamont Brown, op. cit., p. 52.
4. Nelson, op. cit., p. 43; Ó hEochaidh, op. cit., p. 327; Campbell, op. cit. (1860), p. 342.
5. W. Branch Johnson, *Folktales of Brittany* (Methuen & Co. 1972), p. 45, pp. 98 -100.
6. Ó Grady, op. cit., p. 343; Hyde op. cit. (1899), p. 75.
7. Gregory op. cit., (1902), p. 81; Ibid, p. 78; p. 210; Gantz, op. cit., (1976), p. 218; C. O' Rahilly, *The Pursuit of Gruaidhe Griansholus* (Irish Texts Society 1924), pp. 3-5.
8. Curtin, op. cit., (1890), p. 193; Ó hÓgáin, op. cit., (1991), p. 197; William Larminie, *West Irish Folk Tales and Romances* (London 1893), p. 57; Campbell, op. cit. (1980), pp. 297-317.
9. Ó hÓgáin, op. cit., (1991), p. 68.

HAZEL

1. Lady A.Gregory, *Visions & Beliefs in the West of Ireland* (Colin Smythe 1920), p. 158; Ó hÓgáin, op. cit., (1991), p251; Ó Duillearga, op. cit., p292; R.A.S. McAlister, *Lebor Gabála Eirenn* (Irish Texts Society 1938-41, 1956), p. 141; Burl, op. cit., p. 206; Greene, op. cit., (1992), p. 191; Graves R., op. cit., p. 182; Gregory, op. cit., (1902), p. 127.
2. Vickery, op. cit., p. 172; Grigson, op. cit., (1958), p. 248.
3. J.W. Campbell, op. cit., (1902), p. 280; McNeill M, op. cit., (1957),

p. 80.
4. Gwynn Jones, op. cit., p. 187; Graves, R., op. cit. (1948), p. 193.
5. Vickery, op. it., p. 173; Lamont Brown, op. cit., p. 49.
6. Vickery, op. cit., p. 173; Greene, op. cit., (1992), p. 224; McCullough, op. cit., p. 166.
7. Whitley Stokes, 'The Rennes Dinnshenchus' *Revue Celtique* XV (1895), p. 71; Gwynn, op.cit. Part 3, (1913), p. 158.
8. Lucas, op. cit., p. 35.
9. Ó hÓgáin op. cit., (1988), p. 5; Mac Neill, op. cit., (1908), pp. 135-7; Ibid, p. 121, p. 124; Gregory, op. cit., (1902), p. 123; Rees and Rees, op. cit., p. 377; Graves R., op. cit. (1948), p. 182.
10. J.W. Campbell, op. cit., (1860), pp. 378-80.
11. G. Jones, *Welsh Legends and Folk Tales* (Puffin Books 1955), p. 183ff.
12. Jones, op. cit., p. 193ff; Rees and Rees, op. cit., p377; Whitley Stokes, *Tripartite Life of St. Patrick* (London 1887), p. 145; Graves R, op. cit., p. 182; Gregory, op. cit., (1902), p. 62.
13. Gregory, op. cit. (1902), p. 18; Smyth, op. cit., p. 154; Geoffrey Keating, *History of Ireland* (Dublin 1809), p. 221; Rees & Rees, op. cit., p. 112.

WHITEBEAM

1. Kelly, op. cit., p. 118.
2. Gantz, op. cit., (1981), p. 41; C. O'Rahilly, *Táin Bó Cúalnge* (Irish Texts Society 1967), p179; De Barra, op. cit., Vol.1, p. 184; Ibid, Vol 2, p. 154; Gregory, op. cit., (1902), p. 363, p. 424; Gwynn, op. cit., Vol 3, p. 27.
3. Nelson, op. cit., p. 191.

APPLE

1. Vickery, op. cit., p. 10.
2. Grieve, op. cit., pp. 45-6.
3. Lady A.Gregory, *The Voyage of St. Brendan the Navigator and Stories of the Saints of Ireland* (Colin Smythe 1973), p. 113.
4. Ibid., p. 58.
5. MacAlister, op. cit., p. 137; Gregory, op. cit., (1902), p. 36.
6. Ó hÓgáin, (1991), p. 274.

7. D. Ó hAodha, *Bethu Brigte* (Dublin 1978), p. 29; Gerald of Wales, *The History and Topography of Ireland* (Penguin 1982), p133; Stokes, op. cit., (1887), p233; McNeill, op. cit., (1957), p80.
8. Ó hÓgáin, op. cit., (1991) p. 43; Yeats, op. cit.; Jeremiah Curtin, *Irish Folk Tales* (Talbot Press 1964), p. 138; Curtin, op. cit., (1894), pp. 373-4; Gregory, op. cit., (1902), p. 84.
9. Gregory, op. cit., (1902), pp. 62-63, p. 363; Mac Neill E, op. cit., p. 140; Gantz, op. cit. (1981), p. 234.
10. Greene, op. cit., (1992), p. 155, p. 158.

BUCKTHORN

1. Frazer, op. cit., p. 340; Grieve, op. cit., p. 135.
2. Nelson, op. cit., p. 161; Grieve, op. cit., p. 135; Grigson, op. cit., (1958), p. 122
3. Nelson, op. cit., p. 155.

FURZE

1. Ó Eochaidh, op. cit., pp. 347-65; Yeats, op. cit., pp. 183-5; Ó Duillearga, op. cit., p. 359; Vickery, op. cit., p. 157.
2. A.T. Lucas, 'Furze - A Survey of its History & Uses in Ireland' *Béaloideas* 26 (1960), pp. 172, 179-184.
3. Vickery, op. cit., pp. 156-7; Hawkes, op. cit., p. 14 .
4. Gwynn Jones, op. cit., p. 60.
5. Grigson, op. cit., (1958), p. 126.
6. Nicholas Williams, *Díolaim Luibheanna* (Dublin 1993), p. 4.
7. A.T. Lucas, op. cit. (1960), p. 186-7.
8. Grieve, op. cit., p. 367.
9. Gwynn, op. cit., Part 4, pp. 140-3.
10. Lucas, op. cit., (1960), p. 12; Gwynn, op.cit., Part 4, pp. 306-7.

BROOM

1. Grieve, op. cit., p. 126; Hole, op. cit., p. 192; Gwynn Jones, op. cit., p. 185; Carmichael, op. cit., Vol 1, p. 168.
2. Vickery, op. cit., p. 51.
3. Opie & Tatem, op. cit., p. 46.
4. McNeill M, op. cit., (1957), p. 136; Grigson, op. cit., (1958), p. 128.
5. McManus, op. cit., (1959), p. 53.

6. Grigson, op. cit., (1958), pp. 128-9.
7. Grieve, op. cit., p. 125.
8. Ibid., p. 125.
9. Ibid., pp. 124-126; Grigson, op. cit., (1958), p. 129.
10. M. Moloney, *Luibh – Shenchus – Irish Ethno-botany* (Dublin 1919), p. 20.
11. Frazer, op. cit., p. 610.

BLACKTHORN

1. Ó Cróinín, op. cit., p. 491; Gregory, op. cit., (1920), p. 214; William Wilde, *Irish Popular Superstitions* (Dublin 1853), p. 93-4; Ó hEochaidh, op. cit., p. 87; Ibid., pp. 269-71.
2. Carmichael, op. cit., Vol 1, p. 201; Ibid., Vol. 2, p. 275; Lamont Brown, op. cit., p. 48; Graves R, op. cit., p. 245; Vickery, op. cit., pp. 37-8.
3. Lamont Brown, op. cit., p. 48.
4. Frazer, op. cit., p. 560.
5. Evan-Wentz, *The Fairy Faith in Celtic Countries* (Oxford 1915), p. 53; Ó hEochaidh, op. cit., p. 385.
6. Tóibín, op. cit., p. 40.
7. Gwynn Jones, op. cit., p. 114.
8. Gregory, op. cit., (1973), pp. 99-100.
9. Gantz, op. cit., (1981), p. 201; E. Mac Neill, op. cit., (1908), p. 154, p. 160; Ó hÓgáin, op. cit., (1991), p. 286.
10. Gantz, op. cit., (1981), p. 53.
11. Gwynn, op. cit. Part 3, pp. 61-3; O'Curry, op. cit., p. 216; C. Ó Cuinn, *Scian a chaitheadh le tonn - Scéalta Inis Eoghain* (Coiscéim Press 1990), p. 68.
12. D. Ó Baoill, *Amach as Ucht na Sliabh* (Gaoth Dobhair 1992), p. 300.
13. Kevin Danaher, *In Ireland Long Ago* (Mercier Press 1978), p. 149; Gregory, op. cit., 1902, p. 392.
14. Breathnach, op. cit., p. 91.

ELDER

1. Ó Cróinín, op. cit., p. 491; Grigson, op. cit., (1958), p. 352; Williams, op. cit., p. 171; Vickery, op. cit., pp. 118-9.
2. Grigson, op. cit., (1958), p. 352; Graves R, op. cit., p. 185; Wilde,

op. cit., p. 100; Williams, op. cit., p. 171.
3. Grieve, op. cit., p. 266; Vickery, op. cit., p. 121; Lamont Brown, op. cit., p. 53.
4. Grigson, op. cit., (1958), p. 353; Hawke, op. cit., p. 21; Opie & Tatum, op. cit., p. 139; Ó hÓgáin, op. cit., p. 85.
5. McCullough, op. cit., p. 203; McNeill, op. cit., (1957), p. 79; Williams, op. cit., p. 171; Opie & Tatum, op. cit., p. 139; Grigson, op. cit., (1958), p. 352.
6. McNeill M, op. cit., (1957), p. 79; Grieve, op. cit., p. 267; Killip, op. cit., pp. 35-6.
7. O'Sullivan, op. cit., p. 46.
8. Ó Coigligh, *Seanchas Inis Meáin* (Coiscéim Press), p. 180; Campbell, op. cit., (1860), p. 272.

PINE

1. Frazer, op. cit., pp. 122-4; Ibid., p. 311; A. Le Braz, *The Night of Fires & Other Breton Studies* (Chapman & Hall 1912), p. 35; A.T. Lucas, 'Bog Wood: A Study in Rural Economy' *Béaloideas* 23, p. 128; R.I. Page, *An Introduction to English Runes* (Methuen & Co. 1973), p. 82.
2. Vickery, op. cit., p. 68; Ó Cróinín, op. cit., p. 391; Ibid., p. 404; Breathnach, op. cit., p. 72.
3. Frazer, op. cit., p. 561; Hole, op. cit., p. 130; Campbell, op. cit., (1902), p. 213; Gregory, op. cit., (1902), p. 207.
4. Tóibín, op. cit., p. 137; Milner, op. cit., p. 38.
5. Greene, op. cit., (1992), p. 66; Ibid., p. 155; Ibid., p. 214; Frazer, op. cit., p. 120; Ibid., p. 352-3; Graves R., op. cit., p. 191, Ibid., p. 277; McCullough, op. cit., p. 198, Ibid., p. 204;
6. Graves R., op. cit., pp. 190-1; Campbell, op. cit., (1860), pp. 153-4
7. De Barra, op. cit., pp. 142-3; Campbell, op. cit., (1860), p. 44; Burl, op. cit., p. 226.
8. Rees and Rees, op. cit., p. 296.
9. Smith, op. cit., pp. 91-2; Vickery, op. cit., p. 402; Tóibín, op. cit., p. 138; Carmichael, op. cit., Vol 6, p. 83; Le Braz, op. cit., p. 35.

ASH

1. Neeson, op. cit., p. 21; Grigson, op. cit., (1958), pp. 272-3; Rees &

Rees, op. cit., p. 76; Vickery, op. cit., p. 15; Opie & Tatum, op. cit., p. 6; MacGregor, op. cit., p. 274.
2. Lamont Brown, op. cit., p. 53; Burl, op. cit., pp. 150-1; Smyth, op. cit., p. 27.
3. Yeats, op. cit., p. 134; Grigson, op. cit., (1958), p. 272; Frazer, op. cit., p. 683.
4. Grigson, op. cit., (1958), p. 272; Vickery, op. cit., p. 16; K. Crossley Holland, *The Penguin Book of Norse Myths* (London 1980), pxxi ii.
5. Opie & Tatum, op. cit., pp. 7-8; Hawke, op. cit., p. 16; Ibid., p. 8.
6. Logan, op. cit., (1980), p. 91; Ibid., p. 22; Ibid., p. 31; Gregory, op. cit., (1973), p. 95; Mac Neill M, op. cit., (1962), p. 260; Lucas, op. cit., (1963), p. 47.
7. Ibid., p. 23; Gregory, op. cit., (1920), p. 271.
8. Graves R, op. cit., p. 168; Ronald Hutton, *The Pagan Religions of the British Isles* (Oxford 1993), p. 192.
9. Wood-Martin, op. cit., p. 159; Logan, op. cit., (1980), p. 92; Ibid., pp. 42-3; Ó Duillearga, op. cit., pp. 118-9.
10. Smyth, op. cit., p. 100.
11. Ó hÓgáin, op. cit., (1991), p. 120.
12. Graves R, op. cit., p. 192.

ELM

1. Opie & Tatum, op. cit., p. 452; Tóibín, op. cit., p. 78.
2. Frazer, op. cit., p. 120; Charles Graves, 'On the Ogam Beith Luis Nin' *Hermathena* 3 (1879), p. 229.
3. Hole, op. cit., p. 253.
4. L. De Paor, *St. Patrick's World* (Four Courts Press 1994), p. 167; Stokes, op. cit., (1887), p. 111; Ibid., p. 85; Lucas, op. cit., (1963), p. 32.
5. Gregory, op. cit., (1973), p. 30.
6. Greene, op. cit., (1992), p. 213; Wood-Martin, op. cit., p. 158.
7. Grigson, op. cit., (1958), pp. 241-2; Grieve, op. cit., p. 283.

ASPEN

1. Carmichael, op. cit., Vol.2, pp. 104-105; Ibid., Vol.1, p. 201.
2. Lamont Brown, op. cit., p. 50; Campbell, op. cit., (1902), p. 96;

O'Sullivan, op. cit., pp. 28-9.
3. Gregory, op. cit., (1902), p. 286; Ibid., p. 307; Ibid., p. 403.
4. Campbell, op. cit., (1860) Vol 2, p. 138; Burl, op. cit., pp. 150-1.
5. Vickery, op. cit., p. 400.

YEW

1. Lucas, op. cit., (1963), pp. 29-33, p36; Neeson, op. cit., pp. 19-20;
   Ó hÓgáin, op. cit., (1991), p. 19; McNeill M, op. cit., (1980), p. 80.
2. Grigson, op. cit., (1958), pp. 25-6; McCullough, op. cit., p. 203;
   Vickery, op. cit., p. 410; Lucas,op. cit., (1963), p. 29; Ó Cróinín,
   op. cit., (1985), p. 408.
3. Grigson, op. cit., (1958), p. 25; Vickery, op. cit., p. 409; Carmichael,
   op. cit., Vol VI, p. 92.
4. Gregory, op. cit., (1902), p. 78; Elliott, op. cit., p. 72.
5. Ó hEochaidh, op. cit., (1977), pp. 331-3.
6. Ó hÓgáin, op. cit., (1991), p. 43.
7. Mac Neill, E, op. cit., p. 153.
8. N. Ó Dónaill, *Seanchas na Féinne* (An Gúm 1942), p. 27.
9. Neeson, op. cit., pp. 19-20; Myles Dillon, *The Cycles of the Kings*
   (Four Courts Press 1994), pp. 70-71; J.G. O'Keefe, *Buile*
   Shuibhne (Dublin 1913), p. 133.
10. Milner, op. cit., p. 42; Mac Neill E, op. cit., p. 355.
11. Gregory, op. cit., (1902), p. 359; Ibid., p. 69; Ó hÓgáin, op. cit.,
    (1988), p. 205.
12. Mac Neill E, op. cit., p. 176; Ibid., p. 35; Ibid., p. 319; Henri
    Hubert, *The Greatness & Decline of the Celts* (London 1987), p.
    125.
13. Ó hÓgáin, op. cit., (1991), p. 106; T. Ó Cathasaigh, *The Heroic*
    Biography of Cormac Mac Airt (Dublin 1977), p. 126; Larminie,
    op. cit., p. 38; Dillon, op. cit., (1994), p.39.
14. Gwynn, op. cit., Part 3, pp. 238-9; Lucas, op. cit., (1963), p. 18.

SPINDLE

1. Stokes, op. cit., (1895), pp. 68-69; Gwynn, op. cit., Part IV, pp . 214-15.
2. Nelson, op. cit., p. 83.

JUNIPER

1. Campbell, op. cit., (1902), p. 11; Ibid., p. 105; Carmichael, op. cit., Vol IV, pp128-9; Ibid., Vol. VI, p. 92; Vickery, op. cit., p. 207.
2. Lamont Brown, op. cit., p. 49.
3. Grieve, op. cit., p. 682; Smith, op. cit., p. 83; Frazer, op. cit., p. 560; Ibid., p. 610; Hole, op. cit., p. 219; Campbell, op. cit., (1902), p. 257.

ARBUTUS

1. Nelson, op. cit., pp. 91-92.
2. N. Ní Shéaghdha, *Toruigheacht Diarmaid agus Gráinne* (I. T. S. 1967), p. 53.
3. Nelson, op. cit., p. 92.

OGHAM – THE GAELIC TREE ALPHABET

1. Damian McManus, 'Ogam: archaising, orthography and the authenticity of the manuscript key to the alphabet' *Ériu* 37 (1986), pp. 1-31; 'Irish letter-names and their kennings' *Ériu* 39 (1988), pp. 127-168; *A Guide to Ogam* (Maynooth 1991).
2. Ó hÓgáin, op. cit., (1991), p. 184.
3. Nelson, op. cit., p. 161.
4. Lucas, op. cit., (1960)
5. Kelly, op. cit., p. 113.
6. McManus, op. cit., (1991), pp. 27-30.
7. Kelly, op. cit., p. 119.
8. Ibid., p. 122-3.
9. Grieve, op. cit., p. 365.

AN OGHAM TREE CALENDAR

1. E. MacNeill, 'On the Notation and Chronography of the Calendar of Coligny' *Ériu* 10 (1926); P.M. Duval, *Recueil des Inscriptions Gauloises* Vol. 3 (Paris 1986); C. Laine-Kerjean 'Le Calendrier Celtique' *Zeitschrift fur celtische philologie* 23 (1943).
2. K.R. McCone, 'Fírinne agus Torthúlacht' *Léachtaí Cholm Cille* 11 (Má Nuad 1980), p. 140.

POSTSCRIPT
1. Frazer, op. cit., p. 119; Ibid., p. 112; Ibid., p. 115; B. Kingsolver, *The Poisonwood Bible* (London 1999), pp. 238-9.
2. R. Wright, *Time among the Maya* (Bodley Head Ltd.), p. 12; Frazer, op. cit., p. 118, p. 120.

Bibliography

Beresford Ellis, P., (1992) *Dictionary of Celtic Mythology*, London
(1994) *The Druids*, Constable & Co.
Best, R.I. (Ed.) (1910) 'The Settling of the Manor of Tara' *Ériu* IV
Branch Johnson, W. (1972) *Folktales of Brittany*, Methuen & Co. Ltd
Breathnach, P. (1986) *Maigh Cuilin*, Indreabhán
Burl, A. (1981) *Rites of the Gods*, J. M. Dent & sons Ltd
Bord, J & C. (1985) *Sacred Waters*, Granada Publishing Ltd
Calder, G. (1917) *Auraicept na nÉces*, Edinburgh
Campbell, J.W. (1860) *Popular Tales of the West Highlands*, Hounslow
(1983)
(1902) *Witchcraft and Second Sight in the Scottish Highlands*,
James MacLehose & sons
Carmichael, A. (1900, 1928, 1940, 1941, 1971) *Carmina Gadelica*, Vols
1- 6, Edinburgh
Carney, J. (1975) 'The Invention of the Ogam Cipher', *Ériu* 26, pp.
53-65
Chadwick, N. (1979) *The Celts*, Penguin Books
Crisp, T. (1990), *Dream Dictionary – a guide to dreams and sleep
experiences*, London
Crossley Holland, K. (1980) *The Penguin Book of Norse Myths*
Culpeper, N., *Culpeper's Complete Herbal*, Foulsham & Co. Ltd
Curtin, J. (1890) *Myths and Folktales of Ireland*, New York
(1894) *Hero Tales of Ireland*, Macmillan Press
(1943) *Irish Folk Tales*, Talbot Press (1964)
Danaher, K. (1972) *The Year in Ireland – Irish Calendar Customs*,
Mercier Press
(1978) *In Ireland Long Ago*, Mercier Press
De Barra, P. (1984, 1986) *Agallamh na Seanóirí*, Foilseacháin
Náisiúnta Teo.
De Paor, L. (1993) *St Patrick's World*, Four Courts Press (1994)
Dillon, M. (1932), 'Stories from the Law Tracts', *Ériu* 11 pp42 -65

(1946) *The Cycles of the Kings*, Four Courts Press (1994)
Dinneen, P.S. (1927) *Foclóir Gaedhilge agus Béarla*, Irish Texts Society
Duval, P.M. (1986) *Recueil des Inscriptions Gauloises*, Vol 3 , Paris
Elliott, R. (1989) *Runes*, Manchester University Press
Evans, J.G. (1915) *The Poems of Taliesin*, Llanbedrog
Evan-Wentz (1911) *The Fairy Faith in Celtic Countries*, Oxford
Flanagan, D. & L. (1994) *Irish Place Names*, Gill and Macmillan
Frazer, J.G. (1922) *The Golden Bough*, The Macmillan Press Ltd, London
Freeman, M. (ed) (1970) *The Annals of Connaught*, D. I.A.S.
Gantz, J, (1981) *Early Irish Myths and Sagas*, Penguin Books
   (1976) *The Mabinogion*, Penguin Books
Gerald of Wales, *The History and Topography of Ireland*, Penguin Books (1982)
Graves, C. (1876) 'The Ogam Alphabet', *Hermathena* 3, pp. 203-244
   (1879) 'On the Ogam Beith Luis Nin', *Hermathena* 3, pp. 208-244
Graves, R. (1948) *The White Goddess*, Faber & Faber (1961)
Gregorson Campbell, J. (1900) *Superstitions of the Highlands and Islands*, James MacLehose & sons
Gregory, Lady A. (1902,1904) *Complete Irish Mythology*, The Slaney Press (1994)
   (1920)*Visions and Beliefs in the West of Ireland*, Colin Smythe Ltd
   The Voyage of St Brendan the Navigator and Stories of the Saints of Ireland, Colin Smythe Ltd (1973)
Greene, M. (1992) *Dictionary of Celtic Myth and Legend*, Thames and Hudson
   (1996) *Celtic Art*, Everyman Art Library
Grieve, M. (1931) *A Modern Herbal*, Jonathan Cape Ltd
Grigson, G. (1958) *The Englishman's Flora*, Helicon Publishing Ltd, Oxford (1996)
   (1959) *The Cherry Tree*, Phoenix House, London
Gwynn, E. (1903, 1906, 1913, 1924, 1935) *The Metrical Dindshenchus*, Dublin
Gwynn Jones, T. (1930) *Welsh Folklore and Custom*, Methuen & Co. Ltd
Harbison, P. (1988) *Pre-Christian Ireland*, Thames and Hudson,

London

Hawkes, K. (1973) *Cornish Sayings, Superstitions & Remedies*, Penzance

Hole, C. (1978) *A Dictionary of British Folk Customs*, Paladin 1984

Hubert, H. (1987) *The Greatness and Decline of the Celts*, Constable and Co., London

Hutton, R. (1993) *The Pagan Religions of the British Isles*, Oxford

Hyde, D. (1979) *The Stone of Truth and other Irish folktales*, Irish Academic Press

(1899) *The Lad of the Ferule/The King of Norway's Sons*, Vol i Irish Texts Society

Jones, G. (1955) *Welsh Legends and Folk Tales*, Puffin Books (1979)

Keating, G., *History of Ireland* (Trans. by Dermod O'Connor, Dublin, 1809)

Kelly F. (1976) 'The Old Irish Tree List', *Celtica* Vol XI

Kendrick, T.D. (1927) *The Druids*, Methuen & Co. Ltd, London

Kennelly, B. (ed), (1970) *The Penguin book of Irish verse*

Kilgannon, E. (1989) *Folktales of the Yeats Country*, The Mercier Press

Killip, M., (1975) *The Folklore of the Isle of Man*, B. T. Batford Ltd

Kingsolver, B (1999) *The Poisonwood Bible*, Faber & Faber, London

Laine – Kerjean, C (1943) 'Le Calendrier Celtique', *Zeitschrift fur Celtische Philologie* 23

Lamont Brown, R. (1970) *A book of superstitions*, David and Charles Ltd

Larminie, W. (1893) *West Irish Folk Tales and Romances*, London

Le Braz, A. (1912) *The night of fires & other Breton studies*, Chapman & Hall Ltd.

Logan, P. (1980) *The holy wells of Ireland*, Colin Smythe Ltd

(1981) *The old gods – the facts about Irish fairies*, Appletree Press

Lucas, A.T. (1954) 'Bog wood. A study in rural economy', *Béaloideas* 23

(1963) 'The Sacred Trees of Ireland', *Journal of the Cork Historical and Archaeological Society* 68, pp. 16-54

(1960), 'Furze: A survey of its History and Uses in Ireland', *Béaloideas* 26

Macalister, R.A.S. (1937) *The Secret Languages of Ireland* (1938, 1939, 1940, 1941, 1956) *Lebor Gabála Eirenn*, Irish Texts Society

(1945, 1949) *Corpus Inscriptionum Insularum Celticarum*, 2 vols.
McCone, K.R. (1980) 'Fírinne agus Torthúlacht', *Léachtaí Cholm Cille* 11, Má Nuad
McCullough, J.A. (1911) *The Religion of the Ancient Celts*, T & T Clark, Edinburgh
MacGregor, A.A. (1937) *The Peat Fire Flame*, The Moray Press
Mac Neill, E (1908) & Murphy, G (1933) *Duanaire Finn*, Irish Texts Society
(1909) 'Notes on the distribution, history, grammar, and import of the Irish Ogham Inscriptions', *Proceedings of the R.I.A.* 27, pp329-370
(1926-8), 'On the Notation and Chronography of the Calendar of Coligny', *Ériu* 10
MacNeill, M. (1962) *The Festival of Lughnasa*, Oxford
McNeill, M. (1957) *The Silver Bough* Vol. 1 William McLellan
MacKenzie, D.A. (1935) *Scottish Folklore and Folk Life*, Blackie & sons Ltd
McManus, D. (1986) 'Ogam: archaizing, orthography and the authenticity of the manuscript key to the alphabet', *Ériu* 37, pp.1-31
(1988) 'Irish letter-names and their kennings', *Ériu* 39, pp 127-168
(1989) 'Runic and Ogam letter-names: a parallelism', *Maynooth Monographs* 2 pp. 122-143
(1991) 'A Guide to Ogam', *Maynooth Monographs* 4
McManus, D. (1959) *The Middle Kingdom*, London
Maloney, M. (1919) *Luibh-Sheanchus - Irish Ethno-botany*, M.H. Gill & Son Dublin
Milner, J. E. (1992) *The Tree Book*, Collins and Brown
Murphy, G (1962) *Early Irish Lyrics*, Four Courts Press 1998
Neeson, E. (1991) *A History of Irish Forestry*, Lilliput Press
Nelson, E. C. & Walsh, W. (1993) *Trees of Ireland*, Lilliput Press, Dublin
Ní Shéaghdha, N. (1967) *Toruigheacht Diarmaid agus Gráinne*, Irish Texts Society
Ó Baoill, D. (1992) *Amach as Ucht na Sliabh*, Cumann staire agus sean chais Ghaoth Dhobhair

Ó Cathasaigh, T., (1977) *The Heroic Biography of Cormac Mac Airt*, Dublin
Ó Coigligh, *Seanchas Inis Meáin*, Coiscéim Press
Ó Cróinín, S. (1985) *Seanchas ó Cairbre*, Dublin.
Ó'Cuinn, C. (1990) *Scian a chaitheadh le tonn – scéalta Inis Eoghain*, Coiscéim Press
Ó Cuív, B. (1945) *Cath Maige Tuiread*, Irish Texts Society
O'Curry, E. (1873) *Manners and Customs of the Ancient Irish*, Williams & Norgate
Ó Donaill, N. (1942) *Seanchas na Féinne*, An Gúm
Ó Duillearga, S. (1948) *Leabhair Shéain Uí Chonaill*, Dublin
O'Grady, S. (1892) *Silva Gadelica*, Williams and Norgate,
O'hAodha, D. (1978) *Bethu Brigte*, Dublin
Ó hEochaidh, S., Ní Néill, M. Ó Catháin, S. (1977) *Síscéalta ó Thír Chonaill*, Dublin
Ó hÓgáin, D. (1991) *Myth, Legend and Romance - An Encyclopaedia of the Irish Folk Tradition*, Prentice Hall Press
(1988) *Fionn Mac Cumhaill – Images of the Gaelic Hero*, Gill and Macmillan Ltd.
O'Keeffe, J.G. (Trans.) (1913) *Buile Suibhne*, Irish Texts Society, Dublin
O' Rahilly, C. (1924) *The Pursuit of Gruaidhe Griansholus*, Irish Texts Society
(1967) *Táin Bó Cúalnge*, Vol xlix Irish Texts Society
O'Sullivan, S. (1977) *Legends from Ireland*, B.T. Batsford Ltd. London
Opie, I & Tatum, M. (eds), (1989) *A Dictionary of Superstitions*, Oxford
Owen, T. (1959) *Welsh Folk Customs*, National Museum of Wales
Page, R. I. (1973) *An Introduction to English Runes*, Methuen & Co.
Plummer, C. (1910) *Vitae Sanctorum Hiberniae* Vol 1 Oxford
Power, P. (1914) *Lives of S.S. Declan and Mochuda*, Irish Texts Society
Raftery, B. (1994) *Pagan Celtic Ireland*, Thames & Hudson
Randolph, M.C. (1943) *Early Irish Satire and the Whitethorn Tree*, Collectanea
Raynor (1988) *Legends of the Kings of Ireland*, The Mercier Press
Rees A. and Rees B. (1961) *Celtic Heritage*, Thames and Hudson
Rolleston, T.W. (1985) 'Myths and Legends of the Celtic Race',

Constable, London
Ross, A. (1986) *The Pagan Celts*, B.T. Batsford Ltd.
Smith, C.E. & Harvey Kelman, J., *Trees shown to the children*, T.C. & E.C. Jack, Edinburgh & London
Smyth, D. (1988) *A Guide to Irish Mythology*, Irish Academic Press
Stokes, W. (1868) *Cormac's Glossary*, Calcutta

(1887) *Tripartite Life of St Patrick*, London

(1892) *The Bodleian Dinnshenchus*, London

(1895) 'The Rennes Dinnshenchus', *Revue Celtique* XV, pp. 277-289

(1890) *Lives of the Saints from the Book of Lismore*, Oxford

Thompson, F. (1976) *The Supernatural Highlands*, Robert Hale and Co.
Tóibín, S (1967) *Troscán na mBánta*, Oifig an tSoláthair
Vickery, R. (1995) *A Dictionary of Plant Lore*, Oxford University Press
Wade Evans, A.W. (1909) *Welsh Medieval Law*, Oxford
Williams, N. (1993) *Díolaim Luibheanna*, Sáirséal-Ó Marcaigh Teor. B.Á.C.
Wilde, W. (1853) *Irish Popular Superstitions*, Dublin
Wood Martin, W.G. (1902) *Traces of the Elder Faiths of Ireland*, London
Wright, R. (1989) *Time among the Maya*, Bodley Head Ltd
Yeats, W.B., *Fairy and Folk Tales of Ireland*, Colin Smythe Ltd (1973)

Index

Acacia 123
Adonis 50, 117
Ailbhe, St, 138
Áine 142-3
Alder 8, 12 -14, 16, 19, 20, 34-9, 86, 104, 125, 164, 172, 175, 181, 185, 191, 201-2
Anemone 50
Antrim 5, 18, 120
Aongus 26, 27, 48, 50, 87, 117, 146
Apple 5, 11, 13-16, 19, 20, 35, 62-3, 84-90, 104, 141, 166, 175, 181, 185, 198, 201-2
Apollo 56, 60, 117
Arbutus 14, 152-3, 174
Armagh 3, 19
Artemis 117-8
Arthur 79, 84, 198
Ash 6-9, 12, 14, 17, 19, 21, 37, 44, 61, 106, 120-130, 132, 137, 139, 171, 175, 181, 185, 194, 201
Aspen 3, 9, 10, 12-14, 21, 40, 110, 120, 134-7, 172-3, 175, 177, 179, 180-2
Attis 117
Autumn Equinox 198
Avalon 84, 86, 198
Baile Mac Buain 87, 141
Baldur 26
Balor 56, 70, 77
Bealtaine – see May Eve
Beech 15, 17
Belgium 101, 150
Belinus 56
Birch 6, 9, 12-14, 17-18, 21-7, 98, 114, 116, 119, 164, 173-4, 181, 185, 189, 201, 204
Bird Cherry 10, 90, 174
Birds 9, 12, 37-8, 42, 44, 46, 48, 54, 56, 64-6, 94, 104, 108, 125, 191, 204-5
Blackthorn 3, 10, 11, 13-14, 16, 19-20, 32, 36, 86, 90, 102-7, 134, 170, 175, 181
Blodeuedd 100
Bog myrtle 14, 169, 174
Boyne 45, 75, 82
Bracken 14, 15, 92, 169
Bramble (briar) 3, 12, 14, 19-20, 98, 103-5
Bran (king of Britain) 37
Brandon, St, 17
Brehon Laws – see Laws regarding Trees
Brendan, St, 86
Brian Boru 43
Brigid, st, 3, 22, 27, 33, 35, 42, 61, 86, 98, 104, 123, 164, 189-90
Brittany 56, 59-60, 68, 98, 100, 114, 119, 130, 139
Broom 13-14, 18, 22, 98-101, 150, 169, 175, 181
Brú na Bóinne – see Newgrange
Buckthorn 3, 90-1, 168, 181
Bull 31, 44, 64, 125
Cailleach Bhéara 71
Carlow 4, 6, 144
Cavan 18, 114
Cernunnos 64
Cherry 13-14, 17, 19, 31, 46-50, 90, 165, 172-3, 181
Christ (Jesus) 3, 27, 53, 66, 90, 103, 110, 116, 134, 140, 148, 150, 192, 204
Christmas 66, 71, 103, 116, 166, 171, 188-9
Clare 94, 152
Clonmacnoise 3, 55, 132, 138
Colman, St., 123
Colmcille, St, 3, 18, 55, 61, 69, 86, 132, 138
Conchubar 37, 82, 88
Conn Céadchathach (Conn of the Hundred Fights) 6, 32, 62-3, 85, 105, 126, 144

Cork 18, 40, 42, 53, 116, 120, 123
Cormac Mac Airt 62, 84-5, 143
Cormac Mac Cuilennán 35, 86
Cornel tree 17
Cornwall 54, 84, 94, 101, 110, 122, 154
Cow, cattle 3, 4, 15, 22, 28, 30, 42, 45, 52-4, 64, 68, 92, 96, 102, 111, 114, 120, 122, 140, 151, 164
Craebhnat, St, 124
Cúchulainn 26, 32, 37, 59, 64, 69-70, 82, 88, 142
Cypress 37, 125
Da Derga 38, 88, 107
Dagda 59, 65, 79, 87, 126
Dallán 105, 140
Deer 63-5, 73, 87, 195
Deirdre & Naoise 85, 118, 136
Demeter 118
Denmark 34, 110-1, 120, 137
Derry 3, 4, 18, 19, 61, 138
Diarmuid & Gráinne 22, 26, 31, 49, 50, 60, 105, 142, 152
Dog 28, 32, 37, 56
Dogwood 174
Donegal 18, 19, 68, 69, 105-6, 124, 140
Donn 38, 64, 65
Down 18, 55, 138
Druids 3, 11, 31, 60, 61, 73, 86, 96, 140, 146
Dublin 19, 54, 91, 95, 124, 139
Durrow 18, 61, 86
Eamhain Abhlach 84, 86, 198
Eamhain Macha 63, 82, 187
Easter 39, 94, 192
Elder 3, 8, 9, 12-14, 16, 19, 108-13, 134, 170, 175, 181, 185, 199, 202
Elm 8, 13, 14, 17, 42, 130-3, 172, 175
England 2, 4, 8-9, 24, 28, 38, 42, 46, 47, 54-6, 60, 67-68, 72, 79, 82, 84, 88-9, 91-2, 94-5, 98-101, 103, 109-111, 118-20, 122-3, 130, 135, 139-40, 142, 150
Esus 44, 125

Étaín 32, 56, 82, 105, 140
Fairies 6, 8, 25, 29, 34, 52-54, 59, 67, 72, 78, 85, 92, 94, 98, 100, 102, 104, 109, 111-2, 120-1, 130, 165, 183, 189, 192-3, 199
Fermanagh 18, 55, 87
Fintan Mac Bóchna 62, 78, 126, 141
Fionn Mac Cumhaill 31-2, 38, 49, 64, 68-70, 73, 75, 77-8, 87, 108, 118, 141, 197
Fir – see Pine
Fires, bonfires 4, 9, 10, 28-34, 36, 37, 54, 56, 58, 65, 78, 94, 101, 105, 108, 112, 114, 116, 117, 119, 143, 150, 159, 190, 193, 195
France 24, 44, 60, 83, 116-8, 122, 143, 150
Fraoch 31, 48
Furze 13, 14, 18, 92-97, 168-9, 171, 175, 181
Galatia 8, 60
Galway 6, 19, 106, 116, 123-4
Gaul 8, 37, 60, 124-5, 132, 184
Germany 24, 26, 34, 60, 65, 74, 103, 114-5, 140
Glendalough 4, 44, 139
Goat 65, 112
Goibhniú 56, 57
Gooseberry 14, 178-9, 181-3
Greece 50, 65, 90
Gorse – see Furze
Grainne - see Diarmuid & Gráinne
Guelder Rose 174
Halloween 30, 59, 80, 82, 84, 88, 92, 104, 111, 116, 141, 145, 150, 173-4, 183-5,187, 199, 200
Hawthorn 3, 4, 7-9, 12-15, 17-19, 52-57, 61, 94, 104, 106, 110, 122, 134, 165, 193, 202
Hazel 8, 11, 13-17, 19-20, 61-3, 71-81, 87, 122, 125, 157, 166, 173-5, 179-83, 185, 197, 201
Heather 14, 18, 92, 95-6, 171-2, 174,

Index

181
Holly 12-14, 17, 21, 66-71, 94, 159, 165-6, 175, 181, 185, 196, 201
Honeysuckle 10, 11, 17, 141, 168, 174, 177, 181
Horse 28, 32, 43-4, 56, 62, 67, 92, 94, 96, 106, 111, 124, 136
Iceland 116
Imbolc 22, 27, 33, 98, 119, 123, 164, 183, 189-90
India 56, 80, 203
Isle of Man 28, 30, 111, 154
Iubhdan 10-12, 31, 40, 104, 111, 124, 134
Ivy 17, 21, 110, 117, 168-9, 174, 177, 181
John, St, 24, 74, 114, 195
Judas 3, 110
Juniper 14, 19, 101, 148-51, 172-3, 177-9, 182
Jupiter 60, 61, 63, 65, 105, 117
Kerry 42, 52-4, 94, 116, 152-3
Kevin, St, 4, 44, 139
Kieran, St, 55, 123, 132, 137-8
Kildare 3, 6, 18, 19, 33, 54, 61, 123
Kilkenny 4, 7, 19, 55
Labhraidh Loingseach 43, 44
Laburnum 16, 17
Laois 18, 19, 54
Laserian, St, 144
Laws regarding Trees 13-16
Lent 101, 116, 150
Leonard, St 55
Lime 130
Limerick 142
Lucan (Roman Author) 37, 125, 142
Lugh 25, 70, 77-9, 86, 142
Lúnasa 71, 165, 183, 196-7
Mad Sweeny 19-21, 25, 34, 40, 64, 86, 104, 125, 137, 141-2
Mannanán Mac Lir 62, 69, 75, 77, 84, 85, 87-88, 198
Maedhbh 48-49, 59, 82, 105, 106, 124

Mary, (Virgin) 30, 46, 100, 122
May Eve 24, 30, 42, 54, 58, 94, 103, 111, 114, 150, 165, 174, 183, 193
Mayo 19, 32, 124, 131, 152
Meadowsweet 100
Meath 5, 18, 19, 123, 125-6
Medlar 17
Merlin 56, 86
Michael, St, 10, 58, 134
Midsummer 10, 24, 55, 58, 65, 111, 114, 165, 195
Midwinter 24, 27, 119, 166, 171, 174, 188
Mistletoe 15, 26, 60, 103
Mochae, St, 104
Mochuda 86
Molasius, St, 25
Moling, St, 7, 55, 120, 144
Monaghan 18
Monster (Serpent, worm) 32, 48, 64, 105
Moon 42, 43, 94, 181-3
Morrigan 126, 143
Mountain Ash – see Rowan
Naoise – see Deirdre & Naoise
Navan Fort - see Eamhain Macha
Nettle 108
Newgrange 27, 87
New Year's Eve 24, 66-7, 84, 116, 150, 189, 201
Norway 4, 26, 29, 36, 76, 88, 122-3, 125, 136, 140
Oak 4, 6-7, 10, 12-13, 15-16, 18, 19-21, 58-65, 88, 100, 122, 165, 175, 181, 185, 195, 201, 203
Odin 56, 125
Offaly 18, 55, 64, 91, 94, 124
Ogma 157
Ogham Alphabet 154-183
Oisín 64, 136
Olwen 100
Oscar 50, 68, 105, 136
Palm tree 116-17, 119, 170-1

Palm Sunday 42, 45, 140, 192
Patrick, St, 4, 7, 25, 32, 42, 45, 55, 79, 82, 123-4, 131-2, 138, 1911
Peredur 56, 69
Peter, St,114
Pig 50, 64-65, 72, 74, 105, 117, 195
Pine 9, 12-14, 114-19, 171, 178, 181, 185, 188, 201
Placenames 18, 19, 152
Pliny (Roman Author) 60, 61, 67, 122
Poland 115
Poplar 17, 40, 43, 135, 137
Poseiden 123
Privet 174
Quicken/quickbeam – see Rowan
Raspberry 16-17
Red Branch Knights 36, 88, 191
Reed/Rushes 92, 132, 169, 181
Ronan, St, 19, 68
Roscommon 7, 18, 19, 123, 131-2
Rose 14, 17, 170, 174
Rosemary 150
Rowan 4, 9-11, 13-14, 16, 19, 28-33, 37, 58, 61, 67, 72, 105, 110, 150, 152, 159, 164, 170, 181, 185, 190, 201
Ruadhán, St, 131
Samhain - see Halloween
Sally – see willow
Salmon 74-5, 77-78, 177, 182, 197
Scotland 10, 22, 24-30, 34, 42-3, 53, 58, 59, 66-7, 73-4, 78, 86-7, 94-5, 98, 100, 102, 110-12, 116-20, 122, 134, 136, 139-40, 142, 148, 150, 151, 154, 188, 190
Scots Pine – see Pine
Sea – see Water
Senan, St, 77
Servanus, St, 87
Shannon 75-7
Sheep 15, 30, 84
Sligo 32, 123
Sloe – see Blackthorn

Snake 8, 74, 78, 122, 150
Spindle 14, 146-7, 174, 177, 179, 181, 182
Spring Equinox 191-2
Stag – see Deer
Stephen, St, 66, 94
Strawberry Tree – see Arbutus
Suibhne Geilt – see Mad Sweeney
Sun 26-7, 56, 58, 60, 65-6, 79-80, 96, 114, 116-17, 137, 146, 159, 181-2, 189
Sweden 24, 114, 130
Switzerland 143
Tara 6, 32, 84, 125, 141-2, 183, 200
Tipperary 18-19, 123, 131, 138, 143
Tír Fá Thonn (Land Under Wave) 75
Tír Tairngire (Land of Promise) 75, 84, 86, 152
Tree of Daithi 6-7, 125
Tree of Mugna 6-7, 62-3
Tree of Rossa 6-7, 144
Tree of Tortan 6-7, 62, 125-9
Tree of Uisneach 6-7, 125
Tuatha Dé Danann 31, 72, 75, 79, 117, 152
Uisneach 6, 7, 79, 125, 136
Vine 17, 167, 181
Wales 15, 18, 22, 24, 25, 29, 30, 36-7, 43, 48, 54, 56, 58, 61, 65, 66, 69, 74, 78, 79, 91, 94, 98, 100-1, 104, 117, 122, 154, 156-8
Water 8, 32, 34, 37, 40, 44, 48, 72, 74, 75, 86, 122-3, 129-30, 133-4, 159, 172, 182, 192
Waterford 152
Wells 4, 5, 7-8, 32, 36, 55-6, 74-7,104, 122-4, 130-2, 193-5, 197
Westmeath 6, 125
Wexford 19
Whin – see Furze
Whitebeam 14, 78, 82-3, 173
Whitethorn – see Hawthorn
Wicklow 56, 57, 138-9

Willow 5, 8-9, 11, 13-14, 16, 19, 22, 40-45, 98, 125, 137, 164, 175, 181, 192, 201-2

Witch, hag 9, 25, 28-30, 32, 42, 54, 67, 68, 95, 98, 100, 103, 105, 108-10, 112, 120, 122, 124, 137, 140-1, 143, 148, 150, 199, 202

Wych Elm – see Elm

Yew 2-4, 6-8, 12, 14-19, 21, 36-7, 61, 87, 108, 125, 138-45, 148, 160, 173-5, 178, 181, 185-8, 201

Yggdrasill 122, 123, 125

Ysbaddaden Pencawr 56

Zeus 60, 61, 117

Birds of Ireland
GLYNN ANDERSON

An exploration of our interaction with birds, covering mythology and folklore, and bird-related beliefs, proverbs and curses.
ISBN: 978-184889-313-9

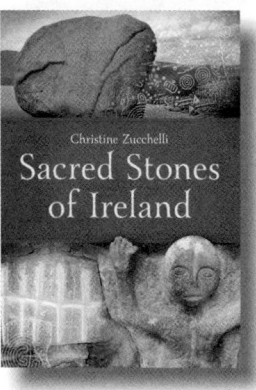

Sacred Stones of Ireland
CHRISTINE ZUCCHELLI

Explore the secrets, myths, legends and folktales of our stone monuments.
ISBN: 978-184889-276-7

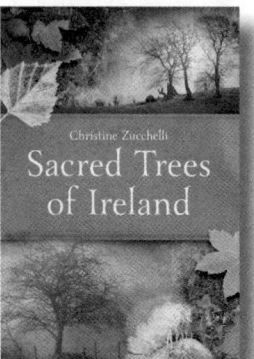

Sacred Trees of Ireland
CHRISTINE ZUCCHELLI

This fascinating exploration of trees' stories and legends reveals their spiritual, social and historical functions.
ISBN: 978-184889-277-4